Praise for

THE MATCHMAKER

"This mystery-romance combo will spice up even the grayest of spring days."
—*Marie Claire*

"Part cozy mystery, part romance, *The Matchmaker* shares a little in common with reality TV shows like *The Bachelor* and *Say Yes to the Dress* in mining the entertainment value found in looking for love and planning lavish weddings. But it's the mystery that really fuels this narrative."
—*The Atlanta Journal-Constitution*

"*The Matchmaker* is the perfect blend of romance and thrill."
—Popsugar

"This romantic thriller reminds us how dangerous falling in love can be, and how fraught weddings get—not just the worry about a dress mishap or seating chart snafu, but actual sabotage and murder."
—*Paste*

"A fast-paced and entertaining read. . . . *The Matchmaker* is a smart, compelling mystery that sparkles with tension—and engagement rings. . . . Romantic suspense at its best."
—*Shelf Awareness* (starred)

"This hybrid romance/mystery takes the South Asian tradition of arranged marriage and works it into a story that delights with its shimmering fluidity, memorable characters, heart-stopping twists, and a happily-ever-after that warms the heart while bringing the narrative to a delectably satisfying close. A warm, winning debut with intelligence and storytelling panache to spare."
—*Kirkus Reviews*

"Saeed's debut adult novel is a romystery, an engaging blend of thrilling action, love of all kinds, and a touch of sweetness."
—*Library Journal*

"Saeed delivers brisk prose and generates sweet chemistry between Nura and Azar."
—*Publishers Weekly*

"An intriguing mystery and a heartfelt romance all in one, *The Matchmaker* is fresh, original, and utterly charming. You'll love this sparkling gem of a book."
—LIANE MORIARTY, #1 *New York Times* bestselling author of *Big Little Lies*

"Aisha Saeed expertly blends romance and mystery in this fun, fresh story that is sure to keep readers turning the pages. Smart, twisty and full of heart."
—AMY TINTERA, *New York Times* bestselling author of *Listen for the Lie*

"*The Matchmaker* combines a page-turning thriller with a sweet romance filled with palpable yearning, adds a dramatic family saga spanning generations, then plunks it into a *Crazy Rich Asians*-esque world of weddings and matchmaking. I loved absolutely everything about it!"
—MIA P. MANANSALA, author of the multi-award-winning *Arsenic and Adobo*

"A stunning blend of enchanting cultural traditions, sumptuous weddings, kidnap, and murder. *The Matchmaker* kept me enthralled and guessing until the very end. Don't miss this gem!"
—LIV CONSTANTINE, *New York Times* bestselling author of *The Next Mrs. Parrish*

"*The Matchmaker* is a magical mix of romance, family saga, detective story, and teeth-chattering suspense. I was swept into the dreamworld of the super-wealthy—a world of beautiful brides, fabulous feasts, shimmering saris . . . and murder. I adored every page, and so will you."

—ROSE CARLYLE, internationally bestselling author of *The Girl in the Mirror* and *No One Will Know*

"*The Matchmaker* is a mystery crackling with tension, both romantic and thrilling. I was swept away by the will-they-won't-they chemistry and the cat-and-mouse mystery, all set amidst a gorgeous backdrop of lavish weddings. This page-turner pairs up the perfect match of romance and suspense."

—JULIA SEALES, bestselling author of *A Most Agreeable Murder*

"I loved *every word* of this novel. Dazzling. I wish I could write like that." —A. J. FINN, #1 *New York Times* bestselling author of *The Woman in the Window*

Advance praise for

THE WEDDING WEEK

"Saeed's portrayal of big, ethnic families is so accurate it is both affirming and triggering. I was equal parts entertained and horrified (but in a really good way). My flabber is gasted."

—JESSE Q. SUTANTO, bestselling author of *Vera Wong's Unsolicited Advice for Murderers*

"A decadent setting, a sisters' story that instantly drew me in, twists and turns for days . . . I couldn't put this book down. Clear your calendar and prepare to be swept away!"

—ALLY CONDIE, #1 *New York Times* bestselling author of *The Girls Trip* and *The Unwedding*

"Set during a lavish wedding where everyone is watching and no one is innocent, this electrifying thriller strips away the glamour and exposes something seedy and vicious underneath. Saeed writes with precision and nerve, escalating suspicion into full-blown paranoia as loyalties fracture and buried secrets surface. Every twist cuts deep, and every relationship feels one step from betrayal. Addictive and unflinching."

—CARTER WILSON, *USA Today* bestselling author of *Tell Me What You Did*

"A treat of a novel! I couldn't put it down, devouring it in less than forty-eight hours. Saeed delivers a propulsively fun mystery full of secrets, wealth, and intrigue set against a lush, Floridian backdrop. With a rich and well-developed cast of characters, mounting suspense, and twisty reveals, *The Wedding Week* is not to be missed!"

—SOPHIE STAVA, author of *Count My Lies*

"In *The Wedding Week*, Aisha Saeed crafts an intoxicating blend of mystery, romance, and family drama, delivering a bingeable thriller that hums with menace. Come for the lush, luxurious setting; stay for the surprises and secrets lurking around every corner." —MEGAN COLLINS, author of *Cross My Heart* and *The Family Plot*

"Aisha Saeed has another hit on her hands with *The Wedding Week*. A lavish destination wedding in the lush Everglades turns deadly in this simmering, twist-filled thriller, with razor-sharp insight into social and family dynamics and tension that never lets up."
—AGGIE BLUM THOMPSON, author of *You Deserve to Know*

"A lavish wedding and buried secrets set the stage for this dazzling novel that I devoured in one sitting. Aisha Saeed delivers a story that's part mystery, part thriller, and part romance—each twist more addictive than the last. She gives chilling new meaning to the vow 'till death do us part.' A must-read."
—ALEX FINLAY, bestselling author of *Parents Weekend*

"The pages just flew by in *The Wedding Week*, a fun read with a charmingly claustrophobic family ensemble and a glittering setting."
—SARINA BOWEN, *USA Today* bestselling author of *The Five Year Lie*

"Set amid the atmospheric Everglades, *The Wedding Week* simmers with complex family and community dynamics. Saeed artfully weaves dark secrets and suspense into the glittery backdrop of a lavish wedding. Full of twists and escalating tension, this novel will keep you turning the pages and checking over your shoulder."
—SARAH FOX, author of *Definitely Maybe Not a Detective*

By Aisha Saeed

THE MATCHMAKER
THE WEDDING WEEK

THE WEDDING WEEK

THE WEDDING WEEK

a novel

AISHA SAEED

BANTAM
NEW YORK

Bantam Books
An imprint of Random House
A division of Penguin Random House LLC
1745 Broadway, New York, NY 10019
randomhousebooks.com
randomhousebookclub.com
penguinrandomhouse.com

A Bantam Books Trade Paperback Original

ISBN 978-0-593-87117-1
Ebook ISBN 978-0-593-87118-8

Printed in the United States of America

1st Printing

BOOK TEAM: Production editor: Cassie Gitkin • Managing editor: Saige Francis • Production manager: Chanler Harris • Copy editor: Cindy Howle • Proofreaders: Cyrus Chin, Andrea Gordon, Russell Powers

Adobe Stock illustrations: Marina Sun (title and part title pages), Leianna (page 11), Katikim (pages 53, 137, 187, 235), Razaul (page 253)

Book design by Jo Anne Metsch

The authorized representative in the EU for product safety and compliance is Penguin Random House Ireland, Morrison Chambers, 32 Nassau Street, Dublin D02 YH68, Ireland. https://eu-contact.penguin.ie

To my aunties,
this book is for you.

THE WEDDING WEEK

SOPHIE,
Cousin of the Bride

66 If I were contemplating murder, there really wouldn't be a better place to get away with it than Florida. *South Florida* to be precise. Home to 1.5 million acres of the Everglades. No matter where you go, from the glitzy art deco of South Beach to the suburban outlet malls, there's no escaping that swamp. It's full of alligators, crocodiles, and exotic pythons that can devour an adult deer without blinking. Don't forget the tannic acid pooling in the waters either. With time, it can dissolve just about anything. Even bone. The Glades have swallowed whole airplanes flying overhead—even with all their fancy GPS and SOS signals, they vanished without a trace.

Now, I'm not saying Hena did anything. Don't put me down as saying that. I'm not. All I'm saying is her fiancé, Nasir Wahidi, disappeared into thin air the night before their wedding. No one's heard a word from him since. And guess what? Her family mansion backs up to that goddamn swamp.

So, I suppose what I *am* saying is, draw your own conclusion. 99

1

Hena sat by her kitchen window, finishing her morning coffee as fog rolled in over the Golden Gate Bridge. As she reached for an envelope from a stack of mail, her phone buzzed. Her book club, she guessed. They were still pinning down logistics for tonight's meetup.

But the number flashing on the screen wasn't anyone from book club. It was her little sister. She was calling. Lulu never called.

Hena's throat caught as she stared at Lulu's goofy grin, lit up on her phone. Her brown eyes partially obscured by a curtain of bangs from her blue-hair phase when she was eighteen. It was when Hena had seen her last. When they were inseparable. When Lulu still loved her.

"I wanted you to hear it from me," Lulu said when Hena answered, sliding past pleasantries. "I'm getting married."

Married? Hena winced as her finger sliced against the edge of the envelope she had been opening. Blood pooled on the tip of her index finger. She pressed a napkin against it to stem the bleeding. Lulu was twenty-one. Nine years her junior. Far too young. But her sister hadn't called for Hena's opinion.

"Who's the lucky guy?" she asked instead, as her tabby, Roscoe, brushed against her leg.

"You know him. Khaled."

Wait. What? Hena sat up straighter.

"Haris's cousin?" she asked. "Did Ammi set this up?"

"This isn't an arranged marriage." Lulu scoffed. "We've known each other forever. I ran into him at Auntie Hanifa's anniversary party last year. One thing led to another . . ."

She filled Hena in on how Khaled had accompanied his parents to their family home for a formal marriage proposal, complete with laddus, gulab jamun, and other desi sweets.

Hena's chest constricted. She knew Khaled. He was the pale-faced kid who'd played football with the other boys at the auntie- and uncle-filled desi potlucks of her youth. His cousin Haris—her first kiss—was best friends with Nasir, the man she'd nearly married.

Hena fled to the other side of the country to escape that world. Her kid sister was hitching herself to it for life?

Lulu had stopped talking. She was waiting for a response.

"Congratulations," Hena managed to say. "When's the big day?"

"Saturday."

"As in three days from now?" she said, half joking.

"Two days, actually. The welcome party is Friday evening. Can you come?"

Hena's cheeks warmed. Why was she surprised? Sure, they exchanged the occasional birthday text, but this was the first time she'd heard Lulu's voice in three years. Why wouldn't she be the last to know about her wedding?

"Thanks for keeping me in the loop," Hena said.

"Don't do that," Lulu warned. "It came together faster than we expected, but it's not like you'd have wanted to come. I can't remember the last time you've been home."

Hena remembered. The last time she'd been in Pembroke Pines was three years, two weeks, and five days ago. Lulu knew why she hadn't been back. Hena was not welcome.

"Why bother inviting me now?" Hena asked.

"Ammi wants you there."

"Good one." They both knew how their mother felt about Hena. *We'll just pretend you're dead*—verbatim the last words she'd spoken to her.

"I'm as surprised as you are."

"Well, thanks for the invite. Work is busy, so I won't be able to make it." Boundaries—she was good at those now. "I wish you and Khaled all the happiness in the world. I mean that."

"Hena—"

"Lulu, I'm in the middle of a major renovation. I can't just drop everything last minute. Honestly, I'm offended you'd ask."

There was a long pause on the other line. Then her sister spoke again.

"Ammi's dying," she said.

Hena gripped the phone tighter. *I misunderstood. I must have.*

"It's lung cancer. Stage four," Lulu explained, to fill the silence. "The doctors said we've run out of treatment options. It's why we rushed the wedding."

She knew people died all the time, but her mother couldn't die. She was a force of nature, her presence and absence in Hena's life equally haunting. She was also her last living parent.

Blood seeped through the napkin. Hena collected herself. Drew in a deep breath.

"I'm . . . I'm sorry to hear," she finally said. "But she doesn't want to see me."

"She does."

"Lulu—"

"Look, she'll never say it to you, okay? But she's been calling out your name in her sleep for days. When I caught her going through your baby album this morning, she admitted it. She wants to see you. She said she wants closure. Regardless of all the shit between the two of you, you're her daughter. She loves you, Hena."

Ammi loved no one. Least of all Hena. She remembered the night in her bridal suite. Her hands and arms adorned in henna. Ancestral gold around her neck. When she told Ammi there would be no wedding. When Ammi took everyone's side except her own.

"I don't think my being there is a good idea," Hena said. "Having the 'killer bride' in attendance might overshadow your big day."

"Don't say that. Everyone knows you would never hurt Nasir. Look, if anyone so much as whispers about you, tell me. I will personally have them booted off the premises."

Lulu fell silent for a moment. When she spoke again, her voice trembled.

"Hena, Ammi's really sick. It's rough. She insisted on sending me off with a proper wedding, so I'm going along with it, but it's a lot to handle. You have to come. Please. I need you."

Hena's eyes welled. Just like that, she was Jell-O. Because Lulu was her baby sister. Hena had changed her diapers. Pureed her applesauce. Walked her to school for her first day of kindergarten. Watched her skip into the fluorescent-lit classroom with the alphabet rug.

She couldn't say no to Lulu's plea. Not when she had already let her down so much.

DAY
ONE

Luma and Khaled

INVITE YOU TO KICK OFF THEIR
WEDDING FESTIVITIES WITH A

Welcome Party

VISTA DEL SOL

345 EUCLID DRIVE

EVERMERE, FLORIDA

Friday, January 9, at 7:00 p.m.
Parakeet Dining Hall

Attire: Florida chic

2

·

t's not too late.

That's what Hena had told herself as she booked her flight. Packed her luggage. Ordered the rideshare to the airport.

It would have been easy enough to cancel. To tell Lulu something came up. To send her regrets. She'd gotten as far as composing the message, her finger hovering over the send button. There was a reason she hadn't been home in three years. But then she remembered the slight wobble in her sister's voice and knew there was no other choice.

Now she was gazing out at the starless night from the back seat of an Escalade, hurtling toward a past she had vowed never to return to.

Hena traced her thumb along her bandaged index finger. Two days later, it still throbbed. She hoped the sharks she was about to see didn't smell blood in the water.

At least it was a quick trip. She'd booked the first flight out on Sunday. And from arranging this car service to putting her up in a resort two towns over from Pembroke Pines, Lulu had been thoughtful. She understood Hena wanted to be as far from the swamplands of her family home as possible.

But looking out at the mangroves swaying in inky waters, she was reminded how much of this state was covered in wetlands. She thought her sister would have booked a swanky beachside resort in Las Olas. Instead, the car continued westward, deeper into the marshy dark.

Eventually, the swamp gave way to a manicured lawn. Ahead, a sign appeared: Vista Del Sol. The hotel loomed in the distance, bone white against the night sky. Spires rose from each corner like watchtowers. Grand arches framed the gilded entryway. More like a castle than a hotel, it glittered beneath the moon.

The SUV rumbled over a drawbridge, then pulled up to the entrance. A dark-haired bellhop in a festive red uniform promptly emerged to gather her things. Hena moved to tip him, but he shook his head, refusing to accept it. Curious.

Stepping inside, Hena felt like she'd wandered into a Moroccan palace. Pendant lights glowed overhead, their tricolor panes casting shadows across the marble floors and jewel-toned couches. Two swans drifted in an indoor lagoon by the glass elevators. Through the transparent back wall, she glimpsed a turquoise infinity pool framed by palms.

The resort was quiet. Almost too quiet. Looking around, Hena realized she was the only guest in the lobby aside from a man in a gray suit by the front desk, a garment bag draped over his arm.

"You should be all set, Mr. Davies," the receptionist told the man as Hena approached. She stole a glance—correction: the very *handsome* man.

The woman handed him a gift bag as his phone buzzed. He stepped aside to check it, and she turned her attention to Hena. She wore a smart red dress, and her chestnut-colored hair was swept back into a neat bun. When Hena gave her name, the woman's eyebrows shot up.

"Ms. Mirza. I'm so sorry, I should have known," she said. "We've been expecting you."

She pulled out a cream-colored envelope from the shelf behind her and handed it to Hena.

"Your key is inside. Wi-Fi info too. I suggest connecting ASAP, as cell service can be spotty. And be sure to download the wedding app for the digital keycard. You'll be staying in one of our VIP suites over at the deluxe tower. Fourth floor. It has a private elevator. The keycards will open both."

"Lucky." The man next to her let out a low whistle as he stuck his phone back in his pocket. "I'm staying at the other tower with the plebes."

He smiled, and Hena felt butterflies, which couldn't be helped. With his broad shoulders, olive skin, and dark hair, he was, simply put, gorgeous. And he had about five inches on her, which meant he was at least six feet tall.

"Here for the wedding?" she asked him.

He nodded. "I'm Reza, one of the groomsmen. And I'm running late."

"Hena. Sister of the bride. Don't worry, desi standard time is taken very seriously in these parts. We're only a touch behind."

"Well, that's a relief." He put out his hand. "It's nice to meet you."

She shook it, ignoring the jolt that went through her.

"Ms. Mirza, before you go . . ." The woman at the counter scrawled something on a notepad and handed it to her. "I'm Lucinda. This is my personal number. If you need anything at all, don't hesitate to reach out."

Reza raised an eyebrow, and Hena pushed back a laugh. Being the bride's sister appeared to have its perks.

"Do you know where tonight's welcome dinner is?" Hena asked Lucinda. "I forgot to ask for the address."

"Tonight's event is in the Parakeet dining hall, just around the corner." She slid a gift bag across the desk. "This will have all the pertinent information you'll need."

Hena peeked inside. There was Voss water. Snacks. La Mer lip balm. Apple AirPods. And a hefty binder embroidered with Lulu and Khaled's names. The first page featured a welcome note from the happy couple. Hena flipped to the next page. And the next.

FRIDAY, JANUARY 9. **Welcome Party**
SATURDAY, JANUARY 10. **Bridal Shower**
SUNDAY, JANUARY 11. **Dholki**
MONDAY, JANUARY 12. **Mayoun**
TUESDAY, JANUARY 13. **Mehndi**
WEDNESDAY, JANUARY 14. **Nikkah**
THURSDAY, JANUARY 15. **Shaadi**
FRIDAY, JANUARY 16. **Walima**

Hena blinked. This couldn't be right. Lulu said the wedding was tomorrow. Didn't she?

Thumbing through the binder, the events were not limited to formal wedding festivities. A million optional ones were packed into each day as well. Spa days. Art deco tours. An on-site class on towel art. A fortune teller reading. A video booth was set up in the business center, and guests were encouraged to record messages for the bride and groom.

And—Hena flipped back to the main festivities and stared at the addresses printed beneath each invitation—the wedding events were here. Every single one took place at this resort.

"See you in a little while," Reza told her.

She managed a limp wave as he headed toward the elevators. A collective burst of laughter echoed from the dining hall. Hena now noticed the edge of orange and yellow flowers peeking out from around the corner. The faint hint of music. They were there. Her family. Her community. She understood now that Lulu wasn't giving her a reprieve from the chaos by putting her up here. She was delivering her straight into it.

"Hi, Hena."

Lulu. She walked toward Hena from the dining hall, and in an instant Hena's frustration was replaced by a lump growing in her throat. Gone were the blue locks and oversized bangs, replaced by her natural dark hair, curled and falling past her shoulders. Her golden kamiz skimmed the floor, a matching veil draped to the side. Her arms were filled with glittering bangles. Lulu was all grown up, but when Hena looked in her eyes, there she was. Her baby sister. As irritated as Hena felt, god, she'd missed her so much.

As Lulu grew closer, instinct kicked in. Hena pulled her into a hug. She pretended not to notice how Lulu's body tensed. How she patted Hena politely before pulling away.

"Thanks for coming," she said.

Hena pointed to the binder of events. "You told me the wedding was tomorrow."

"The wedding *begins* tomorrow. You knew this was a desi wedding, right?"

"I booked my return flight for Sunday morning."

"Change it."

"Lulu, I have work. Clients. You can't just spring this on me last minute."

"If I told you this wedding was a weeklong situation, would you have come?" She leveled Hena with a cool look. "Exactly. I really think you can manage to be around us for that long. I'm sure the yoga studio or whatever you're designing can wait."

Hena's gaze swept over her sister. Her folded arms. Her distant demeanor. It was one thing to hear Lulu's tone over the phone, another to experience it in the flesh. The new Lulu. More like her mother than Hena cared to stomach. As with her mother, Hena saw there was no arguing with Lulu. Hena rarely ever rescheduled; hopefully her clients would understand.

Searching for a neutral topic, she pointed to the indoor lagoon.

"I can't believe you have real swans here."

"Flown in from Scandinavia," she said. "A bit silly, but they came with the property."

"They're beautiful." Hena glanced around. "This resort is . . . wow. It's gorgeous."

Lulu smiled. "Thanks. I wanted something tasteful but tucked away. The wedding will be stressful enough."

"It's definitely your vibe." Hena looked up at the glowing pendant lights. "Reminds me of a vacation we took to Morocco. You were so little."

She remembered hoisting three-year-old Lulu on her back as their family walked down cobbled alleys, the heat beating down on them, Lulu humming songs while Hena prayed their father would not turn and snap at her. Their joy was so often a trigger for him.

"I remember that trip. It's what inspired the theme." Lulu paused. "This is my resort."

"*Yours?*" Hena balked. "What happened to culinary school? Opening a restaurant was your dream."

"Dreams change. Besides, this was important. Hotels are part of our DNA."

Hena shifted. If hotels were part of their DNA, it was their father's half—the part of herself she wished she could scrub away.

"I've been studying hotel management, waiting for the right property to hit the market," Lulu continued. "When this went on sale a few months ago, it was like kismet. It feels like a way to keep Abu's memory alive, you know?"

Hena couldn't blame Lulu for wanting to follow in their father's footsteps. Not when she didn't know who he truly was. Ammi had taken great pains to keep Lulu in the dark. It's why she'd liquidated every last property shortly after—

Nope. Hena shivered. *Not going there.*

She supposed this was what happened when you no longer spoke to your family. You learned everything after the fact. Most days Hena had made her peace with this reality. It was the cost of breaking away. Starting her own life far from this humid, mosquito-filled state and the toxic people who inhabited it. But her kid sister bore no blame for any of the things that happened, and right now, Hena felt it deep in her bones— the cost of being absent.

"When did you buy it?" Hena asked her.

"It's a wedding gift from Ammi. I can't exactly access my trust yet, can I?"

Her tone was calm, but the words landed like a punch. After liquidating their properties, Ammi set up trusts for both Lulu and Hena. There were enough funds in there for neither of them to worry about money ever again. Lulu was supposed to have gained access to hers on her twenty-first birthday, same as Hena, but their mother had delayed Lulu's by five years. Because of Hena. Because of the poor choices she had made.

"Ammi was pushing me to get a beachside property, but I liked the vibe of this place, and ecotourism is all the rage these days. You could call this the soft opening," said Lulu. "The wedding party and most of our close friends and family are staying here. That way Ammi doesn't have to move back and forth. I'm staying in the two-bedroom penthouse suite with her. It's one floor above you."

Ammi was staying here too. This evening got better and better.

Where is Ammi? Hena was about to ask. Before she could, a woman rounded the corner, heading straight toward them.

It was Irum. Nasir's sister.

"Lulu," she said as she breathlessly approached. She wasn't the tomboy Hena once knew. Now she had winged eyeliner and blond highlights in her hair. Her silver dress shimmered beneath the lights. "There's a snag with the table covers for tomorrow's—"

She cut off, taking a half step back, finally noticing Hena.

"What are you doing here?" Hena blurted out.

Lulu gasped. "Hena, really? She's only my maid of honor."

Hena's head spun. Maid of honor? Irum? Of all the things thrown at her tonight . . .

Lulu shot Hena a disapproving look before conferring with Irum. When they were done, Irum gave Hena a tight smile before heading off.

"Great going," Lulu said once she was gone.

Was Lulu serious? "A heads-up would have been nice," Hena managed to say. "I wasn't expecting to see her here."

"We were friends long before you and Nasir were a thing. After everything blew up—the gossip and bullshit—we leaned on each other."

Hena cast her eyes down, chastened. She couldn't imagine the avalanche of whispers following the wake of her canceled wedding. She had fled as soon as she could. Lulu and Irum didn't have that option.

"By the way, I know this is last minute," Lulu said. "But Ammi and I agree you should be a bridesmaid."

"Oh." Hena blinked. "Thanks, Lulu, but you don't have to—"

"I actually do. People are talking."

Of course it was about optics. Hena understood the logic, but that didn't mean it didn't hurt, much like the paper cut that still throbbed along her finger. Was this the real reason she'd been invited? To stave off whispers?

"We threw this week together quickly, so we kept the wedding party small," Lulu continued briskly. "Khaled's got his three groomsmen, and I have Irum, Maheen, and my college roommate Courtney."

"Adding me is going to make your wedding party uneven," Hena said.

"It is what it is." She shrugged. "We're flying by the seat of our pants. We didn't even have time for matching outfits. We're color coordinating instead."

There was no point pushing back, was there? Lulu had clearly made up her mind.

"Sounds good," Hena said.

She was edging toward the flowers and chatter when Lulu stopped her.

"They haven't started dinner yet," she said. "You have time to get ready."

"I am ready," Hena replied. "I changed in the sky lounge."

She had on a silk midi dress with three-quarter sleeves. She'd even stopped by the bank to grab matching gold bracelets and earrings to complement her gold clutch. But Lulu took in her outfit and pursed her lips.

"Too much?" Hena asked.

"Hena. Are you kidding me?"

Ah.

"I don't own anything desi anymore," Hena said.

Lulu sighed but said nothing. Hena followed her toward the dining hall. With each step the laughter and conversations grew louder. Her pace slowed. Her pulse quickened.

Lulu looked back at Hena. Her expression softened a touch.

"Thanks for coming," she said. "I know this isn't easy."

Understatement of the century.

The last wedding she'd attended had been her own. Hena thought of the blood pooling on the carpet of her bridal suite. Blue and white lights flashing outside her family home. The way the police rushed inside the boathouse, guns drawn. The knife still clenched in her hands.

Hena had hidden away from these people for three years. She'd have happily stayed away the rest of her life. But whether or not she wanted to do this, it was time.

3

The dining hall was beautiful, with low-lit chandeliers hanging from the high ceiling and fairy lights that blinked along the windows. Elaborate orchid center-pieces, Ammi's favorite flower, rested on each table. Along the back wall, silver chafing dishes were being set up.

Hena stalled mid-step when she saw a man in a gray shalwar kamiz sitting on a dais, strumming his sitar. He wasn't the same musician who'd performed at her wedding, but the music was achingly similar. In fact, everything here was. The music. The festive colors. The food. It was like time traveling back to a place she'd never wished to revisit.

And the people. They weren't just similar. They were one and the same. She knew everyone seated at these tables—the honorary aunties and uncles she grew up with as well as her actual relatives. Three years ago, they'd been at her own nuptials. Dancing. Laughing. Tonight, they were silent. Their bodies turned in their chairs, staring at her as though she were a ghost returning to haunt them.

She spotted her mother in the crowd and drew in a sharp breath. Ammi had always been a small woman; Lulu and Hena had gotten their height from their father—the only thing of his she was glad to have. But Ammi, in a designer silk shalwar kamiz, seemed smaller than she remembered. As though she had curled into herself. Despite her tastefully applied makeup and concealer, her eyes were undeniably sunken, her lips thin. When her gaze locked onto Hena's, they grew thinner still.

Hena heard whispers of conversation as she maneuvered through the crowds.

"The gall! Crashing this wedding after everything she's done to this family."

"She's hardly crashing it. It's her sister's nuptials. They had no choice but to invite her, didn't they?"

"Not after what she did. Hanifa said they explicitly told her not to come. Poor Irum. This could trigger her all over again. Having to be in the same room while her brother is dead and gone."

"We don't know that he's . . ."

"Don't be naïve. I have half a mind to call the police right now. We don't want a repeat of last time, do we? All that blood . . ."

Hena kept moving, her pace steady, her expression neutral. The police had long ago ruled that the DNA on the bloody knife was not Nasir's. Everyone here knew it. Not that the truth mattered. They were looking for a spectacle, not facts. When the worst night of her life had come to pass, they'd stood on the sidelines as they did now, watching with horrified expressions while trying to mask their delight. Heiress to a family hotel fortune taken down a peg or two.

They wanted to trigger her into turning around. Snapping. Giving them more fodder for gossip. Though their words clawed against her skin, she wouldn't give them the satisfaction.

She was nearly at her mother's chair—

"Shaheen is coming to the shaadi. Can you imagine?"

Hena tensed. Nasir's mother? It was baseless gossip. It had to be. Irum being there was bad enough, but facing her missing fiancé's mother after their last interaction? Her skin prickled at the thought.

One thing at a time. Right now, she needed to face her own mother.

Approaching Ammi, she saw the breathing tube in her nose. The oxygen tank by her side. She was in a wheelchair. Hena felt light-headed. So, this was real. This was happening. Her mother was dying.

Ammi's eyes grew glassy as they met Hena's, but her expression remained impassive. No hint of a smile. Still, Hena had to greet her. Hug her. People were watching this first encounter after three years. They'd be storing every detail to break down later. She put her arms around Ammi and gave her a tentative embrace. All she felt were bones. When she pulled back, her mother's hand lingered on her arm.

"What do you mean, showing up in this outfit?" she asked.

Welcome home, Hena. This outfit cost as much as any designer shalwar kamiz, but it wasn't good enough because it wasn't desi.

"Who is this I see?" a voice chirped.

Khala Simki. Ammi's sister. Weaving between the tables, she hurried toward Hena much like the last time they'd seen each other—when she'd raced up to Hena to wrench the knife from her hands, steering her to the sofa, pressing a glass of water into her grip while Hena sat stunned by the reality of her new life.

There was no hint of that night in Khala's eyes as she drew near. Instead, she pulled her into a tight hug, much like the ones she'd given Hena all her life. With Khala's arms around her, Hena's chest loosened the littlest bit. She had always been the light to her mother's darkness.

"Aren't you a sight for sore eyes?" Khala said.

"Look at her outfit." Ammi jabbed a finger at Hena. "She does it to hurt me, you know."

Hena clenched her jaw. Here she was, trying not to make waves. Trying to make sure the crowd ogling them didn't have more gossip to latch on to. Meanwhile, her mother couldn't care less what people overheard. Fine. If she didn't care, why should Hena? She was about to speak, to let Ammi know that when it came to the ability to hurt someone, she reigned supreme, but her aunt squeezed her shoulder meaningfully.

"No need to get upset," Khala reassured her sister. "We'll go shopping tomorrow. Luxe Boutique has some lovely new arrivals. The bridal shower isn't until late afternoon anyhow, so we'll head over first thing in the morning."

"Luxe Boutique? I don't want to—" Hena began.

"You will," Ammi said.

Just like that, she was seven again, cowering in a corner of her bedroom while her mother berated her for a botched piano recital. Except Hena wasn't a child anymore. She was thirty. Though her mother's voice still lived inside her, she could no longer force Hena to do anything.

Lulu stood a few paces away, her eyes darting between them. Hena bit back her words. She wouldn't add more to her sister's plate. One disastrous wedding in this family was enough. But her hunch had been right. It was painfully clear her mother didn't want her there.

A svelte woman with a shock of pink hair introduced herself as the wedding planner and informed them dinner was ready. People began lining up to eat. Good. The sooner Hena could get a bite to eat and escape to her room, the better. This week would be a marathon, not a sprint.

The musician took a break, and Hena joined the dinner line as Irum adjusted a projector. Moments later, photos of

Lulu and Khaled glowed against the back wall. The proposal at her family home, her mother and his parents, their faces lit up, standing alongside the two of them. A montage of moments Hena had missed. The couple was seated at a table near the front. An attendant brought them their plated meals. Khaled whispered something in her sister's ear. She laughed and touched his elbow tenderly.

A pang went through Hena. She had once been them. Blissfully happy at her own welcome party three years ago. Oblivious to all that was to come.

Pulling out her phone, she downloaded the wedding app. As she waited for it to load, she spotted Haris.

He was here.

Of course he was. His cousin was marrying her sister. She'd known him all her life. He'd been a grade ahead of her in high school. At every childhood potluck. Her first kiss when she was seventeen.

The best man at her wedding.

Nasir's closest friend.

He'd clocked her too and was walking toward her. She braced for impact.

She still remembered the cream kurta he wore at her wedding. The pink carnation pinned to his lapel. The phone pressed to his ear as he kept trying Nasir early on, back when people were more confused and less frantic over his absence. He was as boyishly cute as ever, but clean shaven now, and his light brown hair was longer, a taper cut.

What surprised her more than anything else was that he was smiling. At her.

"It's great to see you," he said once they were face-to-face.

They hugged. When he pulled back, she studied his expression. He seemed genuine. Was it possible he didn't hate her?

"It's great to see you too," she told him.

"I hear you're in California?" At her surprised expression, he laughed. "The CIA wishes they could be as in the know as our community."

He was right. She had scrubbed her personal details from the internet—it was safer that way—but she was back in the land of no secrets.

"I'm in San Francisco," she told him. "No humidity or mosquitoes. Highly recommend."

"San Fran?" He let out a low whistle. "You handling those hills okay?"

"I didn't say it was perfect out there," she replied, to which Haris laughed.

"I'm glad you did it. You'd been wanting to move to the West Coast forever. Nasir used to say—" He paused, and his smile faltered. "Sorry. Seeing you after all this time . . . it's hard not to think of him."

It would have been disingenuous to ignore the Nasir-sized elephant in the room. Especially with Haris. She had braced herself for it, but hearing his name spoken aloud after all this time still sent shock waves through her.

For a beat, neither of them said anything. Hena cleared her throat.

"How's Chloe?" she asked.

He grimaced. "I guess it *has* been a while. We didn't make it. Turns out my mother was right after all. Our divorce was finalized last year."

"Oh, Haris." She reached out and gave his arm a gentle squeeze. "I'm so sorry."

She'd attended his wedding four years ago—an intimate affair on a yacht in Biscayne Bay. She'd worn a pale pink sari and borrowed her mother's favorite diamond necklace. Nasir, in his pin-striped tux, had been best man.

"Don't be sorry," Haris said. "It was rough going at first, but it's for the best."

Haris's mother suddenly came into view as she marched toward them, bunching up her flowing sari to keep it from dragging against the ground. Hena was about to greet her. To congratulate her. Her nephew was marrying Hena's sister. But Auntie Nipa wouldn't meet Hena's gaze. It was as though she wasn't there.

"Your cousin needs you," Auntie Nipa told Haris sharply, wedging herself firmly between them.

"Sure, I'll be there in—"

"You're his best man for a reason. Now, please."

She shot him a look, and it was clear there would be no arguing with her.

"To be continued?" Haris gave Hena an apologetic look before being carted off.

Khaled was currently eating karahi chicken with Lulu, chatting and laughing. Best man or not, Haris was definitely not needed. Hena knew the real reason his mother gripped him by the elbow, dragging him away while whispering furiously in his ear. She didn't want her son anywhere near Hena. If disappearances were contagious, Hena was Typhoid Mary. Even if Haris didn't blame her for his friend's absence, his mother certainly did.

"Is it just me or is this line not moving?"

Hena startled and turned to see Reza behind her. The handsome man from the check-in counter.

"It's not you. It's really not moving," she told him, grateful for the distraction. "And it probably won't anytime soon."

"Not sure I follow."

"Have you noticed you're the last person in line?" she asked him, and he looked back to confirm it. "It's going to stay that way because everyone else is cutting in."

He peered over her shoulder at the single-file crowd ahead of them. Auntie Hanifa, the meddlesome busybody Hena had known all her life, grabbed a plate and slid in with her friends toward the front of the line. Other aunties and uncles were similarly following suit.

"So we're here for the long haul, huh?"

"The line will move. Eventually."

He shook his head and laughed, and Hena's shoulders unclenched. This man was the definition of smoldering. And the jaw on him . . . she was tempted to reach up and graze it.

"Inquiring minds must know," he said. "How fancy is your VIP suite?"

"Haven't had a chance to swing by it yet."

"My room is nice, don't get me wrong, but I'm guessing yours is out of this world."

"I'll keep you posted," she told him. It was refreshing talking to someone unfamiliar with her baggage. "How are you connected to the groom?"

"I was Khaled's RA his freshman year. We only overlapped a year, but we kept in touch. His taste in nineties music is questionable, but otherwise he's a great guy."

"Well, that's good to hear."

"The timing for this wedding was perfect. I caught my flight right before an ice storm hit Chicago. Floridians are not meant to live in frigid temps."

"You're a Florida boy?"

"Orlando, born and raised." He nodded. "I work for a security firm out there. It's great living on Lake Michigan in the summer, but not so much this time of year."

As the line limped forward, he asked what she did for a living, and she told him she was an interior designer. She helped her clients choose the right paint color for their home spas and indoor theaters and sourced the perfect teak table to go with the century-old Persian rug in their library.

"Do you ever do out-of-town consultations?" he asked.

"You interested?"

"I might be."

A smile played on his lips, and there went her butterflies again, fluttering full steam ahead. They finally made it through the line. Holding her dinner plate, she scanned the crowd. Lulu was with her fiancé and his family. There wasn't a single table Hena felt comfortable joining. A familiar feeling washed over her—loneliness, despite being surrounded by people.

"Join me?" Reza asked. He pointed to a quiet table tucked in the corner.

"Feeling sorry for me?"

"More like I want to keep talking to the prettiest girl in the room."

Shameless flirt. She pushed back a smile at his brazenness. Why not? This would be a long week; she might as well make an ally in this sea of side-eyeing aunties.

He set his plate down and promised to be right back before striding toward the bar to get them drinks. Sitting down, she took a bite of biryani and closed her eyes. All right, *this* she had missed. South Florida eats couldn't be beat.

Just then, a voice cut through the din.

"All I'm saying is, her being here highlights the family's poor judgment in allowing this marriage to happen in the first place."

Hena's eyes flew open. A group of aunties were huddled in a darkened corner of the room, not far from her. She recognized them—including Auntie Nipa, Haris's mother, and of course Auntie Hanifa, the leader of the pack.

"Come now." Auntie Hanifa waved a hand dismissively. "How do you turn down the chance to be in bed with the wealthiest family in town? Who wouldn't want to hitch their star to one of those wagons?"

"Money is good and well, but how did wealth work out for the men in their lives?" Haris's mother set her hands on her hips. "Look at their father. Missing. Nasir. Missing. And by missing, we know what that really means."

"Latif died in a boating accident," said Auntie Gudi.

"So they claim. They found the boat, but did they ever find the body? Exactly. We all know they own the police," Auntie Hanifa said. "Besides, how do you explain Nasir? They couldn't even be bothered to make up a story with him."

"Meanwhile, Hena runs off to California. Couldn't get away fast enough," Auntie Usmana chimed in. "You know she's having an affair with a married man? That's what I heard, anyway."

"Is that right? I'd heard it was a married woman," Auntie Hanifa replied.

Hena suppressed an eye roll. Lulu had said to let her know if anyone was whispering about Hena at this event, but if she were to round up everyone, this would be an empty wedding hall. Besides, she'd heard versions of this all before. She had turned her attention back to her meal when Auntie Hanifa landed the knockout punch.

"She fell pregnant. That's what I heard. Didn't want to keep the baby, so she wanted to flee to California. Easier laws there to take care of that sort of thing. Nasir wouldn't dream of it. He put his foot down, and then, well, I suppose he became inconvenient."

Her mouth parted. This one was new. Completely false— but new. She looked over. They were watching her. They'd made sure she heard. They wanted to see how she'd react.

She kept her expression impassive as she stood up. They could say whatever they wanted, but she was done listening.

"Leaving already?" Reza was back with drinks in hand.

"I've lost my appetite."

She looked at him. Hesitated. She'd spent her whole life caring what everyone here thought. But taking in his full mouth and his warm gaze, she felt a rush of boldness.

"Think you can be discreet?" she asked.

He tilted his head. "What do you have in mind?"

"Want to check out my suite firsthand?" She reached into her purse, and pulled out her keycard. "Fourth floor. Private entrance. Finish your meal and join me?"

"Ah." A grin tugged at his mouth, as he took it from her. "I would love that."

She walked over to Lulu. Let her sister know she was exhausted—and she was. It took a lot of energy to pretend that the eyes shooting daggers her way didn't actually feel like they were piercing her.

Her eyes met Reza's, and he gave a subtle nod. She turned the corner and headed down the hallway to the elevators.

One day down. Seven more to go.

MUNAZZA,
Aunt of the Groom

"You want to know about Nasir? Where do I begin? That boy was not just the joy of his family, he was the pride of his community. From the moment he took his first steps to the time he graduated summa cum laude from Princeton University and became a top investment banker at Perth International, he'd had the world at his fingertips. And I'm only being honest here: He could have had his pick of any woman he wanted for his wife.

When he told us he planned to marry the Mirza girl, his mother fainted then and there.

We warned him. He was such a good boy. Kind and thoughtful. Tall, dark, and handsome like his father. We reminded him what everyone here knows—that the Mirza women's reputations precede them. Look at their dear father, who mysteriously vanished. It wasn't a boating accident. Come, now. We saw them around town after he'd gone missing—they carried on like it was business as usual. Hena was seventeen, and she didn't even cry. Not once.

We told Nasir all of this. Begged him to reconsider. He was immune to our pleas. She was the love of his life and that was that. Nothing can stop true love, right? The poor dear. One evening he's dancing at his mehndi, and then—poof—gone. She claimed she didn't know what happened to him, but one look at her and you knew she was lying. And can you believe they actually tried painting Hena as the victim, what with all that drama at the boathouse the next evening? Such a commotion. What was it meant to prove? It was just a distraction and it didn't work. We all know she fled town because she couldn't face what she'd done.

Because let's be honest: When it comes to the Mirza family, nothing is ever as simple as it seems. "

DAY
TWO

4

．

I t turned out Reza did, in fact, just want to check out Hena's room.

Resting her head against the car window, she fought back a yawn the next morning. While the rest of the wedding guests were grabbing breakfast and preparing to head to South Beach for an art deco architecture tour, she sat in the passenger seat of Khala Simki's Toyota Camry, being ferried to Luxe Boutique for her mandatory shopping spree. Her mother sat in the back with her home health aide, Gita, and the car was blessedly silent. Watching the scenery flit past, Hena's thoughts drifted back to last night.

She had never hooked up with a stranger before, but there was a first time for everything. And Reza, with his perfect bone structure and crooked grin, was an ideal candidate. When he knocked on her door and she let him into the foyer, it took everything she had to not draw him to her then and there. She'd restrained herself. Opted to give him the promised tour first. They'd end up where they needed to be.

Vista Del Sol's VIP suite was opulent enough to rival any Hena had ever stayed at. The arabesque touches were ever present here, from the brass fixtures and polished maroon walls to the latticework tracing the ceiling and plush rugs with dizzying geometric patterns. A trio of gold-framed abstract paintings hung above the sofa, their spiraled tilework of red, silver, and gold seeming to shift and swirl of its own accord.

Reza trailed behind her as they walked through the space. He took special note of the chandeliers (tasteful) and the grain of the hardwood floors (high-end). He even knelt and ran a hand along the baseboards, then tapped a knuckle against the wall. "Solid," he said, nodding with approval.

They swung past the kitchen, which would never be used but nevertheless featured stainless steel appliances and marble countertops, before sneaking a peek at the bathroom with its heated floors and rainfall shower. At last, they ended up in the bedroom.

"So this is what luxury looks like." He set her keycard on the nightstand.

Luxury was an understatement. The custom California king was enclosed beneath a thick velvet canopy, its curtains drawn back and tied to each post with tasseled cords. The scent of jasmine clung to the air. Hena traced a hand along the linen embroidery stitched with intricate looping designs.

"Frette," she said with surprise. "My favorite brand."

Could Lulu possibly have remembered?

"You have a favorite brand of bedsheets?"

"Doesn't everyone?"

Reza took a step toward her, his eyes crinkled. "I think I speak from a place of authority that most people definitely do not."

He stood so close she could smell the sandalwood of his aftershave. See the subtle hint of stubble along his jaw. She should have felt apprehensive. Instead, she wanted nothing more than to erase the space between them. But before she could touch him, his gaze shifted over her shoulder.

"I completely missed the balcony."

He strode toward the French doors, opened them and stepped outside. She joined him as he rested his elbows on the railing. The deafening symphony of the swamp—frogs croaking, birds chirping, and the incessant buzzing of unseen insects—filled the night sky.

"You've got total privacy here," he said. "My room overlooks the parking lot."

Hena took in the bougainvillea creeping across the terrace and stole a glance at his profile. What just happened? One minute they were talking about bedsheets, his eyes fixed on hers—and the next, they were looking at the marsh. Had she been out of the game so long she could no longer read the signals?

But the more they chatted, the more her awkwardness faded. As familiar as these swamplands were to her, they were unexplored terrain for Reza, having grown up in a tract home in the suburbs of Orlando.

"Sorry to say, but Orlando is the worst that Florida has to offer," she told him. "Landlocked and ten degrees hotter, no matter the time of year."

"We've got the theme parks, don't we?" he protested. At her side-eye, he laughed. "Fair point."

"I'm just saying, you have the same mosquitoes, the same humidity—but without ocean views or a breeze to make up for any of it."

"I can't argue with that." He grinned, and she tried not to stare too hard at the dimple deepening in his left cheek.

"Are you going to swing by and see your family while you're in Florida?" she asked. "Orlando's, what, three hours from here?"

"It's just my sister and her family there these days," he said. "My mom passed away when I was nine, and I don't really keep in touch with my dad. I should try to head up there, though. It's been a minute since I've seen my nephew."

"I'm sorry about your mother," she said. "I was older—seventeen—when my father died. It was forever ago at this point, but in some ways, I feel like I'm still processing that he's actually gone."

"Right. It's like they're still with you in some way. Though if my mother were here right now, she'd be dragging me back indoors."

"She was scared of the dark?"

"She was scared of jinn."

"Ah yes. The unseen. Of course."

"She took it seriously." He laughed. "She said nighttime was when the veil between our world and theirs was thinnest. You never know when they're listening."

An owl hooted in the distance, deep and mournful, but with the moon shrouded in clouds, she saw nothing but darkness. Feeling his gaze on her, she looked back.

"Do you believe in them?" she asked him.

"No," he said quickly, then ran a finger along his jaw. "I mean, maybe? It's not like you can prove they *don't* exist, right?"

"True. Hard to prove a negative. I guess they could be out there, but honestly, there's so much I *know* to worry about that the unseen gets bumped down my list of fears."

"That's the appeal. Better to be afraid of what you can't see than think too hard about what you can. She died when I was so young, her stories stuck. It's a good thing she'd already debunked the tooth fairy, or who knows?"

He grinned and the softness in his eyes made her breath hitch.

It was easy to talk to him. So easy she barely noticed the hours tick past until pink and lavender streaked across the horizon. But the only time he touched her was before he left—when he thanked her for her company and lifted her hand to kiss it as though they were starring in a Jane Austen adaptation. She pretended the warmth of his lips didn't send shivers through her. Didn't make her want to squeeze his hand tighter and draw him closer. A man like Reza was probably accustomed to women reduced to putty in his presence.

It was just as well. Adding potential drama to what would already be an exhausting week wasn't the wisest strategy. At least there would be a friendly face to chat with during her time here.

"Finally! It took long enough." Her mother's voice rang out from the back seat, dragging Hena into the present. "You drive as slow as ever, Simki."

"I'm following the speed limit," Khala replied, pulling into the parking lot and turning off the engine. "The police around here can be sticklers. You know that."

"I personally think we made good time," said Gita, her mother's aide. "This part of town can get so congested."

Hena surveyed the scene. Except for a Ford Explorer next to a fitness studio two doors down, theirs was the only car there.

"Are you sure this boutique is even open?" she asked. It was early—barely nine in the morning.

"Of course it's open," her mother snapped. "Muni came in three hours early so we could get this matter sorted straightaway."

That tracked. Who would dare say no to her mother?

Khala and Hena got out of the car while Gita retrieved the

wheelchair from the trunk. She was around Hena's age, and effortlessly plucked the steel chair free, setting it on the pavement.

"Stay where you are," Gita warned as Ammi began opening the passenger door. "I'll be there in a second."

"I'm perfectly capable of walking a few paces," her mother retorted.

Except she wasn't. She took one step and lurched forward, but Gita swooped in and stopped the fall, gripping her by the elbow and easing her into the chair.

"I certainly don't need to be strapped in," her mother protested as Gita picked up the seat belt.

"I can't have you flying out, can I?" Gita retorted. "No arguments. Safety first."

Here we go, Hena thought. She waited for her mother's eyes to narrow. For her to fire Gita on the spot. Instead, her mother chuckled.

"I'm seeing things," Hena said as she and Khala walked up the steps to the shop. "I must be. How can anyone talk to her like that and not get swatted at the very least?"

"Gita's a gem," Khala said. "I can't explain it, but she has a way with your mother."

"There must be sorcery of some sort involved."

Gita set Ammi's purse in the back storage pouch, secured the oxygen tank holder, and adjusted her breathing tubes. Looking at her mother, a knot of grief formed in Hena's throat.

She's dying, Hena reminded herself. All of this—the wheelchair, the oxygen tank—was to be expected. Still, her mind struggled to accept it. How had the fierce woman she'd known all her life transformed into this fragile figure?

Turning to Khala, Hena leaned closer.

"What is Ammi thinking, coming out here?" she asked.

"You and I could have sorted this out ourselves. She's in no condition."

"Gita cleared it. Your mother wanted to spend time with you."

"Let's try that again."

"It's what she said," Khala insisted. "Things are complicated between you two, but she loves you, Hena."

First Lulu. Now Khala. Hena wished so badly it were true, but the reality was, the only thing her mother loved was control—especially over her children. When Hena was a baby and not yet something her mother could tame, she'd been off-loaded to her aunt. She'd spent the first five years of her life in Khala's flamingo-pink duplex in Cooper City. That's how much her mother had cared. The official family lore claimed times were tough. Her parents needed Hena properly cared for while they got their first hotel off the ground. It had been for the best. Those first years with Khala were the happiest of her childhood.

A bell chimed overhead as they stepped into the store.

"Be there in a moment!" the store owner called out from a back room.

The interior was larger than it appeared from the outside. Floating shelves were stacked with neatly folded, colorful saris, and mannequins modeled elaborate bridal gowns in the center of the room.

Khala watched Gita adjust the unwieldy oxygen tank by the ramp outside the store. She turned to Hena, her eyes lined with concern.

"How have you been?" She lowered her voice. "Any updates about Nasir?"

Hena tensed. It was one thing to breeze through the topic over the phone from the other side of the country—another to talk about it face-to-face, mere miles from ground zero.

Her brief conversation with Haris the night before had reminded her how fragile her defenses were. One wrong nudge and they could all come crashing down.

"You'd be the first to know if there was any news," she told her aunt. "The police don't even update me anymore about there being no updates. I think they've written it off."

"That's ridiculous. Nasir going missing is bad enough, but they should have at least figured out who broke into your bridal suite the night after. The way that man attacked you . . . it was obviously connected to Nasir." She shook her head. "I'll never understand how hundreds of people missed a masked man skulking about."

"The police said whoever it was had probably been lying in wait for some time," Hena reminded her. "The back window was unlocked, and he spray-painted the security cameras, remember?"

Red. He'd sprayed them red. Like the blood dripping from his midsection. A trail leading to the woods before dissolving into the swamp. The police believed him long dead. The waters he'd fled through were vast—full of alligators, pythons, and water moccasins. Even with the DNA evidence, no one—not the police, not the private investigator her mother hired—had found a single lead.

"I'm sorry, Hena. You deserve closure." Khala rested a hand on her arm.

The bell chimed again as her mother and Gita entered the store, halting their conversation. Hena was grateful. Because the truth was, not everything needed closure. Some questions were better left unanswered.

"Greetings!" The store owner, Muni, hurried toward them. Moments later they were escorted to a dressing room in the back. Thirty glittering outfits—saris, ghararas, lenghas, and kurtas—hung from hooks. Hena inwardly groaned. She would've been fine grabbing a few things in her size and calling it a day, but she'd agreed to come. It was no use arguing now. Best to get this over with as soon as possible.

But as she tried on the selections—and the other clothes Muni continually added to the queue at her mother's direction—she began to understand why attention to detail was absolutely necessary. Lulu said the wedding party outfits didn't need to be identical, but from mandatory pastels for that afternoon's bridal shower to silver and copper tones for the dholki, she'd outlined the group's color coordination with obsessive precision.

"That lengha looks perfect for the mayoun," her mother said as Hena stepped out in her sixteenth outfit of the morning—a flowing, pale blue floral pattern with a chiffon overlay.

"I personally think a deeper blue might suit her complexion better," Gita said. "It would still be in keeping with the seaside theme."

Hena tensed. Giving input on her mother's wheelchair safety was one thing—but offering opinions on outfits? Even Hena wasn't weighing in. Her mother had micromanaged her wardrobe all the way from childhood until she'd left for college.

She waited for Ammi to strike, but instead her mother gave Hena an appraising look.

"You might be right," she said.

Hena glanced at Khala, who shrugged. So miracles did happen. Gita's easy confidence with her mother was astonishing. She really was the perfect caregiver.

Three hours and thirteen new outfits later, she headed to the counter. Before she could reach for her purse, Gita swerved past her, nearly knocking her over as she wheeled Ammi to the register. Handing Hena's mother her wallet, she gave Hena an apologetic shrug.

Gita didn't need to apologize. This was classic Ammi. From the outside, it might look like love—a mother wanting to provide for her daughter. But Hena knew better. It wasn't about love. It was about control.

Driving back toward the resort, her mother leaned forward from the back seat.

"The bridesmaids are wearing peach today," her mother said. "Make sure you get yours to the steamer right away."

"She didn't need to tack me on to the bridal party," Hena said.

"Don't be silly," Ammi replied. "We don't want tongues wagging about you two not getting along."

"Lulu and I are fine."

"Doesn't matter. When enough people say a thing is true, it becomes true, doesn't it? Best not to make too fine a point of the fact that you weren't invited from the start."

Ouch. But fair point. Speaking of bridesmaids—

"I was surprised to see Irum," Hena said. "Someone could have warned me she'd be here."

"Why wouldn't she be here?" her mother retorted. "The two girls leaned on each other after the tragedy. You know the poor thing had a complete breakdown after the situation with Nasir?"

"Her poor mother." Khala clucked her tongue. "That was a difficult time."

"Irum got it in her head someone was hiding something," her mother said. "She'd taken to interrogating people at dinners. Accused them of acting suspiciously. It was awful. Hanifa tried to reason with her at a party early on, gently tried to tell her that she was embarrassing herself, and Irum slapped her! They had to admit her into a wellness center. She's all better now, but it was tough going for a few months."

"Oh, Irum." Hena's voice softened. "I had no idea."

"Why would you?" her mother retorted. "Seeing how you ran as far from us as you could."

There it was. The gut punch. She should've braced for it—but could anyone, really?

"Frida, come, now," Khala said, chiding her sister through the rearview mirror before giving Hena a sympathetic look. "It must've been jarring to see her."

"Jarring or not, it's a wise strategic move to put Irum in a prominent wedding position." Ammi coughed. "The fewer whispers, the better. Her presence shows there are no hard feelings between our families."

Her coughing worsened. Gita patted her back.

No hard feelings? Nasir's mother made clear her opinion of Hena to anyone who asked. And Irum hadn't exactly seemed thrilled to see her last night.

Khala's eyes flicked to Hena's, afraid she was going to push back, but there was no need to intervene. Hena was already surrendering. If keeping her mouth shut brought her mother peace in her final days, so be it.

Hena picked up one of the bags at her feet. She pulled out the folded pastel shalwar kamiz. She hadn't so much as touched a desi outfit since leaving Florida. She'd forgotten how pretty desi clothes could be. She began to remove the stapled tag and say thank you. Regardless of her mother's motives, this was nice. But before she could speak, her mother did.

"I suppose it's best we get this out of the way," said Ammi. "I've received confirmation from Khaled's family that Nasir's parents have been invited to the shaadi."

The staple pricked Hena's finger. It was the same spot as the paper cut from three days earlier. A drop of blood welled.

"I know it's not ideal," her mother continued, "but Khaled's father is Nasir's cousin once removed on his mother's side, so there was no way around it, I'm afraid. I don't expect they'll actually attend, but if they do, I need you to stay away from them. There's no telling how they'll react, but we certainly don't want to risk you upsetting them and causing a scene."

Hena pressed a tissue to her finger. One might think a mother would worry more about her daughter in a hypothetical scenario like this. But then, they wouldn't have known Hena's mother.

Khala patted her arm. *Your ammi loves you.* This had always been her refrain. *Blood is blood. A mother can no more choose not to love her child than she can choose not to breathe.*

Hena wasn't so sure. She remembered the curbside drop-off at the airport when she was heading to Princeton University. Ammi's hands tight on the steering wheel as she admonished Hena to study. To not waste the opportunity. There had been no words of endearment. No emotional embrace. Hena tried to remember a time when her mother had hugged her with tenderness or said she loved her.

She couldn't.

Khala might never have married or had children, but she had been more a mother to Hena than the woman who birthed her. It was for Khala's sake Hena stayed quiet now, afraid of what she might say if she didn't.

And the truth was, if Nasir's parents actually came to the shaadi—if she had to face his mother again—then she had far bigger problems waiting for her.

LUBNA,
Aunt of the Groom

66 It was the flashing blue and white lights that caught our attention. We knew the festivities were delayed, but we hadn't thought anything of it. After all, what sort of desi wedding doesn't run behind schedule?

The police presence at the Mirza residence that evening, though—those cars parked all over the grassy lawn by their family boathouse, where Hena was getting ready for the wedding—well, that changed everything.

We rushed over—to see if we could help, of course. We were nearly at the door when Shaheen, poor dear, shoved past me so roughly I nearly lost my footing. She was trembling head to toe. Irum, her daughter, was by her side.

While police officers crawled all over the place, Hena sat on the sofa, staring at absolutely nothing. We assumed Shaheen had rushed over to check on her. Comfort her. Instead, she surveyed the scene: the officers, the blood droplets splattered on the floor. She marched straight over to a mustachioed detective bagging a reddish-brown knife and jabbed an angry red fingernail in Hena's direction.

"My son is missing. No one has heard from him since last night," she said, her voice catching. "Whatever happened here is connected. And mark my words, she's behind it."

To be fair, Shaheen never made secret her dislike of Hena. When Nasir announced his intentions to marry her, she'd locked herself in her room for a full week, refusing to eat or drink. We knew she disapproved, but the particular fury she unleashed in the boathouse that day? It still makes me shudder. Irum, bless that sweet girl, tried to talk her mother down, but it was like trying to reason with a hurricane.

Here's where things got interesting. Moments later, Hena's mother arrived. She heard Shaheen going on and on with her accusations. I expected Frida to cut her off. To order her off the premises immediately.

Let me tell you: She did neither of these things.

Instead, she walked up to Shaheen and hugged her. Yes, that's right. Hugged her. I swear it on my grandchild's life.

So tell me, can you blame us for our suspicions? How innocent can a woman be when her own mother won't stand by her side?

PLEASE JOIN US TO CELEBRATE
THE BRIDE-TO-BE

Luma Mirza

AT HER

BRIDAL SHOWER

VISTA DEL SOL

345 EUCLID DRIVE

EVERMERE, FLORIDA

Saturday, January 10, at 3:00 p.m.

Cypress Terrace

Attire: pastel

Please note:
The couple is registered at
NEIMAN MARCUS

5

·

Hena had wondered how Lulu was going to keep the wedding events distinct when every single one took place at the same resort, but she shouldn't have underestimated her little sister. Unlike the welcome party, which had taken place in the dining hall, the bridal shower was set on the resort's oversized back patio, flanked with lush, towering palm trees. Round tables draped in pastel linens sat beneath a covered awning adorned with lights and woven through with pale pink flowers. It was well done. Tasteful.

She did her best to ignore the humidity. Thick and heavy. Pressing against her skin.

Hena placed her present on the gift table. It was the only one there, a result of her first misstep of the afternoon: She was on time. Not only was she currently the sole guest in attendance, the venue was still being set up. A dark-haired man in a red uniform—she recognized him as the bellhop who'd collected her things when she'd first arrived—was crouched next to the fondue machine, fixing the wiring. A team of three silently arranged finger sandwiches and cakes on golden tiers for the afternoon's high-tea theme. Two women whispered among themselves as they adjusted the personalized perfume bar, the clear vials set in neat, even rows.

Hena traced a finger along the golden GIFTS sign. Her own shower had been a simple affair. Her aunt had thrown it for her at her duplex. Even now, she could close her eyes and remember the scent of cardamom tea wafting from the kitchen as everyone gave their pointed opinions on the gifts, from the stainless steel cooking spoons to the high-end bed-sheets. They'd laughed at Auntie Gudi presenting Hena with an enormous cooking pot, insisting all new brides needed to know how to cook dinner for a party of fifty.

Hena felt a pang at the memories of her wedding week. They'd been curdled by all that followed.

The glass doors slid open, and Hena stiffened when she saw who it was: Irum, wearing a peach-colored chiffon shal-war kamiz, an Alexander McQueen skull pendant resting against her collarbone.

She held an oversized wicker basket filled with party fa-vors in one hand while scrolling on her phone with the other. Nearing the gift table, she spotted Hena and paused mid-step.

"Oh. Hey," Irum said, her discomfort written across her face.

It hadn't always been like this. Hena had known Irum since she was a baby. Irum had visited their home practically every weekend, raiding Hena's closet alongside Lulu.

She'd been thrilled about Hena and Nasir—the only member of his family who had been pleased. Hena remem-bered Irum's occasional visits to Princeton when she was barely twelve. How the three of them would wander the cam-pus, skip rocks at Lake Carnegie, and grab ice cream from the Bent Spoon. At night Irum crashed in Hena's dorm room, confiding her crushes to Hena like they were sisters. Because they nearly had been. Had life turned out differently, Irum would have been family.

But a lot had changed since then.

Hena steeled herself. As awkward as this moment was, they needed to talk. Better now, without guests to observe them and turn it into fodder for gossip.

"It's good to see you," Hena said. "I'm sorry about last night. I'd come off a long flight, and I was thrown. Of course you'd be here. You should be here."

"Lulu should have given both of us a heads-up."

Hena was about to ask how she was doing, but Irum spoke again.

"Have you heard from my brother? Since . . . you know?"

The way she said *my brother*, her eyes growing bright, made Hena ache. Irum had always adored her big brother. Idolized him.

"I saw him at the mehndi. The night before the shaadi," Hena said, repeating the same words she'd told the officers and anyone who asked. Saying it to Irum though, a pit formed in her stomach. "I wish I had a better answer. I'm sorry."

"Why are you sorry?" Her expression shifted. "Not like you had anything to do with it. Right?"

Her mother's words echoed in Hena's mind: *Irum got it in her head someone was hiding something.*

Given the general consensus of Hena's complicity in whatever happened to Nasir, of course Irum would treat her as suspect number one. And Hena *was* hiding something. If only the truth was an option.

Before Hena could reply, Irum's cheeks flushed.

"That came out wrong," she said. "I'm working on it. Weddings are triggering for me. My mother says maybe it'd be easier to move on if I just accepted he's dead."

Dead? Hena shivered.

"I don't believe that. Not for a second," Hena said. "The police said there was no sign of foul play. Between the emptied accounts, his clothes and luggage gone . . . I don't know where he went"—this part, at least, was true—"but there's no reason to think he isn't out there. I'm not sure I can live in a world where he isn't."

"But Nasir leaving without telling *anyone*?" Disbelief flashed across her face. "You know him. He wouldn't do that."

There's a lot I didn't know, Hena thought. *Not when he was so good at hiding things.*

"One day whatever happened will come out." Irum's mouth pressed tight. "When we finally get answers, whoever did this will pay."

She's a gulab jamun wrapped in a marshmallow and dipped in cotton candy. That's how Nasir used to describe his kid sister. He wasn't wrong. But three years could change many things. Three years of grieving could sharpen anyone's edges.

Irum set the party favors on the table and cleared her throat.

"How are you handling the gossip? It's been a lot, hasn't it?" she asked.

Hena grimaced. "Are people bothering you?"

"It's more faux concern about how I'm holding up. With the two of us here, they're itching for something to happen." She rolled her eyes. "It's going to be a long week."

"People can be ruthless."

"It is what it is. But I say we give them nothing to talk about."

"Yeah?" Hena exhaled. "I'd like that."

Irum's expression warmed. "Good," she said.

One of the perfume hostesses hurried over. There was a snafu with one of the scents. Irum excused herself to help, but they promised to catch up later.

Hena drifted to the terrace. Below her stretched mani-cured gardens, a winding path, a hedge maze just across from her.

Maybe now was the perfect chance to slip away and check out the grounds before the festivities began.

She stepped onto the raised wooden boardwalk running along the edge of the property, a dividing line between two worlds. To her right lay the manicured resort; to her left stretched the swamp—dark and untamed, rolling into the horizon.

Something tightened in her chest at the sight. This was the backdrop she'd grown up with. How many times had she wandered to the marshy water behind her childhood home, plucking reeds like these, thick along the murky shallows? Tucked a spider lily behind her ear?

This place set her teeth on edge. But it was also home.

Farther up, she walked past a metal dock glinting against the sun. A rowboat was tied loosely to its side. The water was deeper here. Darker.

Taking in the property from this vantage point, the glitzy venue seemed so big it felt like it could have its own zip code. She passed three pools, a white-fenced butterfly garden tucked near the parking lot, and a koi pond set toward the back of the premises.

As she walked, her thoughts drifted to her conversation with Irum. She was relieved they'd had a chance to clear the air early on. They hadn't seen each other since that fateful evening in the boathouse. When Irum held her own mother back, tried to talk her down from her torrent of accusations against Hena. This had always been Irum's role in Hena's relationship with Nasir—the peacemaker. When their parents had threatened to disown him, it was Irum who had intervened. Who pushed them to let it go.

It wasn't that his parents had an issue with Hena specifically—more so her family. Wealthy though they might have been, the Mirzas were not respectable in his parents' eyes, having accrued their money through a hotel business rather than something prestigious, like Nasir's father, a vascular surgeon. Hena, they had told him, was not part of the plan.

But Nasir hadn't been part of hers either.

Her goal for college had been simple: to get as far from this place and these people as possible. Princeton's campus, with its Gothic buildings and crimson fall leaves, was the perfect place to escape the never-ending summer of her past.

She couldn't have predicted how lonely she would feel four weeks in, clutching her tray in Frist's food hall, questioning everything. Or that she'd spot Nasir across the room having dinner with friends. That their eyes would meet. That he would smile.

Until then, she'd only seen him as the boy who played football with Haris at childhood potluck parties. Her sister's friend's brother. She hadn't expected him to wave her over. Hadn't expected a friendship to bloom—or for their friendship to grow into something more. Nasir wasn't just the gentlest soul she'd ever known; he had been the first person who made her feel like she didn't have to run from who she was. Who saw her, flaws and all, and loved her anyway. They'd been together nine years. Most of those years were good. The best she'd known. Because she hadn't known what lay beneath the surface—that their foundation was built upon a lie.

The leaves of the mangroves rustled in the distance. Hena shivered. Not for the first time, she wondered: What if she'd declined his invitation all those years ago? What if she could've undone everything that followed?

The boardwalk curved before abruptly ending at a trailhead, where a tilted wooden sign showed an illustrated map of the property. Ten different paths branched off from there, winding past brush and trees. She studied the map as a door at the far end of the resort slid open.

Haris stepped onto the grassy lawn, phone to his ear. When he hung up, he stretched and spotted her. She waved him over.

"Taking a hike?" he asked as he approached.

"Tempted, but not the best idea in these heels." She pointed to her four-inch Aquazzuras.

"Good thinking. Plus, the trails will be crawling with alligators this time of year."

She was pretty sure she'd take her chances with the alligators over the aunties. Though—

"You sure you're okay talking to me?" she teased. "I don't think your mother would approve."

He winced. "I'm sorry about that. I've had a talk with her."

"She's always been super protective of you."

"Doesn't make it right. I hope that's not why you skipped the South Beach outing this morning. This is your family wedding. No one should make you feel unwelcome."

"That's sweet of you, but no. I was busy." She gestured to her outfit. "Apparently the clothes I'd packed weren't cutting it."

He gave her outfit a quick once-over, then met her eyes. "You look nice."

"Thanks." She reached up and straightened the collar of his olive button-down. "Not to be the bearer of bad news, but I'm afraid today's bridal shower theme is pastel. Lulu's a stickler for keeping to theme."

"No men allowed at the bridal shower," he said. "Us menfolk will be at the bro-dal shower. No dress code for us, far as I know."

"The *what?*"

"Right? We gave Khaled shit for it. It's really just a barbecue. Poker table, big screen for the Dolphins game."

Segregated events. It made sense, but she still felt a pinch of disappointment. Between Reza and Haris, at least she had some camaraderie with the groomsmen.

"We'll be competing for best toilet paper wedding dress, so I'm officially jealous of you," she told him.

"Join us?" he offered. "The Dolphins could use all the cheering they can get. It's been a rough season."

"I don't think I've seen a football game since—" She stopped herself.

"Nasir got us great box seats to that game, didn't he?" He smiled.

"And then spent the night complaining we were too far from the action."

"If we were any closer, they'd have kicked us out. For such a clearheaded finance guy, he had no chill when it came to that team."

"He really didn't." She brightened at the memory.

Nasir had been the extrovert in their relationship—always pulling her out for rooftop parties, last-minute concerts, sports events where they barely knew the rules but cheered like superfans. Once they'd moved back to Florida, Haris joined whenever he could—a steady presence, ready to drive her home when Nasir wasn't quite ready to call it a night. But her favorite moments were when she and Haris tag-teamed to convince Nasir to grab takeout and spend the evening at home. Memories of movie nights on the couch came rushing back. The meandering conversations that went deep into the night.

"You know, I still try his number sometimes," Haris said.

"You . . . you do?"

"His father refuses to disconnect his phone line. It goes straight to voicemail, of course, but I keep hoping one of these days he'll answer. Tell me what the hell happened. That he's okay."

Hena had developed a careful stoicism about that time in her life. She had to. It was the only way to keep going. But it was one thing to hold back her memories while discussing the ideal meditation room with a client—another to be back here among the familiar saw grass and salty sea air. Here, she could feel time compressing, the numbness fading. Grief prickling back to the surface. She'd spoken more of Nasir in the past twenty-four hours than she had in three years. It was like memories of the man she loved lingered around every corner.

"I'll never make sense of it." Haris stared out at the swamp. "One morning we're deep-sea fishing at his bachelor party, taking photos of him with the three-hundred-pound blue marlin he caught. Twenty-four hours later, he's emptied his bank account and he's just . . . gone."

It's not a crime to not want to be found, Milcheck—the detective—had said. He'd gone through the motions, though, and come up empty.

"I hired a private investigator," Haris continued. "My law firm has one on retainer. Figured if the police were going to write it off, we had to go harder."

"My mother hired someone too," Hena said. "No leads."

"But people don't just disappear. We leave digital trails. Cash runs out eventually. I can't help but wonder, with the stuff he was involved in . . ." He trailed off.

Oh. She looked at him. "You—you knew?"

"He was my closest friend." He gave her a small smile. "Yeah, I knew."

Some of the tension in her body eased. Of course Haris

knew. He was one of the few people who understood how complicated Nasir was. She was tempted to find out just how much Haris was aware of, but she'd tapped this bruise enough for one day.

"Sorry for bringing it up," he said. "Like you don't have enough going on."

"You're not bringing anything up that's not always in the back of my mind. And hey, at least you're not blaming me like everyone else around here does."

He grimaced. "This community can be the worst sometimes."

"I knew what I was getting into . . . but yeah, it's bad enough to miss him, but then to be treated like I had something to do with it? It's a lot."

Haris wordlessly pulled her into a hug. His warmth, his steadiness—it felt good, and for a second, she let herself lean into it.

"Thanks," she whispered when she pulled back.

"Do you still have his cat?" he asked.

"Roscoe? Of course. He turned five last week." She pulled out her phone and showed him photos of the oversized tabby.

"Hold up." He paused at the most recent one. "Did you really stick a birthday hat on that poor creature?"

"Of course I did. Five is a milestone year! Nasir would approve. He had a whole collection of hats for Roscoe."

"Roscoe hated every single one."

"Too bad he looks adorable in them. Remember the one Nasir got him for his first birthday?"

"The crown?" He laughed. "He had that true-to-life Roscoe cake commissioned too. Poor cat saw it and freaked out. Hid under the bed the rest of the evening."

"Nasir was so disappointed we couldn't get a group picture with him."

Haris's eyes softened as he scrolled through the photos. It wasn't easy to think of Nasir, but it was comforting to talk about him with someone who loved him too.

The scent of barbecue-tinged smoke drifted over, and Haris looked toward the resort.

"Time for me to join the festivities," he said. "I'll see you at tomorrow's airboat excursion?"

"I thought tomorrow was the tour of Las Olas?"

"The wedding party is going on an airboat outing. It's supposed to be some kind of bonding exercise or something."

"Wonderful." Hena sighed.

He waved goodbye. As she watched him walk away, something rustled behind her. She turned in time to see a rabbit—scruffy and gray—poke its head from the brush. It bounded across one of the pathways, growing smaller before rounding the bend. She pictured the alligators lurking along the trail and shivered.

Glancing at the path leading back to the bridal shower, she drew in a long breath. She had her own alligators to contend with, didn't she?

But she had chosen to come. She chose to stay. Icy stares be damned.

6

By the time Hena returned to the bridal shower, the patio was crawling with wedding guests. True to their marching orders, the women around her wore frocks, saris, and shalwar kamizes in varying shades of lavender, pink, periwinkle, and baby blue.

In contrast to the sea of pastels, Lulu wore a low-necked cream kurta and matching tights. Her hair was pulled back in a loose, stylish braid, brown strands framing her glowing face. As uncomfortable as Hena felt about the glances cast in her direction, she couldn't help but brighten at the sight of her sister. Lulu was a beautiful bride.

The bridesmaids ushered guests through the carefully choreographed order of events. Though the bridal shower games were as excruciating as Hena had anticipated—"pass the bridal bouquet" hot potato, toilet paper wedding dresses, and "pin the kiss on the groom"—they kept her distracted. So distracted, in fact, it wasn't until they broke for food that she realized her mother wasn't there.

She found Khala by the punch bowl.

"Where's Ammi?" she asked.

"The morning outing took a lot out of her," Khala said. "She's resting."

"She's not joining for even a little while?"

"She wanted to, but Gita said she should take it easy. A bit of weakness is all."

There was no way her mother was feeling just "a bit" of weakness. "Grit your teeth and push through" might as well have been Ammi's ethos. It's what she told Hena when she dragged her to tennis practice with a twisted ankle. Insisted Hena deliver the school assembly speech despite a raging fever in seventh grade. She had been so concerned with appearances that the night of Hena's wedding, when her world had effectively ended at their family boathouse, Ammi had swept past her to comfort Nasir's mother instead. Hena had understood the gesture—an attempt to placate, to prevent a bigger scene—but it hadn't worked. It had only made the gossip grow louder.

"I don't know why Gita cleared her to come to the shop. Anyone could tell it was too much for her," Hena muttered.

"She wanted to be there," Khala said. "Besides, there will be plenty of other events for her to attend."

Courtney, one of the bridesmaids, clinked a crystal glass and invited everyone to join the bridal party at the gift-opening area. Hena took a seat in the second row of chairs facing Lulu.

Gift time meant the end was near, and all things considered, it hadn't been too bad. The guests seemed to have gotten over the shock of her attendance, and while there were still whispers and lingering looks, things felt calmer now. She was grateful for it.

Courtney handed out party favors—Tiffany key chains engraved with the couple's initials and wedding date. Irum handed Lulu her presents one at a time to open.

"Cartier earrings?" Lulu exclaimed, unwrapping the first gift. "Khala, thank you!"

She gave their aunt a big hug. In fact, after every gift—the custom cutting board, the Le Creuset cookware, a Vitamix blender, an artisanal tea set—Lulu walked over to personally thank and embrace each person.

Then she opened a box, bit back a laugh, and lifted up a sexy black negligee.

"All right, which one of you got me this?"

"That's from me!" Auntie Dilsha called from the back row, setting off a chorus of laughter. "Tradition mandates the bride be mortified by her elder aunties."

"No need to be shy," Auntie Hanifa called out from the front row. "We were all young once."

The gifts dwindled. A spa basket. An iron skillet. A set of knives that made Lulu shriek with joy and turn to Irum.

"These are the Imperion handcrafted ones I told you about!" she cried, reading the card. "I didn't even have them on the registry!"

"Because giving knives to someone on their wedding is bad luck," Auntie Nipa said, shaking her head.

"That's a silly superstition." Lulu scoffed. "If a blender is fine, why can't a knife be?"

Hena suppressed a smile. Lulu lived to cook, and whether or not she ever opened a restaurant, knives were the perfect gift for her. She'd given Hena a set of Shun knives for her own wedding.

One of those knives had saved her life.

Lulu opened each gift until only one remained—Hena's. She unwrapped the striped paper and paused before lifting up the gold necklace with its blue-and-white evil-eye charm. A flicker of nerves shot through Hena when Lulu's gaze found hers.

"Is this the same one?" she asked.

Hena nodded, relieved she hadn't forgotten. Lulu could buy herself anything, so Hena had gone for nostalgia. Their mother had bought both of them these identical necklaces shortly after their father died. It was a silly superstition that the charm could ward off evil, their mother had said. Still, she had insisted they wear them. Given how young Lulu had been, she'd snapped hers in half on the school playground the next day. They'd searched the area in vain. Lulu had wept. Begged for a new one. She'd wanted it to keep her safe, but their mother had refused. She had also refused to allow Hena to give Lulu hers.

Carelessness has consequences, she had said.

Lulu's fingers grazed the delicate gold.

"Thanks," she said.

No hug. No effusive praise. Which was fine. A gift wasn't about the giver, and truthfully, Hena should've given it to her sister long ago. Better late than never. As much as she didn't believe in amulets, she hoped it would keep Lulu safe as she began her new life with Khaled.

"Thank you all for coming," Courtney said as Lulu stifled a yawn. "A buffet will be set up in the dining hall tonight for anyone who's hungry later on."

"What about the marriage advice book?" Haris's mother called from two rows across.

"I think Lulu is pretty tired—" Courtney began.

"Nonsense," Auntie Hanifa protested. "We had such fun filling those out. Let us hear a few, at least?"

Others nodded in agreement. Lulu relented and asked Irum to read them aloud. Irum grabbed the monogrammed white book and took a seat next to Lulu.

"Ooh, this is a good one," she said, flipping to the first page. "It says, 'Habits form early and easily, but once settled, they are impossible to undo. Choose carefully what routines you set at the start of your marriage lest you find yourself stuck with them forever.'"

"That was mine," Auntie Nipa said proudly. "It means if you iron his clothes the morning after your wedding, you'll be ironing them thirty years from now too."

There were nods of agreement. Hena bit back a laugh. Her sister had never ironed an outfit in her life. If someone needed any pressing done, Khaled better know how.

Courtney peered over Irum's shoulder to read the next one.

"'Never go to bed angry.'"

"The next one says the opposite," Irum added. "'Hold your temper before bed. Once words are spoken, they cannot be unsaid.'"

"Absolutely," said Auntie Hanifa. "Cooler heads always prevail in the morning."

Hena couldn't believe she agreed with Auntie Hanifa. She supposed even a broken clock was right twice a day.

Courtney and Irum continued to alternate reading. The advice was mostly standard: the importance of date nights, communication. Hena yawned—her late night with Reza was catching up to her. She would need a nap soon.

When Courtney flipped to the next page, she paused.

"Huh. It says, 'Invest in a good tracker for Khaled. The worst thing you can do is misplace your husband, and we all know disappearances run in the family.'"

Misplace your husband.

The words hit Hena like a gut punch.

Auntie Nipa and Auntie Hanifa covered their mouths and gasped in mock horror. Murmurs spread.

Poor Courtney looked out of the loop, but no one else was

confused. Their expressions said it all: disdain, smugness, delight. These women had never left high school behind.

"Excuse me."

Irum. She was standing, shoulders rigid. A hush fell over the audience. Her lower lip trembled as she glared at the crowd.

"My brother is missing. It's not a joke," she said. "To treat our pain like—" She choked back a sob. Wordlessly, she raced into the resort.

The crowd fell silent as Lulu rose.

"Irum is right," Lulu told the women. "That was awful. We're already navigating a wedding while handling a difficult family health matter. Let's do better. Please."

Auntie Hanifa and Auntie Nipa visibly bristled at Lulu's lecture, but the others seemed to wilt against her scolding, properly chastened.

Hena clenched her jaw. How could these people not understand that their words didn't just hurt her? She wasn't the only one who'd lost Nasir. His absence was more than a punch line.

She returned to her table, grabbed her clutch, and slipped into the resort. The sooner she got back to her room, the better.

Passing the lobby, she glimpsed the men's party through the floor-to-ceiling windows as the football game blared in the background. Her heart leapt when she saw Reza at the front desk. He was chatting with Lucinda. Mansur, another groomsman, was by his side. Something Reza said made both of them laugh before Mansur slapped Reza's back and headed outside.

Lucinda spotted Hena. She waved.

"Ms. Mirza, is everything to your liking so far?" she asked.

"Call me Hena. And everything is great, thank you."

The brown-haired man from the fondue bar, who had initially taken her luggage, hurried over to Lucinda to confer about a parking snafu as she handed Reza a first aid kit.

"Hope you're better in no time," Lucinda told him.

"What happened?" Hena asked Reza.

"Just a little burn." He held out his right hand. An angry red mark ran along the side of his palm.

Hena winced. "What's going on at this party?"

"It's my fault. I was chatting with the pitmaster. I smoke my wings differently—was trying to show him and accidentally grazed the grill."

"You got injured while mansplaining how to cook chicken?"

"Hey now! Is it mansplaining if you're in a room full of men, explaining to a man?"

She bit back a smile. "Fair point."

"It looks worse than it is. What really hurts is getting my ass handed to me at poker. These people are sharks. Now I have to learn how to be a lefty so I can apply this." He opened the kit and reached for the Neosporin.

"Let me do it."

He followed her to the lobby sofas. His hand relaxed in hers as she applied the medicine, unsealed the gauze, and pressed it against his skin.

"You do this often?" he asked.

She didn't look up, but she felt his gaze. "Bandaging up guys who think they're invincible? I guess I'm a certified pro."

"Lucky me."

"I'd say so." She smoothed the bandage in place. "There. All better."

"Thanks, Hena." He gave her hand a grateful squeeze.

Be cool, Hena, she thought, withdrawing her hand from his. "What's on deck for the evening?" she asked.

"Khaled said he's arranging a hookah bar on the back patio tonight. I'm hoping to get out of it. You?"

"Room service and calling it a night."

"Room service sounds perfect," he said wistfully.

"You're welcome to join me."

"Yeah? The dessert menu looked tempting."

She took in his broad shoulders, his almond-shaped eyes, and groaned inwardly. After last night, she assumed he literally meant dessert—but she'd still welcome his company.

They exchanged numbers. He promised to call once his plans firmed up.

Back in her suite, she kicked off her heels. Her phone buzzed. A text from Reza.

> **Reza:** No getting out of the hookah bar. I'll have to hang back. 😞

> **Hena:** Sorry to hear.

> **Reza:** I'm sorrier.

> **Reza:** Rain check?

She thumbs-upped the message. It was just as well. While she would've welcomed another evening in his company, sleepiness was setting in fast. A shower and pajamas were the smarter choice.

She reached into her clutch for lip balm and felt something crumpled inside—a pastel cocktail napkin from the bridal shower. She was about to toss it in the wastebasket when she noticed the handwriting on it.

Unfolding the napkin, she grew still.

The writing was messy, but the words were unmistakable:

Once a slut, always a slut.

DAY
THREE

7

.

Ten different breakfast stations were in full swing the next morning. The air was thick with the smell of fried bread, mangoes, and sugary masala chai. Kids splashed in the infinity pool outside, their shrieks echoing off the glass wall.

Relatives and family friends clutched their plates and milled around the continental bar filled with fruit and fresh-baked pastries set beside artisanal jams. Reza was at the halwa puri station toward the back. Courtney joined him. She gave him a conspiratorial smile and drew close, her mouth brushing his ear. Whatever she whispered made him laugh.

Hena kept moving. Past the omelet station, where two chefs cracked eggs without glancing up. Past the waffle bar with freshly prepared Madagascar whipped cream and sprinkles set in crystal bowls for the little ones. She grabbed a croissant from the pastry tower and carried it to the coffee counter, raising her eyebrows at the familiar dark-haired man behind it.

"You ferry luggage, fix fondue stations, *and* make coffee?" she asked him.

"I'm a jack-of-all-trades," he told her. "And dare I say, I make a mean latte."

Indeed, his creation was lovely, finished with a perfectly swirled foam leaf. She thanked him and took the cup, the warmth seeping into her palm as she studied the crowd.

One of you fuckers slipped that note into my purse.

But who?

She had stared at the note so long, it felt etched into her mind's eye. But the messy handwriting from the bleeding pen gave nothing away.

Who even used the word *slut* anymore? Some auntie catching up on the trending misogynist vocabulary of the nineties? Auntie Hanifa and Auntie Nipa were nestled toward the back, deep in conversation. They were the most obvious culprits. One of them had surely left the "missing husband" remark in Lulu's advice book. But that note had been written for public flogging. Why would either of them bother sneaking her a message when they could just as easily say it to her face?

She turned her head. Another auntie was staring. Their eyes met; the woman quickly looked away. Hena exhaled slowly. If she were to suspect anyone who cast a wary glance her way, then nearly everyone here was a suspect.

It would help if she knew what the note referred to. Was she a slut for the rumored California abortion? Had someone seen her talking with Haris yesterday and jumped to conclusions? Even a simple chat and a hug could be enough for imaginations to run wild.

Or did someone know she and Reza had hung out in her suite after the welcome party?

No. They could speculate, sure, but no one could know. Even if someone had spotted him heading toward the elevators, the VIP tower had six suites, including the one where Khaled—his friend—was staying.

She should probably tell Lulu about the note, but she wanted to avoid adding stress to her sister's week. Besides, she already knew the reason behind it. Someone wanted to mess with her. To remind her she wasn't welcome.

The best response was no response.

Lulu walked over wearing an embroidered kamiz with delicate flowers stitched along the collar. Hena's heart lifted. The necklace she had gifted her sister rested perfectly against her collarbone.

Lulu nodded at her plate. "That's all you're having?"

"Don't go all auntie on me now," Hena teased. "What about you? I don't see you eating."

"We had a food situation," Lulu said. "The chef we hired for the halwa puri station brought in an assortment of nuts for garnish. Almonds, cashews, pistachios, you name it."

Hena's eyes sprang wide. Lulu had a severe nut allergy. "That's a serious fuckup."

"I'm staying far from the kitchen and the food stations until it's all decontaminated," she said. "It's fine. I've been living off my protein shakes anyway. At least now Ammi can't give me grief for not eating a well-balanced meal."

At the mention of their mother, Hena looked around. Ammi wasn't here. Again. Lulu caught Hena's expression.

"She had a rough night," Lulu explained. "We insisted she get some rest so she'll have the energy to attend tonight."

"Can I stop by the room in a little bit to check on her?"

Lulu frowned. "Why would you ask? She's your mother as much as she's mine."

Lulu didn't understand. She couldn't. They were raised by the same woman, but they had different mothers. Hena had been the child who happened to come along. Lulu was the daughter her mother had dreamed of.

Lulu pulled out a key card from her purse and handed it to Hena. "She'd love to see you. Don't worry, you have time. The airboat tour isn't for another few hours."

"Lulu, do I have to?" Hena groaned. "They look so noisy."

"This one isn't!" Lulu brightened. "Seriously. We partnered with Bob's Airboats, and they've got great ratings—guaranteed alligator sightings, and they take you over to their own personal island, which the reviews say is nice as far as gator attractions go. We contracted with them for their prototype electric boats. They're practically silent on the water. I'd love your honest feedback before paying guests arrive."

"Lulu—"

"Think of it as your way of helping the family business. Carrying on our father's legacy and all that."

Hena's stomach turned. Lulu was eight when their father died. A second grader whose biggest worry was figuring out how to tie her shoelaces. Hena and her mother had done everything they could to shield Lulu from the brunt of who he was, but was it possible Lulu didn't remember anything?

Hena wasn't about to poke this hornet's nest now.

"Sounds good," she said instead.

Her sister drifted off to attend to the other guests, and Hena sipped her coffee as Khaled, bleary-eyed, wandered to the juice bar and ordered a kale-and-carrot concoction. Catching her eye, he gave her a wave. It occurred to her now that she had only exchanged a handful of words with the groom since she'd arrived.

"You holding up okay?" Hena asked, walking over to him.

"Barely." He gave her a rueful smile. "It's one thing to *attend* weddings like these, another to be one of the hosts, deciding between pastel blue linens or cerulean. I'm over it and we're not even halfway through."

"It'll be done before you know it," she said. "Then it's Fiji for your honeymoon, right?"

"Yep. I told Lulu I want unstructured beach time and lots of naps. Nothing else."

"Not sure Lulu will let that happen," Hena said. "Knowing her, she's got you scheduled for snorkeling as soon as you deplane."

"You're probably right."

They both laughed as Reza joined them. He was in a plain gray T-shirt and dark jeans this morning, his hair damp.

"Did you find your watch?" Khaled asked him.

"Not in my room," Reza said. "I'll check with the front desk in case someone dropped it off."

"Sounds like you guys had quite the night," Hena observed.

"We were up past three." Reza groaned. "I showered twice, but I still smell like smoke."

Khaled's mother drew him away to discuss the carnation lapels for the evening, and Hena and Reza stepped onto the side patio where a row of iguanas sunned themselves along the back wall, their slitted eyes following the two of them as they sat at a table.

"How's your hand?" Hena asked Reza.

"Much better." He held it out as if inviting her to take it. "You knew what you were doing."

An announcement sounded overhead. Lucinda's peppy voice informed guests that the shuttle for the Las Olas excursion would be departing in thirty minutes.

"There are so many events going on," Hena said. "Even with the binder, I can't keep track."

"This week's giving major summer camp vibes, isn't it?" asked Reza. "There's a seashell necklace class this afternoon. Seashells."

"Well, sorry to disappoint you, but you won't have time to make jewelry. The wedding party's going on an airboat ride, remember? Explain to me how that falls under wedding party duties."

"I'm kind of looking forward to it," he admitted. "I've never been on one."

"I haven't either, but considering alligators are the main attraction, I'm not sure what there is to be excited about."

"Are you scared of alligators?" He tilted his head.

"You're not?" She folded her arms.

"Never met one I didn't like."

"How many have you met?"

"None," he admitted. "At least, never up close and personal in their natural habitat."

"Our family home backed up to a swamp," she told him as a breeze fluttered the fronds of the palm trees. "I promise you, alligators are way more terrifying than jinn."

He laughed at this, and her heart did a little flip. He was far too charming for this early in the morning. She really didn't want to go on an airboat, but with Reza there, the prospect was suddenly a bit more attractive.

"Hena? Is that you?" a voice called out.

Her cousin Maheen strode toward them, her daughter wrapped in a striped beach towel.

"It's great to see you! It's been way too long!" Maheen pulled her into a hug before Hena could reply. "They canceled my flight twice. I told them, I'm a *bridesmaid*. I literally arrived two hours ago. Oh, and the turbulence!" She shuddered. "I threw up three times. You know how I am with anxiety. Anyway, look at you! I've missed you so much. How are you?"

Hena blinked as she tried to keep up with the torrent of words. Maheen's chattiness was a sharp contrast to the coldness of everyone else.

"I'm good," Hena said. "Did Inaya have fun at the pool?"

"I love the pool!" the little girl chirped.

"This is Auntie Hena," Maheen told her. "You were a baby last time you saw her at—"

She cut off abruptly. Her face flushed over the words left unspoken.

The wedding.

"Inaya's all grown up. And she's beautiful," Hena said. "The spitting image of you."

"She's the flower girl." Maheen beamed.

Her daughter tugged at her arm. "Mommy! Look, bunny!" She pointed toward the boardwalk.

"Yes, honey." Maheen cut Reza a look and brightened. "Well, hello."

Hena introduced them. Maheen's grin widened as her daughter yanked harder on her arm.

"Bunny!"

"Go on," Maheen relented. "Stay where I can see you."

Once the girl had darted off, Maheen pulled Hena to the side. Her voice dropped to a whisper.

"I've got to say, I'm impressed. Two suitors in twenty-four hours!"

Two suitors? Hena snuck a quick glance at Reza. He was scrolling through his phone. Hopefully he hadn't heard.

"Maheen, I don't know what you've heard, but—"

"Nothing bad. Weddings are the perfect place to find someone. You know Auntie Hanifa wanted to introduce Haris to her daughter? She's graduating from pharmacy school and they're on the prowl. She was complaining that he was chatting with you an awful lot," Maheen teased her. "And look, I heard Courtney and Reza were flirting at the breakfast bar, but you're the one he's having breakfast *with*, right? My take is they're both cute, so you can't go wrong."

Maheen had arrived this morning and already was up to date on the gossip.

"There's nothing going on, Maheen. Really."

"Well, just so you know, Auntie Gudi cornered Reza yesterday to inquire about his situation. Don't worry—he's definitely single. As for Haris, I'm sure he's over his ex by now, though emotional baggage is always a risk when you're talking about the end of a long-term situation. Did you know she cheated on him with a partner at his law firm? He found their text messages. Poor guy. He was devastated."

Maheen continued talking as Hena exhaled slowly. The note left in her purse made more sense now. Someone thought she was involved with not one, but two men in the span of barely twenty-four hours.

"Don't worry about Haris's mom," Maheen added. "She can be pissed all she wants. That's how moms are. You know she threw a party when his divorce was finalized? Can you imagine? That woman would do anything for her precious son."

"Auntie Nipa doesn't need to worry," Hena said, hoping the words might somehow travel back to her. "We're old friends. That's all."

Old friends who had kissed once. But that was a lifetime ago. Besides, he was Nasir's best friend. Just as critically, he was from this community she desperately wanted to leave behind her. Which meant the door had to stay firmly shut.

"Yeah?" Maheen looked mildly disappointed. "For the record, if I had to choose, I'd pick Reza. He is *hot*. Want me to get some intel for you? I can be subtle."

"Definitely not," Hena said quickly. "I do not want you to—"

Too late. Maheen was already walking over to him.

Hena watched helplessly as her cousin leaned on the table.

"I hear you're single," she said to Reza. "So tell me, who let you get away and why?"

Hena buried her face in her hands. Mortified. She was officially mortified. At least Reza seemed amused.

She needed an exit. Any exit.

"I'll go check on Inaya," she muttered, backing away.

The sun was shrouded in clouds when Hena spotted the girl on the boardwalk, crouched low. Her attention fixed on something across from her.

"Did you find the bunny?" Hena called.

No answer. Inaya didn't move.

"Inaya?"

The girl's eyes lifted to Hena's. Her lower lip trembled.

"Auntie," she whimpered. "Help."

Hena's eyes followed the girl's finger. Her stomach dropped.

Time slowed.

She was seeing things. She had to be.

Except this was real.

There was the bunny. Or rather—there *had been*. An enormous python was currently devouring it in slow, slurping gulps.

And it wasn't alone. Five others slithered nearby. The largest of them—coiled and thick as an old tree trunk—lay inches from Inaya's feet.

Hena's skin prickled. She forced her demeanor as calm as she could make it. "Inaya. Stay still. I'll be there in a second."

She inched closer to the boardwalk across the damp, spongelike ground. Her heels sank deeper with each step. From the corner of her eye she spotted another python slithering in the muck.

The little girl saw it and whimpered louder. She turned toward Hena.

"Inaya—no!" Hena cried out as the heel of the girl's shoe grazed the reptile's tan and black scales.

The creature didn't move.

Not yet.

Hena's pulse skittered. She needed to run forward. Grab Inaya off the boardwalk to safety. Instead, she was frozen in place. Pythons were strong. Their grip tight enough to take down crocodiles without missing a beat. Any wrong move could trigger the snake. If it wrapped itself around Inaya, constricting her body, it was over.

Behind her, footsteps.

Maheen.

"Honey! Let's get you showered. Your dad said the shuttle will be here any minute now, and I have to get ready for my airboat ride."

The footsteps slowed. Maheen drew to Hena's side and stumbled to a stop. Her shoes squished as they sank into the ground.

Her scream ripped through the air.

The snake snapped its head toward the sound. The other snakes stirred.

"Mommy!" The girl broke into a sob and rushed toward her, her foot clipping the snake's side.

There was no time to think.

Hena leapt onto the boardwalk. In one swift motion, she yanked Inaya off, stumbling onto the muck at the base of the walkway. Maheen gathered her daughter into her arms and held her tight, burying her face in Inaya's neck.

"Oh my god," she whimpered. "I'm so sorry, baby."

People flooded the lawn, drawn by Maheen's scream. Aunties and uncles. Courtney. Mansur. Whispers rose to gasps. Reza was there too, his face lined with concern. He took a step forward when Lulu's voice rang out.

"Is everything all right?"

She pushed through the crowd and hurried toward them. Coming closer, she stopped cold. She yanked out her phone and typed furiously.

"Everyone, please go inside," Lulu said sharply. "I'm calling wildlife control. For your safety, return to the hotel now."

The lobby was cool when Hena stepped inside with Reza. Outside, the commotion about the snakes was only growing louder.

"Hate on Orlando all you want," Reza said, running a hand through his hair, "but I've never seen pythons lounging around there."

"That wasn't normal. I mean, yes, pythons are definitely a problem around here, but I've never seen so many in one spot."

He pointed to Inaya sitting across the lobby, now playing with Maheen's phone and swinging her legs from a bench. "She seems to have recovered quickly."

"It's nice to be young, isn't it?" Hena said. "When you don't know all the things that can hurt you."

When they reached the elevators, Reza shot her a sidelong look. "Just so I understand, you're terrified of alligators, but pythons? Totally cool with those."

"You must have missed how I froze up. Every second counts in a situation like that. I was petrified, Reza."

It had been sheer luck the snake hadn't wrapped itself around Inaya. Sheer luck Hena got her away in time.

The elevator dinged and she stepped in. Reza put out a hand to stop the doors from closing. When he spoke again, his teasing tone was gone.

"Petrified or not, you did what you needed to do. She's safe because of you. You were incredible out there, Hena. Really."

She held his gaze until the doors shut. Only then did she release the breath she'd been holding.

What was it about Reza? It wasn't like she'd sworn off men after Nasir. She'd been on her share of dates in San Francisco. Nice dinners at the best spots in the city. Outings to the de Young Museum or the SFMOMA. But even with the neurologist she'd dated for nearly four months last year, going as far as meeting his parents at their Ugly Christmas Sweater party, she hadn't felt the way she did around Reza since the moment they met: butterflies.

It's nothing, Hena firmly told herself. Reza was fun to flirt with. Easy to talk to. Nice to look at. He was also one of the few people here who didn't see her as the enemy.

Reza was a much-needed distraction during a week when she desperately needed one.

Nothing more.

KIRAN,
Family Friend of the Bride

> I'm not trying to be a diva, but seriously—what's with these local tours? I live five miles from Las Olas. Water. Beach. Glitzy shops. Been there, done that. I get the out-of-towners wanting a peek, but couldn't she have organized other options for us local guests?

I got bored halfway through, so I told the group I'd meet them at our pickup spot. Figured I may as well knock out a few errands while I'm here. I stocked up at that Korean skincare shop, grabbed a bite at Havana—still the best Cuban sandwiches in town—then headed to our meeting spot at that new coffee shop that just opened up.

So I'm getting a café con leche (mid, by the way, and of course they spelled Kiran totally wrong. Seriously, three e's?), and just as I'm about to sit down, I saw this guy outside the shop. I know this is going to sound weird, but he was the spitting image of Nasir. You know, Hena's missing fiancé? Speaking of which, poor girl. People act like she had something to do with whatever happened to him, but that's not fair. She doesn't deserve half the crap people say about her.

Obviously, I knew it wasn't Nasir out there today. I'm not a conspiracy theory auntie. And this guy was thinner. Super-short hair, which was never his style. And speaking of style, this guy had none. Zero. Nasir was the sort to turn heads—the man knew how to dress. This dude was straight-up Walmart chic. The Nasir we knew would not be caught dead in those ridiculously oversized sunglasses.

I was going to write it off—too much gossip on the brain—but when he turned and I saw his profile, I'm telling you, I nearly dropped my cup. I scrambled for my phone to snap a picture, but by the time I grabbed it, he was gone.

I hurried out. I scanned the sidewalks. It's like he evaporated into thin air.

I know he was probably just some rando. It was bright outside, so it's not like I could see all that well. We all know Nasir's dead. Even his mother has said it.

Except.

They never found a body, right?

So . . . maybe? 🙶

8

.

Lulu's penthouse suite was silent when Hena stepped inside; the soft hum of the air-conditioning was the only sound. Save the extra bedroom, the space was nearly identical to her own. Same layout. Same maroon walls. Same brass fixtures. Same stainless-steel kitchen—though Lulu's currently had a stunning cream-colored five-tier wedding cake resting on its island.

Hena walked toward one of the bedrooms as Gita emerged from the bathroom, her hair wrapped in a towel. She startled at the sight of Hena.

"I didn't mean to scare you," Hena said. "I was checking in on my mother."

"She actually just fell asleep," Gita told her. "She had a rough night."

"I'll be quiet," Hena promised. It wasn't as though she'd come for a heart-to-heart. The truth was, her mother being asleep was probably for the best.

Gita pursed her lips but said nothing as Hena stepped into the bedroom. This space, too, was an uncanny mirror to Hena's own suite, except for one glaring difference: the stiff hospital bed by the back wall. The one with metal railings and IV bags set on stands beside it. The one where her mother lay motionless as machinery beeped in the background.

The overcast light slanted through the windows, pooling shadows against her mother's sleeping form. Hena took a tentative step toward her and spotted an empty vial on the nightstand. Lifting the bottle, she read the fine print: *morphine sulfate.*

Unease settled in her stomach. Her mother was taking morphine? Growing up, she refused to take so much as an Advil. How much pain was she in?

Hena gripped the cool metal bed railing and, for the first time since she'd arrived, truly took in her mother. Her thin arms. Hollowed-out cheeks. The fragile jawline, once set in stone. It was like staring at a stranger.

She still remembered her final day in Florida. When Ammi had stepped into Hena's bedroom and caught her zipping up her luggage.

"What are you doing?" her mother had asked, her voice sharp.

Hena's insides had knotted. She'd hoped to be gone before anyone noticed. She'd already written a note to stick on the fridge on her way out.

"The police said I'm free to go, so I'm leaving," she said. "My flight is in three hours."

"You're leaving," her mother repeated. "You're running away in the middle of this mess?"

Hena couldn't speak. She watched her mother's face harden.

"No goodbye," Ammi said. "Not even for your sister. She's not here, you know."

"It's better this way," Hena said, knowing it was a lie even as she said it.

Her mother stared at her for a long, silent moment before walking out.

Hena had set her bags down. She'd barely caught her breath when her mother returned, shoving an envelope into her hands.

She looked inside—cash. "I have enough—"

"You want to go? Then go," her mother said. "You want to pretend you're not part of this family, so be it. I told you about that boy, didn't I? I warned you over and over, but Hena does what Hena wants. You have caused me more grief than I ever imagined."

"Ammi—" Hena's anger drained, replaced by a sudden, heavy grief. "I'm sorry. I'll come back. I'll visit—"

"Don't bother," her mother replied. "We'll just pretend you're dead."

She had stayed true to her word. Not a phone call or a text in over three years. Now Hena was back, and her mother lay supine on this bed. Now she was dying. Hena clutched the railing tighter. Just because your mother didn't love you the way you needed her to didn't mean you stopped craving it.

Hena heard the front door open in the distance. Moments later, her aunt stepped inside. Coming closer, she took Hena's hand and squeezed it. Hena gave her a grateful smile.

"Are you all right?" Khala asked in a whisper. "I heard about the snakes. Terrifying. They said the thing nearly squeezed the poor girl's breath away."

Hena suppressed an eye roll. Rumors. Always a pinch of truth with a dash of baseless chatter.

"The snake didn't do anything," she told her. "But a python can kill you even if you're not its natural prey."

"What's this about pythons?" Her mother's eyes fluttered open.

Whoops. Had they been talking too loudly?

"We have a snake infestation. Pythons, Frida." Khala shuddered. "Maheen's daughter was keen on petting one. Hena saved the little girl's life."

Hena expected her mother to be horrified, but instead, she chuckled as she raised her bed with the remote.

"History repeats itself, doesn't it?" she said.

"It certainly does," Khala replied, a knowing look passing between them.

Hena frowned. "What do you mean?"

"You were about three years old when one of those things slithered into the sandbox behind my duplex," Khala told her.

"That one wrapped itself good and well around you," her mother said.

"Me?" Hena gaped at her. "I have no memory of that."

"Count your blessings, because I remember it all in terrifying detail." Khala shivered. "I panicked. Your mother leapt to action. She banged a pot against its head and wrenched it off with her bare hands."

"It was a small snake, as far as pythons go," Ammi said.

A funny feeling passed through Hena.

"You saved my life," she said.

"It's what mothers do," said Khala. "They protect their children at all costs."

"It's what mothers *should* do," Ammi corrected. "A python was simple enough. People were the true challenge."

"Now, now." Khala smoothed her hands over her dupatta. "No need to dwell on all of that."

"I'll be dead soon enough. When else can I dwell?" Ammi replied.

Hena tensed. They were talking about her father. They never spoke of him. She wasn't sure she wanted to start now. Luckily, Lulu stepped into the room, which meant this line of conversation was closed. At least for now.

Her sister walked to their mother's bedside. At the sight of her, Ammi's face brightened.

"Sorry I'm late," Lulu said. "It's chaos out there."

"That is the way of weddings," her mother replied.

"This is extra, even for a wedding," Lulu said. "We have to reschedule tonight's fireworks due to forecasted storms. And Sritala dropped off the shaadi cake four days early."

"Oh dear." Khala's brow furrowed. "I saw it on the kitchen island. I wasn't sure . . ."

"The staff got so flustered they dropped it off *here*. What am *I* supposed to do with it? She said I called and asked her to switch the date! Can you believe her?" Lulu exclaimed. "I went off. Why would you blame me? Mistakes happen, but own it!"

"Could we store it in one of the industrial fridges downstairs?" Hena asked.

"Chantilly cream isn't meant to sit. Besides, the berries will bleed through the sponge by morning," Lulu said. "It's fine. She'll remake it, but between this and the snake situation, I'm ready for this week to be over."

"I heard about the pythons," their mother said.

Lulu shuddered. "I'm mortified."

"There's nothing to be mortified about. Nature happens," Hena reassured her.

"But so many of them?" Lulu said. "The wildlife team is here now. Lucinda's showing them around. Once they remove the pythons, they'll set up a snake gate around the property so it doesn't happen again. I can't imagine if this had happened after we were fully launched."

"Lucinda is lovely," Hena said. "She gave me her personal cell in case I needed anything."

Lulu smiled. "She's great, isn't she? Did you know she used to work for our dad?"

Hena grew still. She looked at her mother, then back at Lulu.

"She did?"

Lulu nodded. "She helped with organizing and bookkeeping. When I saw her résumé, I did a double take. Small world, right?"

"She looks barely older than me," Hena said.

"She started in high school over at his Miramar resort. You know he loved giving kids who needed it the extra boost."

But the hotel in Miramar wasn't just a resort. It was where his side business lived, tucked in the shadows of the palm-lined drive where kids desperate enough for cash did the jobs no one spoke about—delivering envelopes with no questions asked, knocking on doors with threats and ultimatums.

"She's shared so many great stories about him," Lulu continued. "It's a totally different perspective. He was a natural at this business stuff. Hopefully I have some of that in me." She sighed. "I just have the one property, we haven't even opened officially, and already it's one thing after another. Sometimes I miss culinary school, but I'm sure I'll get the hang of it soon enough. I like thinking he's looking down on us. That he's proud we're at least trying to keep his legacy alive."

A doorbell chimed, and she heard Gita go to answer the door.

Hena looked at her mother. Her expression was unreadable. She refused to meet Hena's gaze.

This, this right here, was why Hena had told her mother countless times that Lulu deserved to know who her father really was. No matter how much she'd tried, Ammi wouldn't hear of it. *What's the harm?* Her mother would retort in the face of Hena's arguments. *He's gone. Let her love him.*

But why love a man who didn't deserve it? And Lulu didn't just love their father—she revered him. Or at least the man she believed he was. His absence had only amplified his legendary status in her eyes.

"The steamer dropped off tonight's outfit," Gita said, appearing at the doorway. "She was in a rush, but she'll be back in a little while for tomorrow's clothing. I can put it out for you?"

"No, it's all right." Lulu massaged her temples. "I'll hang it by the service entrance, it's—" Lulu cut off. She touched her throat, blinking fast.

Hena tensed. "Lulu?"

"I—" Lulu coughed. "My throat feels . . . weird."

Ammi gasped. "She's having an allergic reaction."

Hena's pulse spiked. Ammi was right. It wasn't just Lulu's throat—her arms and face were breaking out into angry red splotches.

"I can't—I can't breathe." Lulu staggered backward, knocking a lamp from the side table. The bulb burst into a spray of glass. She clutched at her throat. Panicking. Her lips were already turning blue.

"The EpiPen!" Hena shouted. "Where is it?"

"In her purse!" Ammi cried out.

Before Hena could move, Gita raced to Lulu's bag and frantically rifled through. Loose change, lipstick, and a compact mirror clattered to the floor. At last, she yanked out the plastic tube. Uncapping it, she raced to Lulu's side and thrust the needle into her leg.

It would work. Hena knew it would. But terror shot through her all the same.

Seconds later, Lulu let out a ragged gasp. Hena grabbed her as she sank hard to the floor.

"You're going to be fine," Hena said, soothing her sister, trying to keep her voice from wavering. "Just give it time. You'll be all better before you know it."

Cradling Lulu in her arms, the minutes ticked by. Hena's thoughts flashed to her sister's eleventh birthday, when the server had failed to note her nut allergy. When Lulu bit into the cake, her lips swelled instantly. Hena remembered the panic. Her mother frantically digging through her purse as a crowd grew around their table. Just as before, seeing her sister struggle for air made Hena's own lungs compress with fear.

But Lulu was improving. Hena watched as Lulu's eyes slowly fluttered open and met Hena's.

"Well, that was . . . that was something," she finally said.

"You're okay," Hena said, her stomach unclenching, her own voice growing steadier. "You're past the worst of it."

"Thanks, everyone," Lulu said weakly.

She was better now. Still, the thought of how dangerous the situation was . . . how close she had been to death . . . Hena shivered.

"We should get you to the ER," she said.

"There's no need." Lulu struggled to sit up. She winced as she grazed a hand where Gita had stabbed her. "I'm better now."

"Lulu—"

"If I need the second pen, yes. Fingers crossed this was it."

"How did this happen?" Hena asked. "You didn't touch anything at the breakfast bar, did you?"

"I avoided everything. I've been washing my hands constantly," she said, as Gita swept up the broken glass. "I must have brushed against something allergenic pretty recently—this all sparked after I touched my face."

"Well, you're all right now," Gita said. "That's what matters."

Hena went to the kitchen and grabbed a glass of water for Lulu. She watched as Lulu took a few sips, the color returning to her face.

"Why don't you lie down?" Hena said. "What happened is no joke."

"I'm good. Really," she said. "But I do need a favor."

"Anything," said Hena.

"The airboat ride is in thirty minutes. I forgot to make copies of the waiver. The paper's on my desk. Can you take it down to Lucinda?"

Hena blinked. Minutes earlier Lulu was battling anaphylactic shock. Her arms were still covered in angry red welts. Now she was discussing paperwork?

"Lulu . . . I think you can take a break on wedding logistics for just a second," Hena said.

Her sister's smile was faint but defiant. "I am. It's why I'm asking *you* to take care of this."

"Sure. But I'm going to sit this ride out. I'd rather keep an eye on you."

"Nice try."

"Lulu."

"I mean it. Besides, Gita is here."

"I'll keep an eye on her," Gita promised. "If anything else happens, it's straight to the emergency room."

Hena could see there was no getting out of this. She stood, her legs unsteady. She hated the thought of leaving her sister while she was still recovering, but Lulu was clearly determined. Hena grabbed the waiver and headed to the elevator.

When she got in, she leaned against the back wall. First the pythons, now this. The wedding was off to an unsettling start. It wasn't even noon and she was already exhausted. But all was well, she reminded herself. Inaya was safe. Her sister was fine. Everything worked out as it was meant to.

She was reaching to press the lobby button when something crunched under her foot.

She knelt and picked it up. For a split second she couldn't process what she was looking at.

It was a single crushed pistachio husk.

Hena stared at the empty shell.

Why was it in this elevator?

A guest, Hena told herself. This elevator serviced other suites as well. Khaled's. His parents'. Everyone staying in this tower used the same lift. Someone may not have realized. It's not as though there was an explicit nut ban. They could have been snacking in the elevator and contaminated the buttons as they touched their floor. A contact as faint as this, with Lulu touching her face shortly after, could have triggered a reaction.

However it happened, it was an accident.

No one would purposely hurt Lulu.

But then the thought slithered in, unbidden, as her mind drifted to the note left in her clutch: There were plenty of people who might want to hurt Hena.

People who might try to hurt her little sister to send a message.

Hena shuddered, shoving the paranoia away.

No.

It was an accident.

It had to be.

9

·

"**A**re you sure you don't want me to hang back?" Hena asked again. She stood on the dock with the others as they adjusted their puffy orange life vests. The airboat idled to their right. She knew the threat had passed. She knew Lulu was fine—her hives were practically gone—but worry still lingered in Hena's bones.

"For the thousandth time, I'm fine. I promise," Lulu assured her. "The kitchen's cleared, and since you found that pistachio shell in the elevator, the cleaning crew's wiping down the rest of the property too. We also let guests know they'll have to do without their precious nuts this week. And remember, Gita's going to watch me like a hawk per Ammi's orders. There's a reason the woman's in the will."

"The will?" Hena blinked.

"I know," Lulu said, clocking Hena's expression. "I'd be weirded out too if I hadn't seen what a lifesaver she's been these last few months. Without Gita, there would be no wedding—she goes above and beyond."

"What did Ammi put for her in the will?"

"It's sweet, actually," Lulu said. "Gita wants to go to med

school, and Ammi's been helping her pay for premed classes. She wanted to ensure the rest of Gita's educational journey was taken care of no matter what. As a gesture of her gratitude."

"That doesn't sound odd to you? Sweet isn't exactly Ammi's MO."

"You'd be surprised," Lulu said. "She's getting soft these days."

Judging from Lulu's nonchalant explanation, she clearly seemed fine with it. Besides, it wasn't like helping someone with their education was a bad thing. As fraught as their relationship was, her mother had always cared about Hena's education. She had paid for the best tutors. Encouraged her to apply to as many top colleges as she wanted. *Education gives women choices,* she would say. If her mother was setting aside school funds for Gita, who was Hena to object?

"All right, no more stalling." Lulu nudged her toward the boat.

Reluctantly, Hena snapped on her life jacket. The midday sun was bright overhead; a gentle wind tousled her hair and rustled the reeds along the water's edge. She looked at the murky water and tried to relax.

Lulu is fine, she reminded herself. *This airboat ride will be over before I know it.*

Stepping onto the boat, her shoes skimmed the boat's aluminum floor as she wiped perspiration from her brow. San Francisco had blessedly cool year-round temps that required layers. Here, even in January, the Florida heat was oppressive.

Reza stepped onto the boat after her. He took Irum's hand to help her board. Hena reached down to adjust her shoes as Irum sat next to Reza. He whispered something in her ear

Hena couldn't quite make out, but whatever it was made her smile—a real smile that Hena realized she hadn't seen since she'd arrived.

Courtney hopped in next and slid into the other empty spot next to Reza. She shifted closer, her blond ponytail brushing against his shoulder.

"Look, I love my Lulu," she said in a not-so-quiet tone. "But buying a property in the middle of the swamp and frog-marching us onto an airboat? The beach is literally fifteen minutes away!"

"Right?" Maheen chimed in from across the boat. "I think her eco thing is great and all, but this nature stuff is a lot."

Hena frowned. Swamp chic wasn't exactly her vibe either, but she didn't appreciate the gripe session.

"Gotta disagree. The swamp's growing on me," Reza told them. "It's got character. I think the beach is kind of over-done."

"Overdone?" Courtney pretended to look scandalized as she playfully swatted him.

Heat rose to Hena's face as she watched Reza grin. Just then, he turned back. Catching Hena's eye, he smiled. She returned it before casting her attention toward the water. Reza was friendly. What was wrong with that? The whole point of this trip was for the wedding party to mingle, wasn't it? Looking at Courtney and Reza, though, she thought of the gossip Maheen had shared. Courtney and Reza were getting friendly. Wasn't there always a hint of truth behind every rumor?

She spotted Haris sitting at a middle bench. The sleeves of his salmon-colored shirt were rolled up, and his sunglasses were perched on his head.

"This spot taken?" she asked, walking over to him.

"All yours." He patted the open space.

She sat next to him as Mansur stepped onto the boat; the engine hummed beneath them. The guide, a leathery man with a worn fishing hat and dog tags dangling from his neck, introduced himself as Bob.

"This airboat is the quietest of the fleet, but it's not silent," he warned as he handed each of them ear plugs to muffle the sound of the motor.

"Have fun, guys!" Lulu called from the dock as the boat pulled away. "Soak everything up for feedback later. I want complete honesty—that's how we get better!"

The wind picked up as they gathered speed. Hena tried to steady herself as the boat rocked beneath her. The resort grew smaller and smaller before slipping out of sight.

"Shall we make a bet on who throws up first?" she asked Haris.

"I'll go with me." He gripped the side of the boat, a queasy look on his face.

"Oh, Haris."

He grimaced. "I didn't expect it to be quite this bumpy."

"Me either," she said. "This isn't exactly a luxury ride."

"I guess there's a reason I haven't been on one since we were kids. Remember that?"

She paused, caught off guard. "No?"

"We were, what, eleven or twelve?" He squinted, thinking back. "It was your dad's idea. Lulu was maybe two years old. She kept demanding the captain let her steer the boat."

His words sparked a hint of memory.

"The boat hit a rock or something," Haris continued. "You were at the edge, and the whole bag of snacks you were holding fell into the water."

Hena's stomach turned, the memory flooding back.

"All those cookies and chips bobbing in Ziploc bags in the marsh." Haris laughed. "Your mom's hot mix broke open. The fish were all over it."

"I remember," she said.

How had she ever forgotten?

"Your dad saved the day." Haris gave her a queasy smile. "He had diced Pakistani mangoes stashed in a cooler, and he shared them with all of us. Everyone forgot about the fallen snacks after that."

No, Haris. Not everyone.

Haris didn't know the rest of the story. The silent car ride home. And later, once Lulu was out of earshot and her mother was taking a call with Khala, her father cornered Hena in her bedroom. Slapped her open-palmed across the face so hard she'd stumbled back, her head cracking against the bedpost. He let her know what he thought of her: Careless. Ungrateful. An embarrassment.

Hena's head hurt. Earlier, she'd told Reza she'd never ridden an airboat. But she had. Just as she'd erased the memory of the python her mother had rescued her from, she'd erased this too. When it came to her childhood, all she had to do was tap below the surface to find a painful bruise.

"I'm not going to make it," Haris groaned.

"You've got this." She took his hand and gave it a squeeze. His palms were clammy. "Close your eyes and breathe through your nose. Like in yoga."

He closed his eyes and murmured, "Do I strike you as a yoga guy?"

"You strike me as someone who doesn't want to vomit all over my shoes."

He cracked a smile at this. "No, definitely not."

"Just do it," she insisted. "You'll feel better. I promise."

He did as she suggested. She dug through her purse and pulled out a ginger candy that had been buried in there, handing it to him.

He chewed, and a few minutes later he opened his eyes and exhaled.

"There we go," he said. "I actually feel—"

"Hold on to your seats!" the guide called out.

The boat lurched forward. Hena shot her hand out to keep from crashing into Mansur and the other guests seated in front of her. Murky water splashed onto the boat.

"Hey! Watch it," Haris shouted. He wiped his face.

"Sorry 'bout that," Bob said. "Had to get around old Suzy— she's big enough to topple this boat right over."

As if on cue, they floated past the alligator, deep green and ridged. Only her unblinking eyes were visible above the water, watching them as they passed.

Haris groaned, wiping at his soaked shirt. "This was my brunch outfit."

"It's not too wet," Hena said, brushing his sleeve. "Besides, the resort has dry cleaning, and you can always do a run home if you need. Do you still live in Brickell?"

"Yep. Chloe tried to get the house in the divorce, but that was *not* going to happen. Sometimes I wondered if she married me purely for the real estate."

"Glad you were able to keep it," she said. "Your house is gorgeous."

Gorgeous was an understatement. His beachside estate was worthy of a feature in *Architectural Digest*. Hena remembered it warmly for all the memories it contained. The barbecues and New Year's parties she'd attended with Nasir. It had been along the shoreline of Haris's home that Nasir had taken her hand one balmy evening, gotten down on one knee, and asked her to marry him.

"She said yes!" he'd shouted to their friends peering down from the balcony above, who promptly erupted into cheers.

She smiled at the memory. Although what followed had been painful, this moment remained special. She looked over at Haris and noticed him watching her with an amused expression.

"What is it?" she asked.

"You know you still wrinkle your forehead when you're deep in contemplation?"

"I do not."

"You do. Ever since I've known you. You get lost in thought, and right here . . ." He lightly brushed the spot between her brows. "Every time."

"Hmm. I don't like being easy to read."

"I think it's cute."

Cute? Something fluttered in her at his remark.

The boat veered right, and the marsh opened up before them, a stretch of dark waters and grass swaying in the wind. As they drove past two alligators sunbathing on the banks, she looked at the other guests on the boat. Maheen was regaling the tour guide with an adventure she'd had with her family in the wetlands of Ecuador the summer before. Irum was texting. Reza was chatting with Courtney. Still.

Whatever they were talking about was certainly entertaining, judging by how Courtney was laughing.

At last the boat slowed, pulling up to a forested island.

"Whoa!" Courtney cried out as the boat anchored at a crowded dock. "That thing is *huge*."

She pointed to a massive alligator floating in the water mere feet from them, its eyes fixed on their boat, unblinking.

"Ah. That's Suzy again," Bob said. "See the mark on her left eye? Sets her apart from the other gators. She's our friendliest one."

"Friendliest or hungriest?" Haris remarked.

"Seriously." Mansur side-eyed the reptile. "Is she stalking us?"

"Nah. She's just nosy. She was born on our preserve with her brother, Cox, but she was not one to be contained. She's still a sucker for snacks, though, just like her brother. I like to think she remembers her time here fondly."

Hena stepped onto the dock and breathed in the grass-scented air. She followed the path toward the island's center, where kids clustered around a feeding tank and dangled fishing poles with raw chicken over a pool of snapping gators. Across the way, a woman manhandled a pair of tarantulas next to a tented booth where a man hawked photo ops with a baby alligator.

Reza stood by a metal fence with a sign announcing "Florida's Largest Gator." Hena joined him and leaned over the chain link to take in the enormous alligator sunning near the fence's edge.

"Are the gators as cute as you imagined them to be?" she teased Reza.

Reza's brow creased. "Hmm. Not exactly what I had in mind."

She pointed toward tourists posing with the baby gator. "Interested in a pic?"

"Look at the poor thing." He grimaced. "Its mouth is tied shut."

"So as not to bite your face off."

"If they weren't holding it, there'd be no worry . . ." His words trailed off as Courtney and Mansur jogged up to the vendor, cash in hand.

"Come on, guys!" Courtney waved to them. "Let's do a group pic! He's adorable."

"Wow," Reza muttered.

"Now, that's a big gator," Haris said, joining them.

"Florida's largest," Reza said wryly.

"The fence looks a bit worse for the wear," Haris said, eyeing the rusted metal gate.

"I'll definitely be giving Lulu feedback on this place," Hena said, turning to face them both as a gaggle of children raced past.

"Me too." Haris tugged at his damp shirt. "For starters, I would've liked a heads-up that I should have packed swim trunks."

"I'd also let her know the sun is way too bright," Reza said, squinting, his hand shielding his eyes. "And the ride over here was kind of brutal."

"So the review is, we hate airboats?" Hena retorted.

Reza grinned, and her heart did a little involuntary flip.

Suddenly, he stiffened, his eyes fixed on something behind her. Before she could ask what was wrong, he grabbed her by the waist, pulling her to him. Her foot slipped as she stumbled into him.

"Reza, what—"

Her breath caught.

"Florida's Largest Gator" wasn't enclosed anymore. The gate was open, swinging with a clang against the fence.

The gator shoved through. Lumbered forward. Toward them.

"Fuck." Haris looked around frantically. "We need to run. Now!"

Before anyone moved, the gator hissed, its jaws yawning to reveal its sharp teeth.

"Stay still," Hena said. Gators were fast. Faster than any of them could possibly be. She felt Reza's heart racing against her back—it matched her own frantic pulse. She craned her neck until she spotted their guide. He was chatting with guests by the feeding tanks across the way.

"Bob!" Hena shouted. "We have a problem!"

Looking over, the guide's easy smile shifted to horror.

"Everybody stay back," he barked, charging forward, waving his arms. Then to the three of them, "Back up. Slow as you can."

They gingerly inched away, but the gator hissed again. Its mouth parted. Its tail twitched. It moved toward them. Slow. Deliberate. Her body was locked rigid in Reza's arms. Her heart felt like it was going to explode out of her chest.

"Go on, Cox," Bob muttered. He snatched a pole resting by the fence and nudged the creature, coaxing it with years of practiced calm. He fished in his pocket and pulled out pellets of dog food. He tossed it behind the reptile, toward its enclosure.

The gator didn't move. Its dark beady eyes watched them. Hena swallowed hard as the chain-link fence rattled in the wind.

Then, it pivoted.

Its belly scraped against concrete as it turned toward the snacks. The guide moved, edging closer and closer to the open gate as he kept dropping food, coaxing Cox back inside, until at last, the creature slithered into its enclosure. Bob slammed the gate shut, locking it tight.

Hena let out a shaky breath. Only now did she realize her body was still pressed against Reza's, his arm still firmly around her waist.

She looked up, and his gaze met hers. He flushed and pulled back like she was hot to the touch.

"What kind of operation are you running here, Bob?"

Haris had his phone out. Recording. "That gator could have killed one of us. I need to get this to the authorities."

"That's never—*never*—happened before," the guide stammered, mopping his brow. His attention shifted to something next to Hena.

"Ah." His eyebrows shot up. "Well, there we go. Fishing lure." He walked over and held up a raw chicken wing by Hena's feet. "One of the kids must have dropped it. That's what he was going for. I knew there had to be an explanation. Cox doesn't have a predatory bone in his body."

"Well, he wouldn't have gone for it if the gate wasn't open, now would he?" Haris shot back.

Bob apologized. He promised to review footage and get to the bottom of what had happened. Ensconced in its enclosure, the gator chomped on a raw chicken breast. Hena's eyes drifted to the black waters in the distance.

They were safe now, she told herself. Still, a tremor of unease passed through her.

Pythons. The pistachio shell in the elevator.

Now this.

They were all separate. Unrelated. Coincidental.

But her mind couldn't stop trying to connect dots, to draw a connection.

Just how much could go wrong when the wedding week had only just begun?

ALTAF,
Uncle of the Bride

Call me old-fashioned, but if you don't rein in your girls, you bring what follows upon yourselves. The reality is, Hena was once a very good girl. Things went downhill after my brother died.

Latif was a pillar of our community. A rare breed who, despite the heights he reached, never forgot where he came from. The wealthier he became, the more generous he grew. You know the Pakistani American community center by Boulevard and Tenth Street? The South Asian domestic violence shelter in Pembroke Pines? They were both funded entirely by him. He hired the architects. Reviewed the plans himself. With wealth comes responsibility—it's what he always said.

My brother was not only a financial pillar of our community, he was also its patriarch. People turned to him for counsel. He gave seed money to new entrepreneurs in the community to pay it forward. He was the sort of man who wanted to lift all boats. Even when people spoke ill of him, he paid it no mind. He knew a man of his stature was bound to attract envy.

His death sent shock waves through our community.

I'd long suspected Frida didn't appreciate her husband's way with money. This was confirmed upon his passing. She stopped contributing to any of his causes. It was over. Just like that.

I tried to reason with her. Remind her of the importance of respect and honor, of keeping her husband's legacy alive—but she wouldn't let me begin the conversation. While Luma is a dear girl who has thrived in spite of her family situation, Hena is an example of how the apple doesn't fall too far from the tree. Frida let her run wild, and without her father's guidance to keep her in place, what else could anyone expect to happen?

While I do not condone the unseemly gossip around here, who can blame us for feeling this way? Personally speaking, I believe she and her mother destroyed my brother's legacy. I'm not sure I can ever forgive them for that. ❞

COME DANCE THE NIGHT

AWAY TO THE DHOLAK DRUM

AT LUMA AND KHALED'S

Dholki

VISTA DEL SOL

345 EUCLID DRIVE

EVERMERE, FLORIDA

Sunday, January 11, at 7:00 p.m.

Mariposa Ballroom

Attire: gilded elegance

10

·

ulu's tricolored gown—blending bronze, copper, and silver—glinted in the overhead lights, draped perfectly against her body. She waited for the wedding planner's cue to walk down the aisle, after which the wedding party would follow, dancing down the aisle to their choreographed routine.

All of them, save Hena. She lingered along the sidelines, knowing she'd only ruin the polished routine they'd practiced for the past few weeks if she joined.

Hena's own dholki had been a simple affair at Ammi's home, where family and friends sat cross-legged with a simple drum while singing traditional Punjabi songs. Lulu's dholki, on the other hand, was Bollywood perfect. Fairy lights studded an archway draped with marigolds. The bloodred carpet was framed by flickering lanterns on either side, leading to an elevated stage where a velvet couch rested in front of an intricately carved backdrop.

From the sidelines she watched the wedding planner nod. Her sister stepped into the hall to cheers. Khaled was seated onstage, dressed in a golden kurta with a matching vest. His face lit up when he saw Lulu. He helped her up the steps.

Once they were seated, the DJ lowered the music, and the dhol-walas—the main event—began their drumming.

The groomsmen and bridesmaids entered the hall dancing to a bhangra beat as they made their way toward the dance floor. The music was rhythmic, so loud it vibrated beneath Hena's feet.

She looked down at her freshly painted nails. After the chaos of the airboat ride, Lulu had sent everyone off to the resort spa. The men opted for sauna time and massages, while the bridesmaids chose pedicures, facials, and fruit smoothies. It was a much-needed reset. Hena had even laughed listening to Maheen retell the python rescue, painting Hena more as a superhero than the scared bystander she'd been.

For the first time since she'd arrived, there had been no cutting looks cast in her direction. The group took her in as one of their own, joking about their worst first dates and giving each other skin care pointers. Even Courtney—whom Hena had been a bit wary of, given her snark about Lulu's wedding venue choice—turned out to be sweet, flagging down the server for an extra smoothie when Hena's ran out.

She spotted Courtney among the dancers. She was in a copper-colored sari, sidling up to Reza. He was trying his best, but he was clearly a half beat behind the others. Hena watched as Courtney drifted closer. Brushing her shoulder against his arm, she showed him the move. He tried again, and she patted his arm, nodding encouragingly. *Yep,* thought Hena. *Behind every rumor, a seed of truth.* Really, who could blame her?

Winding her way through the crowded room, Hena found her mother seated toward the front. She was chatting animatedly with Gita, who was leaning in while Ammi laughed. A real laugh, her eyes crinkling. Hena's chest constricted.

When was the last time Hena had made Ammi laugh? Or the last time they had any sort of easy, laid-back interaction? Growing up, she'd attributed their tense relationship to her father. The threat of his unstable mood lurking around every corner. But he had been dead for well over a decade now, and they were no closer than they'd ever been. Maybe the two of them were simply oil and water, never meant to gel.

Both women paused their conversation as Hena joined them.

"How are you feeling?" Hena asked her mother.

"Why does everyone keep asking me that?" Ammi scowled.

"Because you're sick," Gita retorted. "Because we care. That's why."

"Hmm." Her mother said, but didn't say more.

Hena understood. It was one thing to be sick, another for it to be the only thing anyone wanted to talk about.

"How many people are here tonight?" she asked, hoping to steer the conversation elsewhere. "Seems like way more than the previous two days."

"I believe two hundred people RSVP'd," her mother said. "Tomorrow's party will be north of three hundred."

That made sense. The more significant the event, the bigger the guest list. Tonight was mostly a dance party—a light lead-in to the mehndi and shaadi to come. The thought of the shaadi made her shiver as memories of her own doomed event crept to the surface. And she couldn't help but wonder: would Nasir's parents actually show?

"I hope the power holds up," Gita said, nodding toward the window. "The incoming storm looks intense."

She was right. Dark clouds gathered outside. The palm trees swayed ominously.

"They have generators," her mother said. "I think it's just—" She broke off, coughing hard.

Hena pressed a hand to her back. "Does she need an inhaler?" she asked Gita, a knot gathering in her chest.

"This happens sometimes." Gita patted Ammi's hand, though she continued to cough violently. "It will pass."

Her mother's knuckles gripped the wheelchair armrest so tightly, her fingers had gone pale. Guests looked over in their direction. Their worried expressions mirrored Hena's own anxiety. How could Gita be so calm right now?

"I'll get her some water," Hena said.

"S-stop babying me." Ammi wheezed as her coughing subsided. "I'm . . . all right."

Before Hena could protest, Gita spoke.

"Get something to eat," she told Hena. "Have you tried the pakoras? They're fresh from the fryer."

"I'm not really—"

"She needs a minute," Gita cut in. "Please."

Hena bit her lip but relented. Gita was a professional caregiver. She knew what her mother needed. The truth was, Hena needed a minute too. No matter how complicated things were between them, it cut her to see Ammi in such obvious pain.

Heading to the appetizer table, she spotted Haris at the bar. Pivoting, she approached him and tapped his shoulder. His face brightened when he saw her.

"Those were some nice moves out there," she told him. "You've improved since I last saw you on the dance floor."

"I better have. Khaled made me take bhangra lessons."

"I'd say it's a good life skill to have. Though I'll personally be sticking to the sidelines."

"Why? If I remember correctly, you had some good dance moves yourself."

"I'd rather stay as inconspicuous as possible," she replied. "The less gossip I can drum up, the better."

"Why would they gossip about that? I like to imagine people around here are evolving beyond such petty stuff."

"You mean like calling me a slut?"

"Whoa." His brows lifted. "Who said that?"

"They didn't say it to my face. They dropped a note in my purse."

She filled him in on the message left after yesterday's bridal shower.

"That's disgusting." His eyes darkened. "Who would do something that fucked up?"

"It could be anyone," she said. *Including your mother.*

"It's one thing to be snarky, but this crosses a line. Why?"

"To entertain themselves?"

"Well, it's not funny." He scanned the room, his jaw tight. "They should be dealt with. There are lines you don't cross."

Dealt with? He was upset for her sake, but the last thing she wanted was to escalate the situation. Before she could say more, he perked up.

"Wait. I know. They've got cameras all over the property. I bet the footage hasn't been erased yet. We could check—"

"What? No." She cut him off. "That would mean involving my sister. She's already overwhelmed. I don't want to give whoever did it the satisfaction of knowing they got to me. It's not a big deal. This wedding will be over soon enough."

"Hena—"

"It's fine." She reached out and squeezed his arm. "I appreciate you caring."

His expression softened. "Of course I care." He covered her hand with his. "I'm sorry that happened, is all."

"To be expected, honestly. I'm okay. Promise."

A new song came on. He looked at the crowd, then her.

"Are you sure you don't want to hit the dance floor? You said my skills have improved, right?" His eyes crinkled. He looked so earnest and cute. Before she could respond, a familiar voice cut in.

"There you are." Auntie Nipa approached. "I need your help."

Hena bit back a grin. Like clockwork.

"Give me one second," Haris said.

"This can't wait," Auntie Nipa replied. "Now, please."

"Ammi," Haris said, clearly exasperated.

He gave her a pointed look. She stepped back, but it was clear she wasn't leaving.

He turned back to Hena. "I'm sorry. I'll talk to her again."

"She is not my biggest fan."

"She's my mother. I love her." He sighed. "But I don't think she's anyone's fan."

"Except yours?"

"Except mine." He laughed. "To be continued?"

He headed off as Hena ordered a drink. After the song ended, the emcee's voice crackled over the mic.

"Ladies and gentlemen! Khaled and Lulu are ready for their dance-off. Please give them your full attention and cheer for your side. The loudest party determines the winner."

Bhangra filled the air—louder, more upbeat. The DJ raised the music to complement the live drummers. Holding hands, the couple made their way to the center of the dance floor. They squared off, then launched into a synchronized dance, down to the choreographed head tilt. True to their marching orders, Khaled's family whooped and hollered as loud as they could. Hena joined in with the bride's side, clapping and cheering as Lulu's shimmering gown fanned around her as she twirled. The DJ declared it a tie. Khaled drew Lulu into a hug.

The emcee invited the audience to join. Khala was one of the first to hit the floor, her head bobbing as she twirled. When she spotted Hena, she brightened and waved her over. Hena shook her head, but Khala grabbed her hands and pulled her in.

"Your dance moves haven't changed since I was five," Hena shouted over the music.

"Why fix what isn't broken?" Khala winked. "You know you learned everything from me, right?"

Hena had said she wouldn't dance. Didn't want the attention. But with her aunt, the self-consciousness melted away. A new memory surfaced: The two of them in the kitchen, Hena barely in preschool, the bhangra music dialed up to ten. Her aunt twirling her as they cleaned. Even after all this time, these childhood moves came back as if no time had passed.

There was a lull between songs. Hena spotted Reza off to the side in a dark kurta.

"You know how to dance, don't you?" he asked as she walked over to him.

"Want some tips?"

He feigned offense. "I've got moves of my own."

"Prove it. Dance with me."

The beat kicked up. He took her hands and drew her close, matching her beat for beat. Just like that, in the middle of the crowd, everything else faded away. The noise blurred. The lights dimmed. It was just him. Just her.

"I'm not sure I properly thanked you for saving my life," Hena told him.

"I think Bob played a bigger role," he said. "For the record, I've changed my mind. The Everglades are way overrated."

"It's not always fun to be right," she teased. "But honestly, the Everglades can be pretty special. When you see a breeze wave over a wide swath of grassy marsh, it can feel otherworldly. Stumbling across a wild orchid—it's magical."

"That *does* sound nice, but it's definitely time for a scenery cleanse."

"What do you have in mind?"

"I'm thinking of renting a boat and hitting the ocean tomorrow. You know they have an app for that?"

"My parents once had a motorboat. A Chris-Craft Catalina."

For twenty-four hours, anyway.

"I'm thinking more along the lines of a sailboat. It's been a while."

"You know how to sail?" She raised an eyebrow. "Not a lot of ocean in Orlando, last I checked."

"We have lakes. I don't do it much these days, but there's nothing like being out on the water. It really clears your head."

"Sounds nice," she said wistfully. "I bet it's meditative."

He hesitated. Then—

"Join me? It's a three-hour sail out of Key Biscayne."

Her heart skipped a beat, but she did her best to play it cool. "Yeah?"

"Two is always better than one."

"That sounds perfect, but I'm not sure I'd be much help," she said.

"I have plenty of experience for both of us. Besides, Key Biscayne seems like a calm bay—more lake than open sea. A great place to learn. What do you say?"

He smiled. It was the kind of smile that should come with a warning label. And that dimple. That maddening, unfair dimple. What else could she say to a man with a dimple like that except yes?

"I'd love to," she told him.

The song faded. She glanced back at the crowd; she needed to check on her mother, so reluctantly she excused herself. Walking away, she traced a finger along her palm, his touch still warm against her skin.

A sailboat ride.

Just the two of them.

Was this a date? In any other world that's what she would have called it. With Reza, though, she didn't want to prematurely name it something it wasn't.

Nearing her mother, Hena's pace slowed. Ammi was hunched over. Gita crouched by her side.

"I'm fine," her mother said through gritted teeth as Hena joined her.

"Frida. Enough is enough. A bit of Percocet will do the trick. I think—"

"You will not tell me what I can or cannot do. Understood?" Ammi snapped.

Hena flinched at the familiar sting of her mother's words. Judging from the ashen look on Gita's face, this tone was new to her.

"Ammi, it can't hurt to have some pain medication." Hena set her purse on the table and kneeled so they were face-to-face. "Just so you can feel a little better, that's all."

"For the one hundredth time, those medicines put me straight to sleep." Her eyes watered. When she spoke again, her words were barely above a whisper. "I—I want to be here. I'm sick of all these medications."

The plaintive way she spoke, her head bowed, broke Hena's heart. This was the same woman who would roughly march her out of the house barefoot under the cover of night when her father was in one of his dangerous moods. Hena remembered being yanked from sleep, her mother cradling Lulu in her arms and pressing a finger to her lips as the three of them slipped out the bedroom window. They sidestepped snake holes and ducked past dangling black widows before she tucked them into the overgrown shed in the back of their property until the storm passed.

"The Percocet is less heavy-duty. It'll take the edge off," Gita reassured her. "You'll have at least thirty minutes before it makes you drowsy, and you'll be able to actually enjoy yourself. Please, Frida."

"I can grab the medicine," Hena offered.

Her mother didn't reply, but she didn't say no, which was as close to a yes as they'd probably get. Gita handed Hena a key card and reminded her to grab her mother's special filtered water.

Lucinda was by the front desk chatting with the dark-haired "Mr. Jack-of-all-trades" when Hena walked past the lobby. Their voices drifted over to her.

". . . absolutely messed up. I can't believe it," Hena heard the man say.

"They tried to tell me it was a misunderstanding." Lucinda leaned closer to him. "I call bullshit."

"Let me tell you—" The man looked over. Seeing Hena, he abruptly cut off.

"Hena." Color rose to Lucinda's cheeks. "We were being loud, weren't we?"

"You're fine," Hena reassured her.

The man grabbed a set of keys hanging from the back wall. He nodded to Lucinda. "I'll handle that for you."

"You're a lifesaver," Lucinda told him, before turning to Hena. "Are you finding everything okay?"

"Yes," Hena said. "I'm just grabbing something from my mother's suite."

"Fantastic. Let me know if you need anything at all."

Hena hesitated. She could ask Lucinda another time. Her mother needed her medication. But the lobby was empty, this would only take a second, and her question—it was burning inside her.

"Lulu said you worked for my father," Hena said.

At this, Lucinda broke into a smile. "I did. He was a wonderful man, wasn't he?"

Wonderful? Hena blinked. Lucinda seemed utterly sincere.

There was nothing inherently wrong with the sentiment. He had been wonderful to many people. Most people. This many years out, he had practically reached sainthood for some. But if Lucinda worked for him at the Miramar location—where the shadowy parts of his work resided— then surely she had known him better than most.

"Lulu said you did his bookkeeping," Hena said.

"That was my role. Officially, I mean. He said it would look good on my résumé. Honestly, I did a bit of everything," Lucinda replied. "You know how your dad was."

That's the problem, thought Hena. *I do.*

"What do you mean by 'a bit of everything'?" Hena asked.

"Whatever needed doing." She shrugged. "I handled a lot of the paperwork for the side business. Sorting it. Delivering it. Reminding people when they were behind on payments. Your father believed in me. Not many men like him in the world. You were lucky."

Lucky. The word settled in Hena like a stone.

She remembered her father's funeral. Thousands had attended—community members, friends, colleagues, business leaders. So many heartbroken people.

But if they had loved her father, it was because they hadn't truly known him. Over the years, she'd met those who did—

who knew the truth beneath her father's charm. They never spoke a word to her, but their expressions belied their fear. Was Lucinda one of the rare few to have been shielded from it?

A streak of lightning flashed across the glass wall in the background—sharp and sudden. Hena winced. Her mother needed her pain medicine. She was overdue. Hena had turned to leave when—

"You remind me of him, you know?" Lucinda's voice was gentle. Thoughtful. "Every time I see your smile, I think of him. It's nice to know he lives on in his children."

She meant it as a compliment, so Hena did her best not to shiver.

Inside Lulu's suite, Hena flipped on the foyer light. Thunder growled outside—low and guttural. It rattled the windows.

The wedding cake sat untouched on the island, exactly where it had been left that morning, though it was starting to lean. As she walked past it, her eyes landed on the counter next to the fridge. Dozens of translucent orange bottles were lined up neatly along the back wall. A miniature pharmacy.

A heavy ache pressed against her. She had known her mother was on a host of medications, but this many? There was medication for constipation. For diarrhea. For sleep. For pain. So many different pain medications. She picked them up, one by one, reading each label, as thunder boomed outside.

At last, she found the correct one. She crossed over to the fridge, her hand closing around the handle.

Suddenly, a low buzz filled the air, and she was plunged into darkness.

A power outage. Given the storm, it wasn't shocking. But

her mother had mentioned generators. Why hadn't they kicked in?

Hena reached instinctively for her phone to turn on the flashlight—only to remember she had left her purse at the wedding hall. With the curtains drawn and the dark clouds outside, the room was pitch-black. She couldn't even see her hand in front of her face.

She opened the refrigerator and ran her fingers along the shelves until they touched a smooth plastic bottle. She grabbed it, hoping it was the right one, and shut the door.

Then she heard it.

A creak. Long and slow.

"Gita?" she called out tentatively.

No reply.

So not Gita. Probably the wind. The building settling against the storm.

She took a cautious step toward the exit—

Another creak. Higher pitched.

Her pulse quickened. She wasn't afraid of the dark. There was no one else here. There *couldn't* be. But this moment mirrored another. From three years ago.

Her hands fumbled along the wall. Her heart pounded.

Another sound. This time nearer. This time not a creak.

Footsteps.

Blood rushed to her head. She pressed her back against the fridge. Fear prickled the base of her neck. She couldn't see anything, but there was no talking herself down. She *knew*, as certainly as she knew her own name, she was not alone.

"Stay back," she demanded, trying to sound commanding despite the unmistakable quiver in her voice.

Silence.

Then another step. Closing in.

Beads of sweat dotted her forehead. This would not go like last time. She would not wait like a sitting duck until it was too late.

She had to go.

Now.

She lunged forward, fleeing for the door. Her hip slammed into the island. Something crashed to the floor with a sickening thud.

A buzzing sound, and suddenly the lights flickered back on. A smoke detector beeped wildly. The clock on the microwave blinked midnight. Breathing heavily, she scanned the room. Her eyes darted to the corners, searching for a shadow. There was no one there.

But there *had* been someone.

Hadn't there?

Or had she psyched herself out, cowering from ghosts that no longer existed?

Her gaze dropped to the floor. The wedding cake lay smashed beyond recognition.

The front door swung open. Gita wheeled her mother inside.

"Don't worry about the Percocet," Gita called out. "Her coughing is getting worse. I'm going to start a morphine drip now, but we'll need to make an appointment to get her seen tomorrow."

Gita didn't wait for a response before slipping into the bedroom with Ammi. Hena stood motionless, staring at the destroyed cake.

"Lulu has a dress fitting tomorrow," Gita said, once she emerged from the bedroom. "Do you think you can join us at the doc— Oof." She pressed a hand to her temples. "How long has the smoke detector been beeping?"

"Did you see anyone on your way up?" Hena asked, trying to steady her voice. "Anyone out of place? Anyone exiting the elevator while you were waiting?"

"No. Why?" Gita walked toward her—then gasped at the mess.

"I—I'm so sorry," Hena stammered. "When the power went out, I couldn't see where I was going . . ."

"The suite lost power?" Gita asked.

"Didn't the whole resort?"

Gita shook her head. Hena opened her mouth. Then closed it. Because she saw it.

The knife.

It was embedded in the ruined cake.

The one with the glossy reddish-brown handle.

Trembling, Hena knelt and pulled it free. She took in the metal curve of the blade. The hammered finish.

For a moment, it felt as if her heart had stopped.

She knew this knife.

It was a Shun. Lulu had given her a set for her wedding. This particular knife was supposed to be locked away in an evidence bag at the Broward County Sheriff's Office.

Because three years ago, she had sliced that knife into the abdomen of a man who had tried to kill her.

"What a mess," Gita said, shaking her head. "It's all hands on deck with the wedding. I doubt housekeeping will get here anytime soon."

Hena held up the knife, trying to keep her hands steady.

"Why is this here?"

Gita stared at the blade, then paled. "I'm so sorry. I must have left it on the island. I was cutting up an apple this afternoon. I should have placed it in the sink. It could have really hurt you."

"This knife was already here?" Hena asked. "In the suite?"

Gita opened the silverware drawer. There they were. Shun knives. Several of them.

See, Hena? An easy enough explanation. A top-end knife for a top-end suite. One of Lulu's favorite brands, no less.

But no matter how her mind tried to accept this explanation, she couldn't help how seeing the knife made her feel.

Like it had been left there as a pointed message.

Just for her.

TASNIM,
Aunt of the Bride

Don't misunderstand me. I think this is a lovely wedding week. Tasteful, thoughtful. Luma is such a dear putting us up in these wonderful accommodations.

But when I think about the sheer cost of all of this, I can't help but shake my head. Take, for example, the floral arrangements. They swap out new ones for each event. Surely that alone is a year's mortgage for some of us. I heard they flew in the dholki drummers first class from Toronto. And between the welcome bags, the Tiffany key chains, and all the other favors, we're talking thousands of dollars per guest. It's not just wasteful to flaunt one's wealth like this—it can draw the wrong kind of attention.

Take that woman Gita, for instance. That nurse. She is certainly helpful. Always hovering at Frida's side. Ready to address any issue. But might one wonder if she's a touch too helpful? Have you noticed how Frida clings to her every word? She won't take a step without her permission. It's painful to watch a woman of such standing reduced to this. And I'm sorry to say it's the perfect setup for someone less than trustworthy to step in and take advantage.

I tried telling Lulu, but she waved me off. Called Gita a saint. I debated approaching Hena—she's the elder daughter, after all—but that girl is too busy with her romantic escapades to see what's happening right under her nose.

It's a shame money can't protect us from poor decisions. I suppose wealth makes fools of us all. Some sooner than others. ""

DAY
FOUR

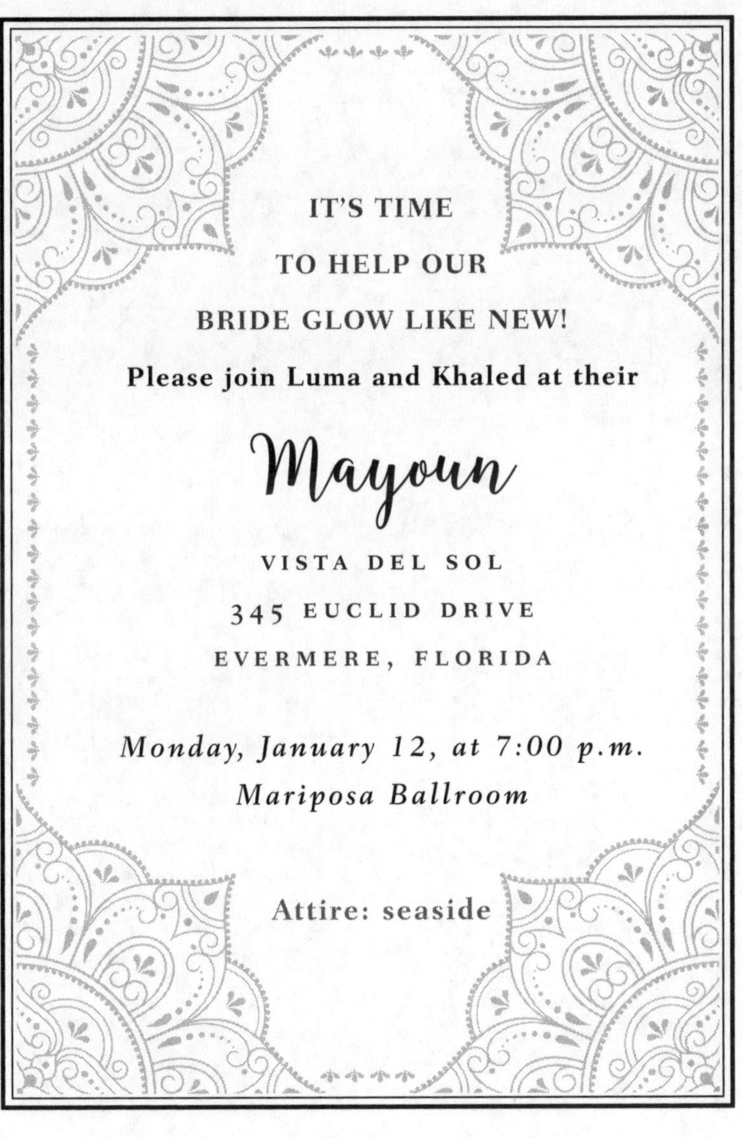

IT'S TIME

TO HELP OUR

BRIDE GLOW LIKE NEW!

Please join Luma and Khaled at their

Mayoun

VISTA DEL SOL

345 EUCLID DRIVE

EVERMERE, FLORIDA

Monday, January 12, at 7:00 p.m.

Mariposa Ballroom

Attire: seaside

ena stepped onto the oversized stucco balcony running the back length of the resort, overlooking the grounds beyond. A cool breeze brushed against her, rustling her dress. Unlike the cloudy, dark skies from the night before, the weather tonight was clear. A crescent moon hung in the night sky.

The mayoun had been underway a few hours, and the ceremony of applying pasted turmeric to Lulu's arms and hands to make her skin glow and shimmer for the wedding was at last blessedly done. Through the oversized windows of the hall, she watched the guests dance. Their indistinct conversations drifted through the windows. A handful of servers methodically arranged the kheer and ras malai for dessert, while others set up the chai table with carafes of polished silver and crystal bowls filled with different types of sugar. On the back lawn, staffers moved about, their figures casting long shadows against the light, as they finalized the rescheduled fireworks display that would conclude the night's festivities.

She shouldn't have been out here, away from it all, but she needed a breather. Despite the twenty-four hours that had passed, she still felt like she was recovering. Her mind tried to unravel what didn't need unraveling—not when the facts lined up exactly as they should.

The storm had caused a power outage. It had only affected the penthouse because—according to Lulu—it had been built on a separate grid.

The creaking sounds she'd heard, creepy as they were, had come from the building's foundation settling against the wind.

And the knife, the thing that had most chilled her to her core, was the easiest to explain. Lulu loved her expensive knives. Hena had checked the cutlery drawer in her own suite. Sure enough, she'd found a collection of Shun knives there too.

She should have been relieved. An easy enough explanation for everything. Nothing shady. Nothing awry. No one had been lurking behind her in the shadows. Instead, she felt unmoored. Because it was like the universe had strung together a maddening string of coincidences specifically designed to torture her over her past.

Or maybe—she gripped the edge of the balcony—the universe was trying to force her to face her past. Because that moment in the darkened penthouse had, for a few terrifying moments, felt like a repeat of the night in her family boathouse—the one doubling as her bridal suite.

She had been so preoccupied she didn't notice at first. Not as he crept closer and closer. She'd been glued to her phone. Texting Nasir. Even though she knew she'd never hear from him again. Not if things went as they should.

The creaking of the floorboards had alerted her to his presence.

"Where is he?" a voice had asked.

When she looked up, startled at the unexpected words,

there he was. The masked man. Inches from her face. Anger radiated off him like heat.

"I won't ask again," he said in a low growl. "Where is he?"

"I—I don't know," she began. "I haven't heard from him since yesterday evening. The mehndi—"

He didn't let her finish. His hands clamped around her throat.

"This isn't personal," he said as her vision blurred. "Just sending a message."

"Please don't do this," she gasped, struggling. Her nails scratched at his hands, but his gloved grip was an iron vise. Tightening with each passing second. Her vision had speckled with darkness. The pain unlike anything she'd experienced before or since. Her body had grown heavy as her back slammed against the dressing table, which cut painfully against her. Useless tears had leaked down her face. The world came in and out as her hands dropped to her sides. This was it. She was done.

Through her hazy vision, her head lolling against the dressing table, her eyes landed on the knife resting on the edge. Lulu's gift. Seconds from blacking out, she strained, inching her hand toward it. Her fingers curled around the hilt. Her body acted on instinct. She lunged forward. The blade found its mark. It was a sharp, clean cut. His grip on her released in an instant as his hands flew to his midsection. He cursed as she fell with a hard thud to the ground.

He had staggered backward, breathing heavily, hatred burning in his eyes. She could tell she had injured him badly, but it hadn't stopped him from taking a halting step forward. To finish what he'd started. Then—

"Hena!" Khala's voice rang sharp and clear from outside the boathouse. "We're running very behind, my dear!"

The man followed the sound. His eyes fixed on the door. Deciding. Debating.

"Please," she croaked. "Don't hurt her. She didn't do anything."

The doorknob began to turn. He bolted. In three long strides, he was at the back window, slipping out into the evening, leaving a trail of blood dripping in his wake.

A rustling sound pulled her back to the present, and Hena shivered. Some people believed it was important to face the past and heal one's trauma, but her? She had no interest in doing so. She would much rather forget.

She heard footsteps. Reza was walking toward her. He wore khakis and a buttoned white shirt with blue embroidered flowers—the uniform for the groomsmen tonight, to complement the bridesmaids' gowns.

"Sorry I couldn't join you on the sailboat," Hena said. "Lulu was tied up with wedding stuff, so I needed to go to the doctor's appointment with my mother."

"Family first," he said. "How is she?"

"The doctor thinks this new combination of medicine they've started her on will do the trick, but she's well beyond the highest doses for most of what she's taking at this point." Hena swallowed as she thought back to the cold, sterile room. The doctor's grim expression. "Hopefully, this new prescription does the trick. The cough is completely tapping her out."

"I'm sorry, Hena. I can't begin to imagine."

"Yeah. Well." Hena forced a shrug. "How was sailing?"

"I didn't go."

"Why not? You were looking forward to it."

He shrugged. "Figured I'd wait for you."

"Aw, I'm sorry."

"Why?" He tilted his head and gave her a smile. "I'd say you're worth the wait."

"Good to know," she said, keeping her tone light, hoping he didn't detect the flush in her cheeks. She looked out at the hedge maze across from them. Reza followed her gaze.

"Have you tried going through it yet?" he asked.

"I know myself. I'd get lost."

"Why don't we check it out together?"

"Yeah?" She turned to look at the wedding hall behind them. "I think the fireworks are set to go off soon . . . and the maze looks a little creepy at night, doesn't it?"

"Don't be scared." He gave her a solemn look. "I'll keep you safe."

She arched a brow. "Cheesy much?"

"A little?" he admitted. "Seriously, it's all lit up. Looks fun."

What was the harm? Besides, she wasn't about to pass up a chance to spend time with Reza.

They walked down the steps and crossed the lawn. Up close, the maze was taller than it had appeared from the balcony. The hedges towered over them, and the leaves were sharp and spiky. The path inside was paved and narrow. But with the unexpected twinkle lights threaded throughout the interior of the maze, and Reza by her side, it felt like they'd left the Everglades entirely, crossing into a place that belonged only to them.

"I think Lulu took the maze concept a little too seriously," Hena said as they walked. "This thing is *intricate*. Is there an actual way out?"

"I have a feeling we're almost through. Let's go left," Reza said, confidently leading them to a dead end for the second time.

"Wrong again." She poked him. "Some protector you are."

"Maybe I overestimated my navigation skills," he conceded.

"If it wasn't spiky, we could've cut through here." Hena pointed to the gaps in the hedge maze to their right, where bits of brown leaves and dead branches had splintered and fallen to the ground. Through it she could see hints of light from the resort.

"Are you suggesting we cheat our way out of this?" Reza looked scandalized. "We got this, Hena. I believe in us."

They strolled down side alleys, doubled back to the main arteries, and eventually glimpsed the end in sight. Their shoulders brushed as they reached the other side. The swamp glimmered beneath the moonlight.

"I need more wealthy friends," he said, looking around. "A week here and I feel properly spoiled."

"I tend to get cabin fever at all-inclusive resorts," she said. "Places like these were my mother's vacation of choice—she'd drag me along to massages and mud facials with those cucumber slices on your eyes. I hated every second of it."

"Massages and facials. Sounds rough." Reza raised an eyebrow.

"World's tiniest violin for me." She elbowed him playfully. "Were your family vacations more nature-based?"

"We didn't take vacations. I'd say the closest we ever got to resorts was working at them."

"Yeah?"

"They were nice resorts, a lot like this one. Ours catered to the Disney tourists. My dad tended the gardens. My mother cleaned rooms. My two older sisters did odd jobs—towel duty, shifts at the kids' clubs. They toiled seven days a week, but we still lived paycheck to paycheck."

"That sounds really hard."

"It was. Especially after my mother died. My dad shut down, so my sisters had to keep everything running. I was the baby, so they basically raised me."

"I'm guessing they were probably too young to take care of a child."

"They tried their best." He smiled faintly. "My oldest sister used to make Mom's favorite omelets each Sunday all the way until she graduated and moved out. My other sister would swipe gummies from the kids' club. She'd hoard them all week, then leave little stashes on my bed if I had a rough day."

Hena felt a tug of familiarity. "It was KitKats for me. My aunt raised me when I was little. Whenever I had a bad day, one of those bars would magically appear on the kitchen table."

"That couldn't have been easy, not having either of your parents around."

"It was the best thing that could have happened to me."

The admission startled her. She didn't talk about her family. Not even with her family. But Reza was a good listener. There was something about him that made her want to tell him. Except she couldn't tell him. There were some things she was meant to keep to herself.

She was thankful he didn't press.

They fell silent for a few moments, the scent of night jasmine lingering in the air. She needed to change the topic. Back to something lighter.

"You said you like this resort," she said. "What's the best part?"

He thought for a moment. "Hard to narrow it down. The service is unbeatable. You already know how good the food is. I tried the Jacuzzi the other day, and it's top-notch. The swans, though . . ." He shook his head.

"What about the swans?" she asked.

"One of them tried to bite me."

"You weren't trying to pet it, were you?"

"They're cute." He flashed her a sheepish grin.

"Reza, no! Swans are notoriously vicious."

"Trust me, lesson learned."

"So I guess it's safe to say the swans are out of contention."

He was still smiling, but a look passed over him as his eyes held hers.

"I'd say my favorite part of being here is pretty obvious, don't you think?"

"Yeah?" she asked, the word coming out lower than intended.

He didn't look away. "Yeah."

Crickets chirped in the darkness. The air between them felt like it was shifting. Only then did Hena realize how close they were standing. So close she could feel the heat of his body, inches from hers, his breath warm against her skin. His gaze drifted from her eyes to her lips. It lingered there. Her heart fluttered. Because she saw it then: the wanting. The same want she felt, written all over his face.

She touched his shirt sleeve as his hand grazed her wrist. Goosebumps trailed her arms. She took one small step closer and lifted her gaze to his. Leaning closer, she almost forgot to breathe.

"The button goes here," a nearby voice burst out.

They jumped apart.

"I know that!" a man retorted. "It's literally what I'm doing!"

A group of people were adjusting wires for the fireworks show a few paces away. They tested the platform and tapped the mic, not even noticing Hena and Reza in the darkness.

She felt jolted awake as though from a dream, except her skin still tingled from where his hand had grazed her. It wasn't a dream. It had been real. But the moment had passed.

"We should—" she started.

"Yeah." He nodded to the resort.

They sidestepped the maze and walked across the grassy lawn back to the festivities. They exchanged no words, but she could feel his eyes drifting toward her.

Hena steadied herself. She tried to make sense of the emotions coursing through her. That she longed to kiss him was nothing new—she had since she'd first laid eyes on him at the registration desk.

It was the other emotion that was more complicated to sift through: a sensation like she was standing on the precipice of a skyscraper, staring down.

They stepped into the hall. The up-tempo dance music had slowed—now classical sitar music played softly in the background. She ignored the curious looks as people noticed them entering together. No doubt it would fuel speculation. If only they had given the crowd something real to talk about.

She grabbed a ceramic cup and poured herself chai from the carafe. Reza stood beside her. His fingers trailed the rim of a cup.

"Should I pour you some too?" she asked, reaching for his cup.

Reza didn't respond, his attention elsewhere. Toward something at the entrance.

In fact, everyone had stopped talking and was looking in the same direction. At him. The man with the dark mustache and stoic expression.

Dread washed over her.

Was she seeing things?

No. She wasn't. She knew this man well.

A manila folder tucked under his arm, he surveyed the room.

His eyes landed on hers, and he walked up to her.

"Hena Mirza?" Detective Milcheck asked. "We need to talk."

NIPA,
Aunt of the Groom

"Haris says I'm going too far. He insists Hena is a great girl. That she's misunderstood. Do you know he had the nerve to ask me to stop worrying so much? Sweet boy, this is just his way—honest and trusting. But how am I not to worry? How can I not be protective? He's my only son, and we've seen what happens to the men in their life. Look at Nasir. Look at her own father.

They say Latif Mirza was a good person. It's what everyone says, including my husband and Haris himself. I shall not speak ill of the dead, but I will say I know the family well enough to know they are trouble.

It's why I'm not surprised by the police presence. We're at a Mirza wedding. This is how they go.

I'm not being cruel. It's simply fact. Whatever that detective hauled her away for? Mark my words, she's guilty."

12

This couldn't be real. This couldn't be happening.

Hena stepped into the conference room adjacent to the mayoun hall. The long oak table gleamed beneath the recessed lighting. It was a sleek, modern space—designed for CEOs who had chosen a tropical location for their annual board meeting to sneak in some sun. It certainly wasn't meant for whatever this conversation was about to be.

The detective shut the door and sat down across from her. He wore khakis and a linen shirt, ostensibly to avoid drawing attention to his presence, though the odds were everyone in attendance had already figured out exactly who he was.

She was afraid to know why he was there.

Folding his hands on the table, he leaned forward.

"I'm not sure you remember me. Detective Milcheck," he introduced himself. "I've been investigating your fiancé's disappearance."

"I remember you," she said. "I thought the case had gone cold."

"Interesting assumption." He studied her like she had given something away. "Why would you think that?"

Was he serious? "It's been three years," she said slowly. "That's why. I've received no updates."

"Just because we don't call doesn't mean we let things fall to the wayside," he said. "And when we get new information, we act."

Her breath caught. "You found something new?"

"We received a tip, yes." His eyes were trained on her. "It's about you."

"Me?"

"Someone reported you have information pertaining to his absence," he continued. "That you might know where he is."

The timing of this "tip" meant whoever phoned it in was at the wedding. She wasn't surprised, but the disappointment stung. It was one thing to gossip with one another, but to bring the police into this?

"I wish I knew where he was," she said. "It's why I called every week for years trying to see if you all might do your jobs. Last I remember, you said disappearing isn't a crime."

"Ms. Mirza, we have been doing our jobs. As you can see, we are still doing our jobs." He frowned. "While going missing is not a crime, we take it seriously if there's suspicion of foul play. If you know something about what happened to him, it's important you share it with us."

The door swung open.

Haris. He stepped inside, closed the door behind him. Before the detective could speak, he drew to Hena's side.

"She won't be answering any questions without me present," Haris told the detective. "I'm her attorney."

His presence alone was enough to shift the air in the room. Hena gave Haris a grateful smile as Milcheck leaned back.

"That was fast," he said.

"Lulu filled me in just a second ago." Haris gave Hena an

apologetic look before turning back to the detective. "We don't want any misunderstandings."

"Of course not," Milcheck replied, but there was something smug in his tone. "Funny thing, though—misunderstandings usually start when people have something to hide."

"What do you think I'm hiding?" Hena's voice rose. "If I knew where he was, why would I have kept it secret all these years?"

Haris touched her knee gently beneath the table—a reminder to stay calm. A reminder he was here to help her, and she needed to let him.

"Detective, if you have something to say, say it," Haris told him. "This is a family wedding, and we would like to return to the festivities."

As though on cue, there was the crackling sound of fireworks. Brilliant orange and green sparks burst into the night sky through the windows.

"Ms. Mirza, we recently got a ping from a cell tower near Homestead," said Detective Milcheck. "We have reason to believe the device belonged to Nasir Wahidi."

Homestead? Her pulse quickened. Homestead was here. In Florida. Only an hour south of them. Looking at Haris, he was processing this as well—the news clearly a shock to him too. He nodded, signaling for her to answer.

"I don't know anything about that," she said truthfully.

"You don't know," he repeated. "Let me be honest. Here's what we do know. We know he didn't arrive for your wedding. We know he turned off his phone the morning of the nuptials. We know his accounts were emptied. So we know there was premeditation in his leaving."

"None of this is new," she said, her frustration leaking out.

"We received a tip that you saw him—in fact, *spoke* to

him—not just the night before, but the morning of his disappearance. Which means you would have been the last person to have seen him."

Shit. This *was* something new. Something that sent ice down her spine.

"We also have reason to believe the quarter of a million dollars he removed from his account was yours," he said.

A wave of nausea passed through her. How would he know? No one knew about that.

"I don't appreciate this fishing expedition, Detective." Haris's tone sharpened. "Gossip isn't a justification for harassment."

"This isn't a fishing expedition. It's a tip." Milcheck's voice grew clipped. "A guest at this wedding reported their concerns, and we're obligated to investigate any new information that comes to light. Ms. Mirza, it's a simple question. And I'm assuming it would be all right if you shared your bank statements with us for the relevant time period? A quick look at your records from that time frame will put this particular theory to bed."

She opened her mouth to speak, but nothing came out. This was déjà vu. They had asked to see her bank statements three years ago. She had demurred. They hadn't pressed.

That part of her life was supposed to be behind her.

But if they saw her records, nothing would be behind her at all.

"We are done here." Haris pulled out a business card from his wallet and slid it across the table. "If you have cause to bring my client in for questioning, or if you have a subpoena to request her records, contact me. Otherwise, we invite you to leave the premises."

Milcheck pursed his lips, but he took the card. He studied Hena as he stood. "Thank you for your time, Ms. Mirza."

He was nearly at the door when he looked at the card. His focus shifted to Haris. Something flickered across his face.

"So, you're Haris."

Haris's face remained unreadable. "Is there something else?"

"Well, it's interesting." The detective studied the card. "I wasn't going to mention this as it hardly seemed relevant, but the tip we received mentioned you. Or rather, the two of you."

He gave them a knowing look. Hena stiffened. Was he accusing them both of conspiring to get rid of Nasir?

"If it's of relevance, please share what you've heard," Haris said calmly.

The detective looked from her to Haris. "I'm still figuring out if it is."

"Excellent," Haris said. "Once you're done enjoying all the gossip our guests can regale you with and are actually ready to find Nasir, get in touch. Until then." Haris gestured to the door.

When he was gone, Hena pressed her back against a wall to get her bearings.

"Wh-what was that?" she stammered. "Was he implying we did something to Nasir?"

"He's throwing darts in the air," Haris said. "Hoping to touch a nerve. That's all. If they had anything real, we'd be having a different conversation."

She should have felt reassured by this. But she wasn't. Because someone had called the detective with this information. And whether they were speculating or not, what they told him was true.

She *had* spoken to Nasir that morning.

The money Nasir withdrew *had* been hers.

"Now what?" she asked shakily. "Are they going to go through my accounts? Are they going to—"

"Not without legal justification they won't," Haris said. "First thing tomorrow I'll head to the police station and find out what is going on. If there's new information, if they really found his location, you deserve the full picture. Don't worry, Hena. We got this."

We. For the first time since Milcheck arrived, her chest loosened. Haris was right. She wasn't alone in this. Despite all the years that had passed, here he was, helping her carry this weight.

"I don't know what I would have done without you," she said.

"I'm happy to help."

"I'm sorry, Haris," she said. "For leaving the way I did. Khala . . . Lulu . . . you. None of you deserved that."

"No one could blame you." He put a hand on her shoulder. "We're glad you're back, though. *I'm* glad you're back."

She met his warm gaze and something stirred in her. She quickly pushed it away.

They walked toward the large oak doors. She braced herself for a sea of wedding guests on the other side trying to listen in, but only Irum was waiting in the hallway for them. Arms crossed, she wore a grim expression. Before Hena could say anything, Irum spoke first.

"Lulu told me to come find you," she said. "I'm so sorry, Hena, but it looks serious."

"What is it?" Hena asked.

Before Irum could reply, Hena saw red and white lights flashing outside the hotel entrance.

She rushed through the sliding doors. Partygoers were gathered around the ambulance. Before she could ask what happened, she heard the sliding doors part behind her. Two medics wheeling a stretcher hurried past as bits of conversation wafted over to her.

The stress was too much . . .

The officer . . .

The shame of it all . . .

That poor thing, after all she's been through . . .

Their words surrounded Hena, but all she could focus on was her.

Ammi.

Lying motionless on the stretcher.

13

•

Hena hated hospitals. And today was the worst experience to date. Ammi lay sound asleep on the bed. The heart monitor beside her beeped in tune to the throbbing inside Hena's own head.

But the beeps meant Ammi was alive.

It meant she was still here.

It had been two hours since she was stabilized. Khala yawned from where she sat on a stiff-backed chair by the wall. Gita, who had been standing guard by her mother's side since they'd arrived, was curled up on the ledge of the cushioned bay window now, drifting in and out of sleep.

Hena hadn't stopped pacing. Her body was restless, as if constant motion could hold off whatever was coming. She walked to her mother's side now. Gingerly, she touched her mother's sleeve and braced. For her mother's eyes to fly open. For her to scowl at Hena. Ammi didn't so much as flinch. Thanks to the wonders of morphine, she wouldn't be waking anytime soon.

"I don't understand," Khala said. "Today was a good day. The new cough suppressant was working wonders. This

coughing fit came out of nowhere. When I saw the blood—"
She paused. "I was preparing for the worst."

A nurse came to check Ammi's vitals. Hena stared at the
IV delivering the morphine. She thought of the rows of pain
medications lining the counter of her mother's penthouse
suite.

"Is this level of morphine safe?" Hena asked the nurse.
"She's on constant pain medication, and the dosages are high.
People can get easily addicted, can't they?"

"Oh, hon." The nurse looked at her sympathetically.

Ah. There was that knot in Hena's chest again.

When the nurse left, Hena glanced at Khala. Gita rubbed
her eyes and yawned. She finally asked the question she had
been avoiding since she arrived.

"How long does she have?"

Gita and Khala exchanged concerned looks.

"Please," Hena said. "Don't sugarcoat it."

"Soon," said Khala.

"Soon, as in . . . ?"

"It could be weeks. Or it could be any day, really," Khala
said softly.

Any day. Hena looked at her mother as the words sank in.
She had known, hadn't she? Deep down, she knew. All she
had to do was look at her mother's skeletal frame to know she
was barely holding on.

"The goal is to keep her as comfortable as possible," Gita
said. "The pain is the hardest thing to deal with."

Pain so brutal that her mother—who hated hospitals,
doctors, medication—was letting Gita and the medical team
load her up with whatever it took to dull the agony.

"This is the worst time to throw a wedding," Hena said.
"No matter how comfortable we make her, the schedule is

grueling, and the exertion is wearing her out. She can't keep going like this. Someone should have talked her out of it. It's—it's killing her."

"We tried our best to reason with her. All of us did," said Khala. "But your mother said seeing Lulu off in a grand wedding was her dying wish. You know your mother. If she sets her mind on something, there's no stopping her. She's difficult to counter on an ordinary day, but once she pulled the 'I'm dying' card, how were we to refuse?"

"She's the most stubborn person I know."

"You have no idea," Khala said.

But Hena did have some idea.

Looking at her now, a strange sort of grief climbed up Hena's throat. It wasn't just sadness for Ammi. It was for herself. Deep down, a part of her had hoped there would come some kind of turning point for the two of them. Their relationship. A moment where her mother would have a realization. That things didn't have to be the way they were between them. That maybe there would come a day where they would mend things. But sometimes there was no fixing what was broken. Sometimes you ran out of time before you could.

Hours passed. Hena was perched on the edge of the bay window next to Gita, her eyes drifting closed, when Lulu burst into the hospital room. She'd been in and out since Ammi had been hospitalized. Now she stepped inside with their mother's favorite pillow. Her special filtered water. All these hours later, she'd still not changed out of her mustard-yellow mayoun outfit. Her makeup was smudged. Her hair, half-unpinned, fell haphazardly down the sides of her face.

"How is she? Any updates?" Lulu began, but she stopped abruptly when she saw Ammi. A sob escaped.

"She's all right. Just sleeping," Khala reassured Lulu. "I told you to get some rest. She's stabilized now."

Lulu shoved down the side railing and squeezed into the bed next to her. She wrapped an arm around Ammi's frail body. "You'll be okay, Ammi," she said softly.

Her mother's eyes fluttered open. She looked at Lulu. When she spoke, her words were barely a rasp.

"You're going to ruin your outfit."

Everyone froze for a moment, before bursting into laughter.

"You fainted," Hena told her mother, once the laughter subsided. "They're running tests to see what's going on, though the current guess is severe dehydration."

"I've been hydrating as much as I always do," Ammi said. "And you have me on those godforsaken IVs each day."

"Even so," Gita said, "a full desi wedding schedule is exhausting even if one is fully healthy. You need to pare down how much you're doing. Your body can only handle so much stress."

"I'm done. We can't keep going like this," Lulu said suddenly. "Khaled's coming in a little while. I'll call the imam. He can marry us here."

"What are you going on about?" Ammi asked.

"I'm saying we'll make it official and call it a day," said Lulu. "The guests will understand."

"The mehndi is this evening," Ammi said. "You can't miss it."

Lulu looked at her, incredulous. "Are you kidding me?"

"Where is the joke? I certainly didn't make one." Ammi pressed a button on the remote and adjusted her bed upright. "A mehndi is one of the most important days of a wedding. You told me yourself it was the mehndi you were most excited about."

"Ammi," Lulu said slowly, as though she couldn't believe she had to explain this. "Things have changed since then."

"I will not have tonight's festivities canceled on account of me." Her voice took on more power. "I mean it, Lulu."

Lulu continued to argue with Ammi, but Hena could already see there was no sense trying to fight this. As weak as she was, her mother was refusing to take no for an answer.

"I'd like to be discharged," she said when the nurse returned to check her vitals.

"I understand," the woman replied. "It's difficult to be cooped up in this room. Dr. Kao will be here in a little while. We're waiting on a few more tests, and then he'll go over the results of everything and—"

"He can phone me with whatever updates he needs to relay," she interrupted. "Where do I sign the forms to leave?"

"Ammi." Lulu was clearly exasperated. "You can't just leave."

"I can do as I wish," Ammi retorted. "I'm a dying woman, and I get the final say with how I spend my final moments, don't I? Isn't that the least I deserve?"

"Ms. Mirza, I understand the urgency, and we will discharge you as soon as we are able," the nurse hurriedly assured her. "But we need the doctor to go over your results. It won't be much longer, I promise. I'll ping him as soon as I step out."

After everyone forcefully and firmly sided with the nurse, she relented, requesting her favorite peppermint tea and the metal bracelet to help her nausea while they waited for the tests to come back.

"Let me get it," Hena offered.

Lulu handed her car keys over, and Hena headed down to the lobby as the sliding door opened. Khaled, Haris, and Irum hurried inside.

"How is Auntie Frida?" Khaled asked worriedly. "Lulu said . . . she thought . . ."

"She's awake, and she's in good spirits," Hena told him. "Lulu's there with her right now. They'll be happy to see you."

"I'll catch up," Irum told Khaled. She turned to Hena. "Lulu texted me the mehndi was off?"

"It's back on," Hena said. "Our mother is insisting we keep everything as scheduled."

Irum balked. "Is she joking? I saw her pass out. She's in no condition."

"I know, and mehndis can go on for hours. There's no reasoning with her. We tried."

Irum considered this. "How about we shorten it?" she asked. "We can push it to an earlier start time. Maybe four o'clock?"

"Good idea," Hena said. "And we can cut some of the rituals as well."

"I'll set a strict schedule. Every ritual will have a hard end time. We can make sure she's in bed by eight."

"Sounds perfect." Relief swept through Hena. "Thank you, Irum."

Irum headed down the hallway, but Haris hung back.

"Glad to hear your mother is doing better," he said. "You doing okay?"

"Define *okay*." Hena gave him a weary smile. "I'm relieved she's hanging in there, but she's also currently planning her own hospital jailbreak."

"I'm not sure whether to be impressed or horrified."

"I'm a little bit of both, to be honest."

"Between your mother and that detective barging in . . . it's a lot."

"I'm grateful Lulu's got some great bridesmaids to help. And you, Haris. I can't thank you enough for your help with the detective."

"I'm heading to the police station right now," he told her

as they walked out to the parking lot. "I want to see what Milcheck has, and if it's as I suspect—nothing—I plan to file a complaint. It's fucked up to intrude on your family wedding like this."

"I'd love to know who called it in," Hena said.

"If I can get any information, I will, but tips are normally anonymous."

A car zoomed by in the distance. She heard the sound of distant honks.

"I don't even get the implication he was trying to make about us." Her voice faltered. "They think we colluded to hurt him? What would our motive be?"

At this, Haris winced.

"Uh-oh. What have you heard?"

"You don't want to know. Trust me."

"Haris . . ."

"It seems like someone started a rumor." He exhaled. His ears turned a subtle shade of pink. "About us. About a romantic past."

A romantic past. A strange weight settled over her. "Are they saying I cheated on Nasir? That you and I . . . ?"

"Not exactly." He rubbed the back of his neck. "They're referring to Auntie Hanifa's potluck. Not sure if you remember . . ."

"The kiss when we were teenagers?" Now it was her turn to feel heat rising to her face.

He gave her a sheepish half shrug.

"Someone reported that to the police?" Then, in a smaller voice—"Someone saw us?"

"Big Auntie is always watching, right?"

Their kiss was a lifetime ago. During one of the lowest moments of her life. Mere weeks after her father's death, her mother had dragged her and Lulu to a dinner party, insisting enough was enough—it was time to move on. But Hena couldn't bear to be around the easy banter and chatter while her emotions were churned up and spinning. Seeking a reprieve, she'd wandered outside after dinner and sat on a bench overlooking the retention pond. Haris had found her there. Asked if she was okay—the only person who had. And when she cried, he'd sat beside her, silent, his arm around her shoulders. He hadn't said much. Hadn't tried to fix anything. He just listened. She couldn't even remember how the kiss had happened, exactly, except it had been sweet. By the following year, she was with Nasir. They never spoke of it again.

But someone had spied on them all those years ago. Someone had stored up the memory, and they decided now was the time to share it?

"That's sick," she muttered.

"It's ridiculous," Haris agreed. "Milcheck knows it. He's just fishing. But we do need to discuss some things. Later, when you have the headspace. I know you're already dealing with enough."

"No, go ahead," she said.

He hesitated. "To be clear, if you're not comfortable discussing it, I completely understand. Just know whatever you do tell me stays between us. Attorney-client privilege."

"I appreciate everything you've done," she told him. "Ask me anything."

"They can't access your financial records without a court order, so no need to worry for now," he said. "But if they do gain access, and the transactions indicate the money withdrawn was yours, I want to warn you it'll get messy fast. So if any money was exchanged, it would be better to tell me sooner rather than later, so we can get ahead of it and plan accordingly."

Her eyes slid to the pavement. She had told Haris he could ask her anything. She couldn't talk about this, though. She couldn't.

They were silent for a few moments, and then Haris spoke again.

"In case it helps," he said gently, "I've lent him money too."

She looked at him with a start. Of course. And the way he was looking at her—he already knew.

"There was this person," she said, her voice catching. "Someone Nasir owed money to. They're the one who . . . who started it all, really."

"Nasir told me someone was harassing him," Haris said. "He'd clam up when I asked for details. Said he didn't want to put anyone in danger."

"He wouldn't tell me much either," Hena said. "They're the ones who got him caught up in the high-stakes tables. When Nasir lost, they gave him credit. Over and over again. I didn't know about it for years, until he was in too deep."

She pressed her back against the car, trying to steady herself. "I don't know why he kept going back, even after he'd swear he was done. I told myself if he wasn't done, then I was. I must've made that promise a dozen times. But when it came down to it, how could I leave him? And how could I say no when he needed money? Especially when it was a matter of life or death by the time he came to me."

She shivered, remembering the black eyes. The dislocated shoulders. The broken ribs. Unlike her father, Nasir didn't have a mean bone in his body. It was what had drawn her to him. It was also what had made him such easy prey.

"But he was done with all that. He'd moved on," Haris said. "Work was going good. We were hitting the gym every week. I saw it in his eyes. He was getting his life back on track."

"I thought so too. It's why we set our wedding date. I believed him."

"Of course you did. From what I saw, I think he believed it too. Look, you don't need to feel bad for lending him money. It'll raise questions with Milcheck because it wasn't disclosed earlier, but it's understandable why you were hesitant to share. And giving him money isn't a crime."

This was the painful part to admit. Even to Haris. Especially to Haris.

"I didn't lend him the money this time."

Haris tilted his head.

"You didn't lend him the money," he repeated. He paused for a moment. When he spoke again, his voice was lower, as though he was afraid to say the words. Afraid to hear the answer. "Are you saying he stole it?"

"I don't know if it's stealing." She wrapped her arms around herself. "We were going to be married soon, right? He didn't clean me out completely. I'd transferred a bit of my trust into an account for the cottage we were about to close on. He knew where I kept my log-ins and passwords."

"How much did he take?"

She paused. Then—

"All of it," she whispered. "He emptied the account."

The corner of his mouth twitched. He took a second before speaking.

"Unbelievable," he said. "Even for him."

"I should've been more vigilant. I knew he had a problem. He didn't mean to—"

"Hena . . . no. This was a bridge too far. I loved him too, but this?"

"Something was off with him all week. I should've dug deeper," she said. "He was getting paranoid. Looking out the windows constantly. He started talking about getting a gun. Can you imagine Nasir with a gun? I pressed him on it, but he swore he wasn't gambling anymore."

"But he emptied your bank account. So . . ."

"Someone *was* after him," she told Haris. "The person who tried to kill me—he said the attack was a message."

Haris exhaled. He gazed at the road in the distance.

"He really fucked up," he said quietly.

"He tried so hard. I know he did. He couldn't kick the habit."

"I meant with you, Hena." His eyes locked onto hers. "What more could he have wanted? How could he throw it away? He betrayed you in the worst way possible. It's unforgivable."

Hena moved to speak, to defend him, but she stopped herself, afraid she might start crying. Haris was right. Nasir may have had his reasons, but there was no getting around the fact he had betrayed her. Over and over again. She had loved Nasir, loved him with everything she was, and love had blinded her to the truth of the situation. Love had fooled her into thinking it was enough. And it wasn't.

She laid her head against Haris's chest. He put his arms around her shoulders, resting his chin on her. He was warm. Comforting. He smelled like lemons. Her thoughts drifted back to their kiss beneath the lemon tree.

It was a road not taken, wasn't it?

What if she *had* taken this road?

How different would her life have been?

She started. The thought felt treasonous. To whom? To Nasir? The man who walked away three years ago and never looked back?

There was no use dwelling on what-ifs, she reminded herself. It was too late for all that.

Still, with Haris's familiar arms around her, the ache in her chest eased. Not gone. But for now, a little easier to bear.

And for now, it was enough.

DAY
FIVE

14

·

Two trips to the hospital and back, and Hena finally returned to her suite. The adrenaline that had kept her functioning all night had fully drained out of her system, leaving her hollow.

She dropped her purse on the kitchen table and texted Lulu for an update on their mother. The sun was steadily rising in the sky. It was nearly ten o'clock in the morning. Waves of exhaustion rippled through her so strongly she considered collapsing then and there. She wanted nothing more than the oblivion of sleep.

She kicked off her shoes and walked toward the bedroom.

Suddenly she heard it: a creak.

Hena froze.

The noise sounded again.

Just like last time.

Which means it's nothing, Hena told herself. Buildings settled. It was what Lulu said. And this one, built over the wetlands, likely settled more than most. Her nerves were frayed and she was exhausted. The sooner she slept, the better.

A knock.

Hena paused. She edged to the door. Peered through the peephole. No one. Cautiously, she cracked it open. The hallway was empty. But she'd heard a knock.

Hadn't she?

Shutting the door, Hena latched the bolt. She moved to grab her phone to call the front desk, when—

Footsteps.

The undeniable sound of heels clicking against tile. Someone was here. They were in this suite.

Shit. She needed to leave. *Now*. She yanked at the doorknob, ready to flee, when—

"Hena?"

Lucinda. She emerged from the kitchen holding a vase of flowers and a wrapped gift.

Seeing Hena's stricken expression, her face flooded with color.

"I'm so sorry," she said quickly. "I thought you were at the hospital. I'd have rung the front door otherwise."

"Wh-where did you come from?"

"The service entrance."

She led Hena to a laundry room tucked behind the kitchen. Hena hadn't noticed it before, but sure enough, there it was: A narrow white door opened onto a landing. A metal staircase across from it led to the ground.

"I had no idea there were two entrances," Hena said.

"It's a fire code thing," Lucinda replied. "Lulu also prefers staff use the back entries so as not to jam up the elevators for our guests."

She apologized again for giving Hena a scare.

"It's okay," Hena said, her pulse settling down.

"I'm glad to hear your mother is better." Lucinda handed

Hena the flowers and gift. "It looks like someone was thinking of you."

She headed out the back entrance, and Hena tried not to flinch at the way the stairs creaked with each step Lucinda took.

The same creak she'd heard the night of the storm.

Was it possible it *hadn't* been in her head? And if so . . .

Stop.

Hena tried shaking it off. This was the exhaustion talking. That was all.

But.

The man who'd tried to kill her had never been caught. The police had insisted he'd likely died. Swallowed by the swamp behind her family home.

But likely was not definitely.

There was a chance he was still alive. There was a chance he knew she was back in town.

Maybe he was looking for her.

Maybe he had already found her.

Or maybe it really was the wind. Maybe I should calm down. This place had security, Hena reminded herself. Multiple cameras. So many people. She just needed to get through a few more days.

Hena set the flowers on the kitchen table—gorgeous pink peonies. She opened the note.

Thinking of you and your family—Reza

Her heart lifted as she unwrapped the gift: a KitKat bar.

Pulling out her phone, she texted him.

Three bubbles appeared. Then—

> **Reza:** There's more KitKat bars where that came from 😊

> **Hena:** Thank you, Reza. This is so sweet and thoughtful.

> **Reza:** The least I could do. And if you need a break, the boating trip is still on the table . . .

Hena's smile lingered. Before she could reply, the phone lit up with an incoming call—Lulu.

"Is Ammi all right?" Hena asked as soon as she answered.

"She's fine," Lulu said. "Turns out the initial guess was right—severe dehydration. They've got her on a higher level of electrolytes, and she's perking up. We'll probably get the discharge paperwork in a little bit. She'll be back in time for the mehndi."

"I'm happy to help," Hena offered. "Whatever you need, don't hesitate."

"I was hoping you'd say that. I do need help. Not with the mehndi, though."

"Uh-oh."

"It's simple, I promise. The men are on their deep-sea fishing excursion, but the charter bus for the women's outing is set to leave at noon. It's the Bartelo House."

"What is this one?" Hena grabbed the wedding binder from the coffee table and paged through it. "I can't keep track of all the events you've got going on."

"How have you never heard of the Bartelo House?" Lulu exclaimed. "It's that cute little boho chic place by the water where Mariela shares her visions."

"So, she's like a fortune teller?"

"Not *like* a fortune teller, she *is* a fortune teller. Mariela? She's got three million followers on TikTok!" Lulu sounded personally offended. "She can read people's fortunes without ever having met them. You choose the topic you want her to explore, and she takes it from there. It's uncanny how good she is. She predicted I'd meet Khaled. She knew it down to the month. I told her to keep today's fortunes strictly peppy and upbeat so everyone can leave in good spirits. They'll have tea and sweets followed by the palm reading, and everyone gets to take their fortune home memorialized in a cute little typed-up scroll. It should be fun."

"So . . . what's the favor?"

"I need you to go."

"Lulu—"

"We need a representative from the family," she said. "Khala won't leave Ammi's bedside, and Ammi doesn't want me to go. Besides, I have the power of attorney, so I should be close by. You know, in case."

In case she had to use it. This really could be any day now, couldn't it?

"Please, Hena?" Lulu pleaded on the other end of the line. "I promise it won't be too painful."

"Of course I'll go," Hena told her. She would take a quick catnap. She'd much rather crash for a few hours—her body was almost demanding it—but this was what family did. They showed up for each other.

"Thank you!" Lulu said. "Lean into the kitschy, okay? It'll be fun."

Lulu and Hena clearly had different definitions for what constituted kitschy.

The three-story moss-lined Bartelo House perched on the edge of a sleepy inlet was over-the-top extravagant. Banana, orange, and guava trees framed the lush grounds. Actual peacocks strutted across the lawns. Gentle instrumental music wafted in the background.

Servers in full livery carried trays of pastries and crystal glasses filled with something pink and fizzy. Courtney and a few aunties made affirmation bracelets at a high-top strewn with beads and crystals.

Irum was getting a tea sandwich when Hena joined her at the snack table.

"How's your mom?" Irum asked.

"She should be getting discharged from the hospital any minute. Thanks for handling the mehndi stuff today."

"It's all set," she said. "We'll stay strictly on schedule. I'm making sure of it."

"Thanks, Irum," Hena told her.

Irum pressed her lips together. "The detective who came by last night. He was the same one from your wedding?" When Hena nodded, Irum's expression grew clouded. "Was he here about Nasir?"

Things had been so chaotic since the detective had swung by, Hena hadn't found the right time to bring it up. Of course Irum had questions. Of course she wanted to know. She deserved to know.

Hena told her what little relevant information Detective Milcheck had shared: The phone ping. That it had come from the Homestead area. That it may have been Nasir's phone. Maybe.

Irum's lips parted. The hope blooming across her face broke Hena's heart.

Before Hena could tell her that Haris hadn't put much stock in it, that he suspected this was the detective's ruse to get her talking, Irum spoke again.

"Was Kiran right?" she asked, almost to herself. "Did she *actually* see him?"

Hena stiffened. "What?"

"Kiran. She said she saw him," Irum said, excitement rising in her voice. "A few days ago. At Las Olas."

"Sh-she saw Nasir?"

"Well, she said she saw someone who looked like him. I didn't think anything of it. She didn't talk to him or even get a picture, and she said he was dressed like a hobo with over-sized sunglasses. Does that even sound like Nasir?" She shook her head, half laughing. "I figured it was Kiran being Kiran. You know, gossip for gossip's sake. I didn't even dare tell my mother. I wouldn't want to get her hopes up." Her eyes were brighter. "But, maybe? Maybe it was him?"

Hena's pulse ticked up. Could Milcheck have been telling the truth? Did he really get a ping from Nasir's phone? And if they traced him to Homestead . . .

She pulled out her phone. She scrolled to his name in her contacts. Three years later, there he was. Brown hair parted to the side. A photo she'd captured mid-laughter. She pressed the call button. Held the phone to her ear.

"Straight to voicemail."

"But it could have been on for a little while." Her smile wavered. "It's why my father won't cut the line. He said he'd leave it just in case. So . . . maybe?"

A dull ache throbbed in Hena's head. She needed to tell Haris about Kiran. What she thought she'd seen. Soon. But before that, there was something else Hena needed to know.

"The detective said someone at the wedding accused me of being involved in Nasir's disappearance," she said.

She studied Irum's face as this sank in.

"Are you serious?" Irum said, blanching. "Does Lulu know?"

"I haven't had a chance to tell her yet. With everything going on, it's hard to find the right time."

"She needs to know. This . . . this is beyond the pale. Isn't there enough for them to gossip about? There has to be a limit."

She seemed genuinely surprised. And angry. Which meant she probably hadn't called in the tip.

"I'm scared to ask, but . . . how deep in the hole was he?" she asked Hena. "My brother?"

"The hole?" Hena repeated.

"His gambling. Whatever happened was related to that, right?" Taking in Hena's surprised expression, Irum sighed. "I knew," she said. "My parents did too. They'll deny it if you ever ask them, but he'd skimmed money off them when I was in high school. I'd hear the fights."

It seemed Nasir's gambling problem was the worst-kept secret there was.

"He swore he was clean," Hena told her. "He'd given me no reason to doubt his word."

"Hard to trust an addict, though, right?"

Hena flinched at Irum's harsh tone. "He wasn't—"

"He was." Irum's eyes grew moist. "Sometimes you have to call things what they are. It pisses me off sometimes. How everyone refused to face facts, indulging him like they did, forgiving him each time he fucked up. It led to everything getting worse."

Her words landed like a punch. Because by "everyone," Irum included Hena too. Which was fair. Each time Nasir vowed to do better, promised he was done, she allowed her-self to believe it. What if she'd put her foot down the first time she'd learned of his addiction? How different could things have been? Maybe he could have gotten the help he'd needed sooner. Maybe things wouldn't have gotten as bad as they had.

A bell chimed. A woman in a flowing red dress informed them it was time for their session. They stepped into the low-lit home draped in gauzy fabrics and decorated with murals of seascapes.

Mariela was in her fifties, plain-faced but with piercing green eyes and blond hair pulled back in a low knot. On each wrist, she wore an assortment of bangles. She had a feathery shawl draped over her shoulders and a cream blouse with a flowing skirt. She'd leaned so deep into her fortune teller persona, it was like she was cosplaying one. This must have been what Lulu meant by kitschy.

Mariela pulled out a leather-bound book and a pen, setting them on her table. Clasping her hands together, she addressed the crowd.

"Welcome, welcome. Please take any open seat. I am honored to have you in my home." She gestured to the woman to her right, seated by an old-fashioned typewriter. "Colette will be memorializing your fortunes so you may take them home with you as a memento. Now." She swept her gaze toward the audience. "Who shall we bring up first?"

Colette consulted the notebook. "Maheen."

Hena's cousin bounced up to the dais and sat across from Mariela. She placed her palms on the low-seated table.

"What topic would you like insight on, my dear?" Mariela asked.

"I'd love to know about my job. Specifically, what is to come," Maheen said. "Will we succeed?"

Mariela studied Maheen's hands. She pursed her lips. "I see you're in business with someone?"

Maheen gasped. "I literally opened the practice with my best friend two months ago."

"A medical practice."

Maheen was beside herself. The women around Hena chatted excitedly, and she had to fight the urge to roll her eyes. (A) They were desi, so the odds of someone being a doctor were pretty high, and (B) Maheen had left enough context for Mariela to make an educated guess.

"Is it sports medicine?" Mariela asked.

Hena blinked. All right, that was specific.

"How did you guess that?" Hena asked her.

Mariela jerked her head up, narrowing her eyes at Hena.

"I don't guess, my dear," she replied, before turning her attention back to Maheen. "You and your business partner went to medical school together. I'm sensing a landlocked city."

"University of Chicago. Yes. Wow."

The crowd was mesmerized, and Hena made sure to bite her tongue. These details confirmed to Hena this was more a party trick than any real intuition. Mariela had their names in her ledger. She must have looked them all up online. Scoured their social media.

But did it matter? Everyone was enjoying the show. Lulu had hit it out of the park with this one. Hena would be sure to let her know.

The fortune teller informed Maheen her business would prosper. Word of mouth alone would propel them to greater heights. She'd have a waiting list this time next year, with patients clamoring for a spot.

Next up was Auntie Hanifa.

"All right, let's hear it," she demanded, once seated. "When is my daughter going to get married?"

Mariela studied the auntie's hands. She trailed a finger along her palm. "Your daughter will be engaged by year's end."

"Wonderful." Auntie Hanifa's eyes lit up. "Now let's hope I can find her a groom soon."

"No need," the fortune teller replied. "She's already in love. There's a woman with a T name. Tammy? Tabatha?"

"Tamara?" Auntie Hanifa gasped. "I thought it was over!"

"Not at all." The woman clucked her tongue. "I see them together right now. A mountainous horizon . . . a cabin of sorts."

Auntie Hanifa drew a hand to her mouth.

Laughter. Whispers. Claps. They were eating this up.

The time passed swiftly as Colette invited people one by one to have their fortunes read. Everyone was amazed at the accuracy, even though Hena remained skeptical.

"And last but not least: Hena," Colette called out.

"No, thank you," she said quickly. "I'm just here taking it all in."

"Nonsense," Mariela replied. "You're our final client. We must read all fortunes so I can close the aura."

"Go on," an auntie insisted. "You had fun listening to all our stories. It's your turn."

She was nudged—gently but firmly—toward the dais. She didn't want to kill the mood, so she might as well get it over with.

"What would you like guidance on?" Mariela asked once Hena was seated across from her. She took Hena's hands in hers and studied the lines. "Your love life, perhaps?"

"We don't have all day." Auntie Hanifa chortled.

Hena ignored her. There had to be something she could ask. Something harmless. Something innocent. Maybe about her job—some insights on who her next interior design client might be. Before she could say anything, Mariela's grip tightened. She slid a finger over Hena's palm lines. Her lips pursed.

"I see darkness," she said.

There was laughter from the audience. Hena looked at the woman in disbelief.

"I thought Lulu asked you to keep our fortunes happy," she said.

"You betrayed someone," Mariela continued, undeterred. It was as though she hadn't even heard Hena.

The good-natured chuckles were gone. An eerie silence settled over the space.

"Just as you betrayed someone, soon you too will be betrayed." She lifted her eyes to meet Hena's. Her expression was troubled. "I'm sorry, dear. I was commissioned for happy fortunes, but I cannot ignore danger."

"So I'm in danger too?" Hena said sarcastically.

Mariela closed her eyes. When she spoke, her tone was hushed.

"So much anger. Directed at you. They believe you have wronged them." Tiny beads of sweat dotted Mariela's forehead. "Has anyone given you reason to think they mean you harm?"

"With a girl like Hena, the list might get long," someone quipped.

Hena jerked her head back. Auntie Nipa. She smirked in Hena's direction, pleased to have gotten a rise out of her. Anger bubbled up, hot and fast. Hena yanked her hand from Mariela's. She understood what was going on.

"My mother is in the hospital." She glared at the women. "She's dying. But it's not enough to keep you all from having your fun with me?"

"What are you accusing us of?" Auntie Nipa's eyes flashed. "Why on earth would we ask her to give you a bad fortune?"

Entertainment.

She was just a story to these women. A source of endless speculation. It was all her family's pain had ever been to them.

"Simply because you don't like what I say doesn't mean what I have shared is false." Mariela's eyes flashed with indignation. "I had no intention of sharing such a dark fortune. Do you know how much energy it takes out of me? But when I get a premonition like this, it's my professional obligation to disclose it."

"Then be specific," Hena said evenly.

"I'm not a genie." The woman scowled.

"Give me a name. A detail. Anything."

She took one of Hena's hands and closed her eyes.

"Darkness obscures their face," she said at last. "I see they have already made an attempt. Someone tried to hurt you before."

She was referring to the assault in her family's boathouse. Anyone could look that up. The police report was available for anyone who knew to ask. Before Hena could cut her off, Mariela spoke again.

"A flash of lightning. A darkened room." She concentrated. "Rattling. Metal stairs."

Her words turned Hena's blood cold. This wasn't about the boathouse. She was talking about the other night. When Hena had gone to retrieve her mother's medicine. When the power went out. When Hena had sworn someone was in Lulu's suite with her.

She couldn't possibly know about that.

Could she?

Seeing Hena's expression, she gave her a sympathetic look.

"No one likes the messenger, but it doesn't change the

message. I must urge you to exercise caution, my dear. Some- one means you harm. Hold on . . ." She concentrated for a moment before speaking again. "They have done dark things to survive. They will do what they must. I'm seeing some- thing about a knife . . . something about how the knives are out for you."

The knives are out for you.

The air in the room suddenly felt much too warm. It was just a phrase. A warning, a metaphor. But for Hena, there was only one association.

Mariela couldn't see the future. No matter how noble she held herself out to be, someone must have paid her an amount she couldn't say no to. Fed her details to get under Hena's skin.

If that was the goal, it was working.

LUMA AND KHALED INVITE YOU

TO PAINT HENNA AND DANCE

YOUR HEART OUT AT THEIR

Mehndi

VISTA DEL SOL

345 EUCLID DRIVE

EVERMERE, FLORIDA

Tuesday, January 13, at ~~7:00~~ 4:00 p.m.

Mariposa Ballroom

Attire: your mehndi best

15

ehndis were meant to take place at night.

At least, Lulu's was. The whole aesthetic— bridesmaids carrying glowing votives on gilded plates to the vibe of nostalgic Bollywood songs—relied on a dark sky. Instead, it was late afternoon. The sky was wide and blue and the sun beamed bright through the windows, which meant the candles would flicker, but they could not glow.

But at least it was happening. There was still a mehndi. Her mother was here, alive, wearing a pale silk kurta with a trail of pearls around her throat. No one would ever guess she had been discharged from the hospital barely an hour ago. Aunties hovered around her, complimenting her bangles, asking too many questions. But she was smiling, and for that Hena was grateful.

She tried to push away the memory of the fortune teller. Her final words:

The knives are out for you.

She wanted to dismiss it as nothing more than cheap theatrics to close the session out with a bang. The event was meant to entertain, wasn't it? And these women found nothing more entertaining than digging up more dirt on her, no matter how real or imagined it might be.

Except how did Mariela describe the night in Lulu's suite with such accurate detail? The flash of lightning. The creaking of metal steps. She recited it as though she'd been standing off to the side watching everything unfold.

She headed to the bridal suite tucked away next to the mehndi hall. She walked past the trays, the golden palanquin set by the door that her sister would soon sit in as she was carried into the hall.

When she stepped inside, Irum, Courtney, and Maheen were already there. Lulu was at a makeup table and caught her eye through the mirror.

"Is it time?" she asked.

"Almost. The guests have arrived."

The other bridesmaids headed outside to light the mehndi trays, leaving the sisters alone.

Lulu was in a flowing emerald gown. The dupatta draped over her head was threaded with intricate mirror work, and with her sparkling jhumar and golden tikka framing her face, she looked like royalty.

"You should join them," Lulu said. "You're a bridesmaid too, remember?"

"I wanted to make sure you're all right," Hena said.

Lulu studied her lap, twisting the edge of her gown with her finger.

"What's the matter?" Hena asked. "Ammi's doing great out there, I promise."

"It's not that . . ." She was quiet for a moment. "I wanted to say I'm sorry."

"For what?"

"You should have been in the bridal party from the start. Honestly, you should have been my maid of honor."

"Don't worry about that. It's fine."

"It's not fine. I hate all these rumors. People saying you're a wedding crasher. But I gave them the fodder, didn't I?"

"Who cares what they have to say?"

"Even if they weren't gossiping, I shouldn't have invited you last minute. Gossip or no gossip, it was wrong."

"Lulu." Hena drew closer to her sister. "Given everything . . . I don't blame you."

"The truth is, I was pretty pissed at you."

That tracked.

"I can't imagine what you dealt with," Hena said, and then she pushed past the knot in her throat. Because it was time to say the words she'd needed to say for far too long. "And the trust—Ammi delayed your trust because of the mistakes I made. You have every right to be pissed. My mistakes cost you. I'm so sorry."

Lulu's eyes welled with tears.

"Is that why you think I've been upset? The trust? I mean, yes, I wish Ammi hadn't delayed it. It's millions of dollars, stuck. That sucks. But no. Hena, you just . . . you left." She sniffled. "You didn't even say goodbye. It's like you couldn't wait to be done with us. With me."

"That was never true," Hena began, then corrected herself. "I mean, I did want to get away from this place. Our community. There were too many painful memories, and the gossip was so hard to deal with. But done with you? Never. Leaving you was the hardest part. And it never got easier. Ever."

"It's like one minute you were my best friend. I told you everything. And the next . . ." Lulu trailed off.

A bird trilled outside the window. Hena took a seat across from her sister. "I tried to call you early on, but you never answered. I decided to give you space. I thought it's what you wanted. I didn't want to make things harder. Especially since you lived with Ammi. You were still part of the community."

"When I got engaged, I knew I had to tell you, but I didn't know how." Lulu sniffled again. "So much time had passed. Then Ammi's diagnosis . . . I shouldn't have waited so long to reach out."

"I'm here now, right?" Hena said, squeezing her hand.

"You *are* here." She drew a steady breath. "Not sure how I'd have made it through this wedding week without you."

"I'm glad I could help."

Lulu dabbed her eyes with a tissue and adjusted her makeup.

"What do you think of Khaled? You haven't said much about him."

"I don't know," Hena said honestly. "I haven't spent much time with him. He seems nice, though, and you both look happy together."

"Maybe you can come back for a visit? That way you can actually spend time with us and get to know him."

Hena's heart lifted at the invitation. "I'd love that," she told her.

Lulu smiled. "You know he's all in with my dream of rebuilding the hotel empire?"

"Rebuilding the *empire*?" Hena repeated, hoping she had misunderstood her. "Beyond this resort, you mean?"

"This resort is only the start. I told you, I'm rebuilding a legacy," she said. "It's awful how Ammi sold every last building. They'd spent years, decades, creating this dynasty and then—poof—it was gone. Lucinda told me how it was so much more than hotels."

"Like what?" Hena asked cautiously. "What did Lucinda share?"

"Well, I'd obviously heard about his charity work, but I

didn't know the extent of it. Did you know he had a whole side business helping people struggling financially?"

Helping people. Hena almost laughed. She wasn't sure if the people on the receiving end would describe a loan shark quite that way.

"What Ammi did was wrong. I was too young to get a say, and I'm working on forgiving her," Lulu said. "But when I turn twenty-six and get access to my trust, I'm getting it all back. I've already got a wish list of properties to buy. You know the Miramar resort is coming on the market soon? Wouldn't it be amazing to grab it? You could come in on this with me. Help with the redesign. Wouldn't that be great? We could make it a proper family business again."

Until that moment, their conversation had been so heart-warming and healing, but now a prickle of unease crawled through her. Her father's legacy was best left where it was. In the past.

It wasn't her sister's fault. Her mother chose not to give Lulu the full truth. After his death, they'd argued about it. Back then, Hena could hardly blame her mother. Lulu had been so young. But as the years went by and her mother refused to address the elephant in the room, Hena worried it would become a problem.

And it was a problem now, wasn't it?

There was a knock on the door. The wedding planner popped her head in. It was time.

Hena helped her sister into the golden palanquin. Reza and the other groomsmen and relatives lifted it up, carrying it on their shoulders. Hena took a spare lit votive from Irum and slid into formation alongside the other bridesmaids and cousins. They entered the hall to a romantic Bollywood ballad; the guests clapped and cheered as Lulu was taken to the stage.

As Hena set her votive on the stage alongside the other bridesmaids, she spotted Reza off to the side.

"Thank you again," she said, walking over to him. "For the flowers. The gift. It was the nicest thing anyone's done for me in a long time."

"My pleasure. How's your mother?"

Hena looked in her mother's direction. Her eyes sparkled as she looked at her younger child.

"She's better—" Hena began, but the weight of Khala's words pressed against her.

It could be any day now.

Reza seemed to understand. Quietly, he reached for her hand. Gave it a reassuring squeeze. "I'm not sure I've ever seen a family hold it together like you all are."

"Glad to hear it looks like we are. I guess there's not really an alternative to keeping it together, considering it's a wedding, right?"

"Maybe," Reza said. "But you don't have to hold it alone."

"You're sweet."

"Just being honest. I'm here if you need to talk."

"Thanks," she told him. "You look nice, by the way."

An understatement if there ever was one. In his cream-colored sherwani with gold accents on the collar, he was perfect. Painfully so.

"As do you." His dimple deepened. "But what else is new?"

Yeah? she wanted to say. *Then why haven't you done anything about it yet?*

The music grew louder in the background. From the periphery, Hena saw the bridesmaids readying the henna to apply to Lulu's hands. Already the crowd was lining up for the ritual.

Hena cleared her throat. Excused herself to help.

Get it together, she told herself as she walked away.

After the rituals concluded, friends and cousins of the bride and groom took to the dance floor for choreographed routines. The afternoon went smoothly. So smoothly that when the emcee announced the final slideshow before dinner, she was pleasantly surprised at how punctual they'd been. This was the first event of the week that had stayed perfectly on schedule.

She searched for Haris and spotted him sitting with his mother. It seemed like Auntie Nipa was keeping a tight watch on her son tonight, which meant Hena wouldn't be able to sidebar with him quite yet, but they did need to talk. She was sure the piece of gossip Irum had shared—about Nasir wandering the streets of Las Olas—was baseless chatter. But given what Milcheck had said about Nasir's phone pinging an hour south of the hotel, they needed to take it seriously.

"Hi, everyone," Courtney said, taking the mic. "Thank you for your patience while we shuffled things around today. We are excited for the nikkah tomorrow, where Khaled and Lulu will finally make it official!"

The audience cheered, and Hena joined them in applause. Courtney held out the mic for Irum, but Irum's eyes were fixed on her phone.

"Okaaaaay," Courtney said slowly. She turned to the crowd. "Well, this has been such a fun week celebrating our bride and groom, but tonight we're flipping the script. Khaled and Lulu put together something special—not about them, but about you. Thanking you for being part of their journey."

The lights dimmed. The monitor hummed to life and music swelled through the hall as a video overlaid with nostalgic music played.

The first photo was of Khaled grinning toothlessly in front of a birthday cake with his parents. Khaled's family clapped. They laughed at the other photos popping up. His parents in

Star Wars outfits for Halloween alongside seven-year-old Khaled. His cousins and him in jerseys at a YMCA basketball game. His aunts and uncles at a reunion party.

Soon the photos shifted to Lulu's side of the family. Khala's eyes glistened as she looked at the photo of herself from twenty-one years earlier, gazing down at baby Lulu swaddled in pink. There was Hena, barely in the double digits, pushing Lulu's stroller down their sun-drenched sidewalk. Her mother appeared on-screen next, regal in her sleeveless sari and smiling down at her beloved Lulu, then a toddler, tightly holding her hand.

Lastly, her father. His wavy hair was parted to the side. Words appeared over his photo: *Gone, but never forgotten.*

The audience clapped. Hena kept her expression blank, willing her face not to betray her.

The video ended. The lights flipped back on. The wedding planner informed them the buffet lines were open for dinner. As Hena made her way toward her mother to see if she could fix her a plate, the lights abruptly turned off again. Against the same wall, a white screen appeared, with black text in a vintage typewriter font:

```
There's more.
```

Laughter bubbled from the crowd—good-natured. Curious. Courtney was a few paces away from her. She frowned at Irum.

"I didn't do this part," she said. "Did you add something?"

Irum didn't respond.

Another click.

```
There are people who make us. But there are
also the people who break us.
```

Another click.

The Truth About Hena Mirza.

Hena's breath caught.

There she was. Smiling into the camera. She was wearing the red veiled gown from her wedding day. These were professional photos she'd taken that morning. The caption beneath it:

Once upon a time, there was a girl named
Hena.

The next photo.

And a boy named Nasir.

There he was. His hair brushed back. In his mehndi clothes—light gray, a white vest. What was happening? Why was this projecting on the screen? Her shoes felt made of lead. Why couldn't she take a single step toward the projector to unplug this nightmare from the wall?

She tore her gaze from the screen and looked at Lulu, who stood equally frozen—her attention riveted to the footage.

Photos of Nasir and Hena flashed by. There they were at a Princeton college basketball game. A selfie from the Mumford & Sons concert during her junior year. At a Dolphins playoff game when they'd moved back to South Florida. There was a photo of them on the shoreline when he asked her to marry him—the ocean waves in the backdrop frozen in time. Her arms draped around his shoulders.

She'd scrubbed these photos from the internet when she

deleted her social media accounts three years ago. But here were those very pictures. Blasted on this screen for the world to see.

She had to shut this off.

She rushed to the projector. Yanked the plug from the wall.

Nothing happened.

Her heart pounded. She looked around frantically. The images were coming from somewhere . . .

There.

The stream of light projecting from a high window on the back wall. She was racing toward it when a hand roughly gripped her arm.

Irum.

"Don't," she said.

"Irum, you don't understand. This is—"

"Let it play." She fixed a glare on Hena, as though daring her to say another word. Something cold lodged in the pit of Hena's stomach.

A new image appeared.

```
Boy meets girl. Boy falls in love with
girl. Tale as old as time. But there's
always more to every story.
```

The next slide was not an image. It was a video.

Filmed at a high angle, it was grainy, as though pulled from security footage. There she was in her wedding red. Nasir wore scuffed pants. A plain shirt.

Her stomach lurched.

It was footage from the boathouse.

The morning she last saw him.

Her arms were clamped against her sides, her eyes narrowed at Nasir, who was studying the ground. She knew this moment. She'd never forget it. It was seconds after she'd learned what he had done. What he had taken. What he had cost them.

"I'm sorry," said Nasir.

"Sorry?" she repeated. "Sorry isn't good enough."

"Hena. You have to understand—"

"I don't have to understand a fucking thing, do you hear me?"

He moved toward her. She took a step away.

"Don't touch me." She wiped away tears with the back of her hand. "Tell me something. Did you ever even care about me? Or was it always about my money? Was that what all of this was about?"

"What? Hena. No! Look, I know I don't deserve you. I never have."

"You're right. You don't deserve me. We were a mistake from the start."

"Let me explain," he begged. "Please."

"No. No more excuses. I don't want your apologies or explanations. Why can't you get that through your head? I don't want to hear from you ever again."

"I was trying to fix things. I wanted to—"

"Fix things?" She let out an angry laugh. "You ruin everything you touch. Just go and stay gone. I wish I'd never met you."

The audience gasped as the footage ended—which only happened because she had run out of the boathouse.

Thank god she had.

Thank god the rest of their conversation—when he stopped her outside, wrapped his arms around her, told her everything in lurid detail—hadn't been captured.

But they weren't done.

```
Surprised?
   You wouldn't be if you knew who Hena
Mirza really is. She hasn't changed one
bit. Not in three years.
   Remember the pythons? So many snakes, all
in one spot. What are the odds . . .
```

A new video appeared, of a ginger-haired man in fatigues holding a machete.

"I was happy to help with the python party. Why wouldn't I be? Hold up, you asked who placed the order. I got it right here. Here it is. Heena? Meerza? Nice lady. Good tipper. Sure, it's a weird ask for a wedding surprise, but it's Florida, man. And when someone offers you that kind of money, you don't ask questions, do you?"

A new slide. A photo of a delivery bag set by the lobby door. A close-up of the receipt showed an order of pistachios. Hena's name printed on it, clear as day.

A new slide. New text.

```
Luma nearly died. How far will someone go
for attention?
```

A screenshot of the website for *Cakes by Stritala*. A recorded phone call blasted through the speakers.

*"I'm meticulous about my orders. I knew when the shaadi
was, but when she called and asked for it to be delivered
sooner, I moved heaven and earth to get it done in time,
only to get yelled at for sending it early. I have a reputation to maintain, so I backed off. But maybe you're
right . . . maybe she's not the one who called to change
the delivery date. I will say she certainly sounded like
Lulu. So yes, it may have been her sister."*

The slides were coming and going so fast it was hard to
keep up.

```
She's always said she saw him last at the
mehndi. We know now that is false.
   Why did she lie?
   Why did she wish she never met Nasir?
   Was it because she had moved on?
```

A photo of Haris and her. The two of them on the boardwalk. Here. At this resort. The air stuck in her throat. It was
taken from a distance, but there was no denying it was them.
It was from the afternoon they caught up, right before the
bridal shower. When they spoke of Nasir. Of how much they
missed him.

But taken at this angle—his hand on her arm while she
gazed up at him—it looked like a different kind of moment
entirely.

```
You might be surprised to learn who the
real Hena Mirza is. That's only because you
didn't know.
   Now you do.
```

A knife appeared. That knife. The same one.

We will never forget.

The lights turned back on. A hushed silence filled the room.

"Someone sent me a sneak preview." Irum glared at Hena. "I guess we all know the truth now, don't we?"

Beads of perspiration dotted Hena's forehead. The fortune teller had said this, hadn't she? She said someone would betray her. Whether she conjured it from her own premonition or was paid handsomely—like the python hunter must have been—to say those words, it didn't change the truth.

"Hena . . ." It was Haris. He was hurrying over. "Are you all right?"

She wanted to reply, but she couldn't stop looking at Lulu. The hurt, so clear on her face. Wordlessly, Lulu ran out of the room.

Only moments earlier they'd talked. They'd cleared some of the pain and complicated feelings between them.

Hena felt broken. Truly and utterly broken. A tear slipped down her face. She moved to follow her sister, but Haris stopped her.

"We need to talk," he said. "That slideshow—"

"Not another word!" Auntie Nipa shrieked, rushing up to them.

"Mom," Haris began in warning. "Don't."

Auntie Nipa lunged toward her. Haris gripped his mother by the elbow, holding her back. Her face was red with rage.

"It's one thing to draw your own family's name into the mud," she shouted. "But to bring my son into this? How dare you!"

She wanted to defend herself. She couldn't.

It was as though the slideshow had taken everything out of her. She needed to go. Haris argued with his mother as Hena raced out of the hall. Toward the suites. She jabbed the elevator button.

She'd talk to Lulu. Explain.

The elevator pinged. The doors slid open. She stared at the gaping space.

What if Lulu refused to speak to her?

What if she didn't believe her?

Tears slipped faster down her face as a hand rested on her shoulder.

It was Reza. He eyed her quietly.

"Do you want to get out of here?" he asked.

The thought of leaving sounded good. Actually, it sounded perfect.

She met his gaze. "How about that boat trip?"

USMANA,
Aunt of the Groom

Oh. My. Goodness.

You can use many words to describe the Mirzas, but *boring* is certainly never one of them. The fortune teller predicted this, didn't she? We were all there, we heard it with our own ears, and look how quickly her vision came into reality. Betrayal, indeed.

What are my thoughts about the slideshow? Someone had to do it. Did you see that video? The way that poor boy's shoulders drooped as she screamed at him? He was clearly used to her abuse. At least now she can't hide behind her innocent doe-eyed looks.

Who do I think created the slideshow? Sorry. I'm not smiling. Really, I'm not. When I'm stressed, my reactions can be a bit off. I think the answer is obvious, though. It's Irum. Poor girl probably cracked under the pressure of having to play nice for so many days. Good for her. She's a brave soul to speak truth to such a powerful family.

And if I had to put money on it? I'd say there is more still to learn.

16

·

The boat rocked gently as Reza took her hand and helped her board. She braced a hand against the rail unsteadily, her mind replaying the slideshow—the images, the accusations, the knife. They had been quiet on the drive over, but he watched her now with tense concern.

"You okay?" he asked.

"No," she told him. "It's fine. Let's just go."

Reza chatted with the owner of the boat before they took off. They were checking the sailboat—it was a classic wooden one, sleek and simple. Reza's hands moved with practiced ease, testing the ropes, the rudder, making sure everything was in place.

She scanned the landscape for anything—or anyone—suspicious. Because if someone had been watching her in the boathouse . . . If someone had gone through the trouble to show the video to everyone at the wedding in order to frame her . . . Who was to say they weren't watching her right now?

A lighthouse stood tall off the peninsula. Even in the middle of January, the air here was thick with salt and humidity. The water glistened under the lights of the dock. There was nothing amiss. Nothing awry. She tried to draw a deep breath but couldn't push away the unease pressing against her ribs.

She looked down at the clothes she had hastily changed into—a thin-strapped sundress that cut at her knee. Sandals. Not exactly sailing gear, but better than the flowing gown she'd had on earlier. Reza was in a simple T-shirt and track pants.

While Reza chatted with the boat owner, she checked her phone.

Haris had called twice. There was a text from him now:

> Are you all right? Call me.

She let him know she would. Soon. But all she could think of was how his mother had screamed at her in front of hundreds of people. How he had to physically restrain her. How could she ever return to that resort?

The note slipped into her clutch at Lulu's bridal shower flashed before her eyes. She'd dismissed it as snarky aunties. Now every unsettling event, from the pythons to Lulu's allergic reaction to even the misdelivered cake, had proven to be a carefully choreographed attack against her.

By whom? Auntie Nipa? Auntie Hanifa? Both of them together?

She tried to shut down her thoughts before they could spiral. She'd escaped the resort because she needed space to breathe.

But as she finished scrolling her messages, a cold weight settled in her stomach. She'd texted her sister on the way here. Told her they needed to talk.

Lulu still hadn't responded.

They pushed off the pier. As the dock slipped from view

and the city faded behind them, something in her unspooled the slightest bit. Closing her eyes, she drew a deep breath. The discordant hum in her head quieted a notch.

"Can I help?" she asked, walking over to Reza.

The muscles in his forearms were taut as he fixed up the sail. Knotted the rope.

"We're all set," he told her. "The wind will do its thing."

The sail caught and they moved effortlessly, the only sounds coming from the creaks of the boat, the rustle of the sails, the splash of water against the hull, and the distant cries of seabirds.

"So, this was teenage Reza?" she asked. "Other kids sneak beer. Meanwhile, you're mastering sails and knots."

"I didn't get out as often as I'd like," he said. "But it's nice, isn't it? Being out here, navigating the boat yourself. It stills the mind."

"It really does."

Her stomach growled and Reza grinned.

"The cabin came stocked," he said. "Let's see what they've got."

She followed him to the compact but cozy wood-paneled space.

"Watch your head," he warned as she stepped inside.

They pulled out crackers, cheese, and fruit from a mini fridge. Hena sank onto the built-in berth. It was thickly padded like a bed—so soft she could have lain back and fallen asleep with the sway of the sea. Instead, she sat on the edge, stretching out, pretending not to notice how his eyes flicked to her legs, then quickly back to her face. He waited a beat.

"We should talk about what happened. Are you all right?"

"I'm fine," she said automatically.

"Hena."

She looked out at the water. Exhaled.

"I'm better now," she said. "I needed this even though I know everything is waiting for me when I get back."

She checked her phone. Still nothing from Lulu. The moment of peace she'd found started to fray.

"If Lulu thinks I could have done all that . . ." She blinked quickly. "Whoever it was made sure to have receipts. Literal receipts."

"It's bullshit. Come on. Anyone can make up a delivery receipt. I didn't believe it. Not for a second."

"Does it matter if it's unbelievable? My mother always says if enough people say a thing is true, it might as well be. She's right. Those videos. Those accusations . . . You don't know the people around here like I do. If you knew what they say, all the things they think they know . . ."

"Like what?" His gaze held hers.

"I'm sure you've heard plenty about my family at this point."

"I've heard bits and pieces. I much prefer this, though. Hearing about you, from you."

He was being polite. She was sure he'd heard far more than bits and pieces. The truth was, she'd rather he know about her in her own words too.

So she told him.

About her father's towering reputation—the way their standing crumbled after he vanished. She told him how her community reacted when they learned Nasir was marrying her—as though she were Hades luring Persephone into the Underworld.

As she talked, he drew his arm around her. Warm and solid. The more she told him, the lighter she felt.

"That's a lot to carry," he murmured when she finished. "I'm so sorry."

A tear slipped down her cheek. He reached out, brushing it away.

They sat in silence for a few moments. She let out a breath and turned to him.

"I've been going on and on," she said with a half smile. "I'm kind of sick of hearing myself talk at this point."

"I think given the events of this afternoon, it should be all about you, don't you think?"

"Still," she insisted, "I want to know about you. Tell me something."

His eyes searched hers. "What would you like to know?"

Everything. The thought startled her. *I want to know everything about you.*

"Anything you want to share," she said instead.

He considered this, then nodded.

"I guess when you were talking about your father, I could relate."

"You said he shut down after your mother died, right?"

"Those were the good days. Once my sisters grew up and moved out, he decided to get angry instead."

His expression darkened. She took his hand.

"Using fists was his go-to," he said. "Sometimes he got creative, though."

He raised his shirt, revealing a faint but visible scar across his abdomen.

"Reza—"

"Metal hook. From a fireplace poker. Sophomore year of high school. I forgot to take the trash out on time. Like I said." He looked at her stricken expression. "Creative."

"That's awful."

"That one actually got him in trouble when a teacher noticed me bleeding through my shirt. Christian Davies got himself a little mug shot. He was more careful after that."

Reza shrugged, but she recognized the hurt behind his eyes. It was the kind of hurt only a parent could inflict. The kind that stuck to you like a second skin.

"My father could get creative too," she said. "He mostly hurt my mother. But as I got older, I became a punching bag as well. I couldn't do anything right because I couldn't be the son he'd wanted."

The last time she saw her father, she had come home ten minutes late from school. Her study group had gone over. She'd made sure to get a teacher's note confirming it because her father valued punctuality. He hated when people "wasted his time." She'd shown him the note. He didn't care.

Excuses, he'd sneered. *That's all you ever have.*

And then, before she could reply, the punch. Straight in the abdomen.

She'd dropped to the floor. The rest was a blur. Still was. She only knew he'd beaten her so badly she coughed up blood. She knew from the urgent care visit that she'd suffered three broken ribs, a concussion, and two black eyes from her "fall down the stairs."

She also knew he had been thirsting for more. Had her mother not come into the room when she had, she was sure she'd be dead.

"Sailing saved me," Reza said. "One of the deckhands at the hotel I worked at in high school offered to teach me. Being out on the water reminded me there was more to life. That I could leave one day."

"And you did."

"I left as soon as I could. I haven't spoken to my father in years. Still, when I talk about that time in my life, it all hurts like it happened yesterday. So how far did I really move on, you know what I mean?"

Hena nodded. She'd moved to the other side of the country to put as much space between herself and this place as she could. But even with the rolling hills out west, these flatlands of her childhood, these memories, still held her in their vise.

"Too bad a KitKat bar can't make it all better," he said with a soft grin.

"It helps." She smiled at him.

A seagull soared overhead, settling onto a buoy. She leaned down to pluck a grape from the small table. From the corner of her eye, she noticed Reza's gaze. How it lingered on her neckline as the fabric dipped down. He looked away quickly, but not quickly enough.

Hena leaned back and crossed her arms.

"I thought I was good at reading people," she said. "But I can't read you, Reza."

His eyes flicked to her mouth before meeting her eyes. A million thoughts seemed to race through his head. He shifted closer. She felt the sweetness of his breath against her face.

"What are you reading?" he asked.

They sat so close, their foreheads were practically touching. She took in his full mouth. His jaw, chiseled from stone. She wanted to kiss him so badly she ached.

"I don't know if I want to say," Hena said. "What if I'm wrong?"

His eyes held hers so intently Hena could barely think straight. His jaw twitched.

"You're not wrong."

His hand dropped to her knee. Before she could reply, he kissed her.

It was a gentle kiss. Tentative. Slow. His mouth was soft and sure. The hint of stubble on his face brushed against her skin, sending shivers down her spine. His hands glided to her waist as she drew her arms around his neck, erasing any space between them. His mouth felt made for hers.

She moved closer. Traced her hand along his jaw. She kissed him again. Harder now.

His breath hitched, and then—it was like a dam had burst. Any restraint he had dissolved. His arms circled her tighter. His mouth pressed insistently against hers. Hungry.

She tasted the salt of the sea on his tongue. She closed her eyes as his kisses traveled downward. They trailed her jaw. Her neck. Sending goosebumps down her body. He brushed aside the strap of her dress. His lips pressed against her bare shoulder and she could scarcely breathe as he eased her back against the berth. His hand skimmed to the zipper on the side of her dress. He paused, searching her eyes. For what? Permission?

She grazed the hem of his T-shirt. With one yank, she slid it over his head. Let it fall to the side. He breathed heavily as she traced her fingers over his jagged scar, pressed her palms against his bare chest. She met his eyes.

"Don't stop now."

So he didn't.

The boat swayed beneath them. The world outside vanished.

It was just Reza and her. Nothing else.

DAY
SIX

17

·

Hena woke past nine o'clock the next morning, the hazy maroon walls of the bedroom sharpening slowly in the soft morning light. For a surreal moment, she wondered if last night had been a dream. They'd returned to the resort late. When Reza suggested he stay over, for safety, she hadn't disagreed.

She replayed their night together in her mind's eye. His mouth on hers. His body pressed against her, his arms around her as they drifted off to sleep in this very bed. The deepest sleep she'd had in days. Years, really. She reached over to the spot where he'd been, only to feel the cool touch of linens.

Oh.

Before she could dwell, she heard the front door open and shut. She grabbed a plush robe, cinched it at her waist, and stepped into the main suite. There he was, standing at the kitchen island, a brown paper bag in his arms.

"You're up early," he observed.

"Later than you," she countered, eyeing the bag. "Where did you go?"

"Thought I'd make us breakfast. I left a note." He gestured to the fridge. "Figured you wouldn't see it since you were snoring when I slipped out."

"I resent that. I do not snore." She feigned offense.

"You absolutely do." He stepped closer, tilting her chin up to meet his eyes. "And it's very cute."

He kissed her—a slow, lingering kiss. She draped her arms around his neck as she drew him closer. This moment felt suspended, free floating above all that weighed on her.

"You don't need to make us breakfast," she said when she pulled back. "There's enough food downstairs to feed a small nation many times over."

"Well, first, I'd rather stay here with you. Second, you need to try my omelet. It's way better than the ones they have here."

"The ones made to order by Michelin-rated chefs?" She gave him a look. "That's quite presumptuous."

"Tells you how confident I am." His dimple deepened. "It's my family recipe. Figured you should try it."

She tried not to melt on the spot. And though she offered to help him prep, he insisted he only wanted her company. She watched him chop onions and sweet peppers, season and stir. The rhythmic clatter of knives and pans filled the space. God, he looked so sexy cooking.

They sat down to eat. She was about to take her first bite when his phone rang. He checked it and placed it back on the table.

"Do you need to get that?" she asked.

"It's my nephew, Bilal. He likes to randomly video call sometimes."

"You should answer it."

"I can chat later."

She insisted he take the call, and though she stayed out of

frame, she couldn't help but listen in, warmth filling her at how gentle he was with his nephew.

"Did you see an alligator?" the little boy asked.

"More than one," he said. "I took photos."

"What was their names?"

"Hmmm. Well, one was Suzy. And Cox, who could forget him? The others . . . I don't know." He seemed truly troubled at this realization. "Maybe you can help me name them?"

Bilal loved this idea and rattled out ten options. When they hung up a few moments later, Reza looked at her apologetically.

"Sorry about that."

"For what? He sounded so sweet." She took a bite of her omelet. "Wow. This is good."

His expression fell. "Good?"

"Wait." She frowned. "I mean it's very good. Why do you look disappointed?"

"Good isn't great."

She suppressed a laugh and stood up, settling onto his lap. "What I meant was, this right here is the best omelet I've ever had in my life."

"See? Now, that's more like it."

His finger traced her collarbone, sending shivers through her. How did he do that? How did one touch light her entire body up? The first night she laid eyes on him, she'd hoped Reza would be a good distraction—perhaps a fun fling with a stranger. But he was no longer a stranger. And this was not a fling. Whatever this was between them, it felt real.

He kissed her. His hands skimmed her waist, tugging at her robe.

"Shall we take this to the bedroom?" Hena whispered.

"Those *are* some really nice sheets."

"Told you."

His hand slid up her leg. "Just not sure I can wait that long."

She reached for his waistband just as the doorbell rang.

Housekeeping? Hena groaned. What even was the point of a Do Not Disturb sign if they still disturbed you?

"Come back later!" she called out.

"It's me," said the voice on the other side.

Lulu. Shit.

She jumped up quickly.

"Go to the room," she whispered.

His eyes widened. He slipped away as Lulu knocked again, more insistent this time.

"Hurry up, Hena!" she shouted.

She tightened her robe and barely got the door open before Lulu brushed past her and stepped into the sitting room.

"Where have you been?" she asked.

"I was out. I texted you."

"This isn't a text conversation. We need to talk. Face-to-face."

Just like that, the magical spell of the last twelve hours broke—reality crashing full force.

"I'm so sorry, Lulu." Her composure slipped. "What happened yesterday. The things I was accused of . . ."

Lulu's expression darkened. "It was something."

A quiver of fear sliced through Hena. Was this the moment when Lulu cut her off once and for all?

"I know how it looked." Her lungs constricted. "But all I've ever wanted to do my whole life was to protect you and keep you safe. I would never hurt you, Lulu."

Lulu regarded Hena. Searched her face. Then—

"You wouldn't," she said. "I don't know how to explain

what the hell is going on, but there's no way any of it was true."

A wave of relief washed over Hena, and she hugged Lulu. Her sister's body reacted with surprise at first, before she hugged Hena back just as tightly.

"We'll get to the bottom of it," Lulu said when she pulled back. "There will be hell to pay."

"Did the security team get any footage for who set up the second projector?" Hena asked hopefully.

Lulu's expression fell. "It was running on a separate system the previous owner had integrated into the space. The team says it was operating remotely. We'll dig into it. There must be some way to trace it."

Even with this chilling information, that someone had gone through the trouble of hacking into the resort's tech equipment with the singular intent to destroy her, Hena felt lighter. Because Lulu didn't buy it. Right now, this was everything.

"We'll deep dive into this as soon as we can, but I'm freaking out right now because I can't find Gita," Lulu told her. "You haven't heard from her by any chance, have you?"

When she said she hadn't, Lulu's forehead creased. "She left the property to replenish Ammi's water and refill some prescriptions, but the rideshare app shows her returning over an hour ago. I've called her a million times, but it goes straight to voicemail."

"That's weird," said Hena. Gita was like their mother's shadow. Why was she suddenly unreachable?

"I'm sure it's fine. She probably got sidetracked, but after the video hack I'm on edge. Lucinda's arranging more security on the premises ASAP. We should be set up by this afternoon."

"Let me change and help you look for her," Hena offered.

"Great." Lulu looked relieved. "Haris was looking for you too, by the way. I think the detective wants to follow up."

Of course he did. Whoever shared the slideshow at the mehndi likely would have sent it to the detective as well. It would explain why Detective Milcheck had been so confident about knowing she'd spoken to Nasir the day he was reported missing.

"I'll call Haris after we find Gita," she said.

"I'll meet you in the lobby." Lulu headed to the front door. "We can . . ." Her eyes had dropped to the floor, landing on the pair of men's shoes tucked neatly on the side.

She stiffened. Her gaze flicked to Hena, then to the closed bedroom door.

Hena opened her mouth to say something, but Lulu was already moving.

"Hey!" she called after her. "Don't—"

Too late. She pushed the door open.

Reza was sitting at the edge of the bed. He saw her and jumped up.

Lulu exhaled, low and sharp. "What the fuck?"

"I can explain . . ." Hena faltered. Lulu wasn't looking at her. Her eyes were locked on his.

"What are you doing here?" She glared at him.

Reza didn't answer. His face had gone pale, his lips parted, as if the question had sucked the air out of his lungs.

A prickling unease crept up Hena's spine. Her eyes darted between them. What was going on? Why was Lulu looking at him like that? Why did he look so scared?

"Last I checked, I'm the big sister here," Hena said. "Can we be grown-ups about this?"

Reza shifted. "I should go."

"Yes," Lulu replied. "You should."

"What? No." What was Lulu doing? "You can stay, Reza."

But he was already walking to the foyer. He slipped on his shoes. In seconds, he was gone.

She stared at Lulu. They'd been getting along so well. But the way she spoke to him—

"What the hell was that?" Hena asked.

Lulu opened her mouth. Closed it. Then said, "Let's find Gita first. We'll talk about this later."

Hena released a sharp breath. Lulu was stressed. They were all barely getting any sleep. But they would definitely need to address this.

She quickly changed, and they headed downstairs. Lulu asked Lucinda to make an announcement, and seconds later, her words rang through the hallways, asking Gita to join them in the lobby. Asking for anyone who saw her to alert them.

Lulu rushed off to talk to a security guard by the front door, and Hena heard a sharp voice.

"You have some nerve showing your face here."

Hena turned. Auntie Hanifa. Her lips were pressed into a thin line, her eyes narrowed. She wasn't the only one. Other aunties, including Nipa, were there alongside a few uncles. They all watched Hena, unsmiling. Hena's face grew hot. These people would grasp at anything to hate her, but now they had received a perfectly tailored slideshow complete with accusations and "visual proof."

"Aren't you going to say anything?" Auntie Hanifa snapped.

Every muscle in her body told her to look away. To let it go.

Except.

She hadn't done anything wrong. Over and over, both at this wedding and for decades longer, Hena had bitten her tongue. So as not to make waves. So as not to feed the flames in the furnace.

But enough was enough. Auntie Hanifa didn't get to shame her. She didn't get to make her feel unwelcome at her own sister's wedding. If the gloves were off—if Auntie Hanifa wanted to do this—Hena could hold her own.

"The accusations were false. You of all people know how gossip works," Hena replied.

"Nice try," Auntie Hanifa retorted. "The slideshow didn't have rumors. It had proof."

"If you want to believe what it said, go ahead." Hena's eyes narrowed. "But you're welcome to keep your opinion to yourself."

"We saw your fight with Nasir." Auntie Hanifa snorted. "Are you asking us not to believe what we witnessed with our own eyes?"

Hena flinched. The fight was real and true. Stripped of all context, but still true.

"It must hurt to have the world see who you really are." Auntie Hanifa took a step closer to her. "And what you did to your sister, that's low. Even for you. Thank goodness for the good Samaritan who exposed you."

"I wonder who the 'kind soul' was," Hena said, using air quotes. "I'm guessing someone with a lot of free time and a small, hateful heart. Someone who enjoys entertaining themselves at the expense of other people's pain."

"Are you implying I did it?" Auntie Hanifa chuckled. "I'm flattered you think I know how to turn on a projector, let alone orchestrate that spectacle."

"I have no idea what you're capable of," she said icily. "For the record, you don't know anything about Nasir or me, or that moment."

A crowd was steadily gathering around them, surely drawn to the lobby by Lucinda's urgent message but sticking around for the show. Once again, she was the main event.

"Maybe not," Auntie Hanifa conceded. "But we'll get to the bottom of it soon enough. I've let the detective know. Poor Nasir's fate may already have been sealed, but we can at least save Haris before you sink your claws any deeper into him. It's like I've always said—once a slut, always a slut."

It was Auntie Hanifa. The note slipped into her clutch at the bridal shower. Hena's shoulders went rigid, fury rising sharp and fast. Before she could reply—

"Out."

Lulu. She was marching toward them. Her expression was cold. Furious.

Upon seeing her, a gentler look crossed Auntie Hanifa's face.

"Sweetheart, are you all right?" she asked. "You poor dear. I'm so sorry you—"

"Not. Another. Word. You are gone." Lulu's words sliced through the air like steel. "Someone will collect your things and send them to your home."

A stunned hush fell over the room. Auntie Hanifa stood stock-still. It was like she hadn't processed Lulu's words. The truth was, Hena wasn't sure she had either.

"Luma, darling," Auntie Hanifa rushed to explain, "I was defending you. I understand she is your sister, but what she has done—trying to sabotage this wedding. The cake. The snakes. My dear, she nearly killed you! None of this is something anyone should defend. Family is family—but we must be clear-eyed."

"I want you off the premises," Lulu said evenly. "Now."

Auntie Hanifa scanned the audience, searching for anyone to intervene. Surely *someone* would speak up for her, among all these friends she'd gossiped and whispered with all week.

No one did. Even Auntie Nipa stayed silent.

Auntie Hanifa's eyes flew to Hena, then Lulu. "Neither of you took after your father," she spat. "God knows I have tried to be magnanimous. I have tried to stand by your family. To support all of you despite everything. What has it gotten me? Absolutely nothing."

"Safe travels," Lulu said.

One of the security guards strode over to Auntie Hanifa. She mumbled under her breath before stalking out the sliding doors.

Lulu leveled a warning look at the crowd. "Does anyone else have anything they'd like to air out? Now's the time."

Everyone took their cue, promptly dispersing. Murmurs flitted through the air. There would be plenty to unpack once they were safely out of earshot, because when it came to drama, this wedding was certainly delivering.

Hena's eye caught Irum's. She stood off to the side, her expression unreadable. Hena tentatively approached her.

"Irum," she said once they were face-to-face. "I'm really—"

"You have some nerve talking to me right now," Irum said.

"Irum—"

"You lied."

"I—"

"You lied. I asked when you last saw my brother. You looked me in the eyes and said you saw him the night before, at the mehndi, like the rest of us. You said it back then. You said it again this week." She let out a bitter laugh. "Silly me, falling for your bullshit."

"Irum, it was complicated—"

"The way you screamed at him." Irum's voice shook with rage. "You told him to leave. He left."

"It's . . . it's not what it looks like."

"Are you saying it was a fake video?"

"The footage was real. But there was more going on."

"Well, I'm all ears. Go ahead. Fill me in."

The truth hovered at the tip of Hena's tongue. She wanted to tell Irum. She wanted to tell her everything.

But she couldn't.

"Like I thought," Irum said. "Sorry, Hena, but it didn't look complicated to me."

"I loved your brother," said Hena. "I miss him every day. He was my best friend. Every day I wish things didn't go down the way they did. What you saw was a fight. People fight. I never would have wanted him to disappear."

"That doesn't change the fact that you lied," she said. "You lied to the police. To my mother. To me. You knew where he was the morning of the wedding. All these years you kept it to yourself. What if we'd known everything? What if that could have helped us find him?"

Hena didn't reply. She couldn't. She *had* lied. Because she'd made a promise to Nasir. To keep him safe. Because the whole point had been for no one to find him. But it didn't mean Irum's stony face wasn't tearing her apart.

Before she could say more, a scream pierced the air.

Both women whipped around. The side door next to the reception desk was parted open. Hena raced through it and found Lucinda around the corner by the service entrance. She was hunched over, shaking from head to toe.

Then Hena saw. Lying near a shadowed corner by the resort's air-conditioning units. A body. Motionless. Blood slicked the pavement beneath her.

Hena's knees buckled as she realized who it was.

Gita.

18

The ambulance had left moments ago. Two ambulances in the span of a few days—except this time they had come for a woman who had been left for dead.

But Gita wasn't dead. A faint pulse had fluttered beneath Hena's fingers while they waited for the medics to arrive.

The police were everywhere. Their heavy boots echoed against the polished hotel floors.

Lucinda sat across from an officer at one of the lobby chairs where days earlier, Hena had helped Reza apply a bandage to his burned palm. That moment felt like it was from a lifetime ago. The glass of water in Lucinda's hand sloshed as she tried to compose herself.

"There was a phone call." Her voice was thick with emotion. "He said he was with our AC repair company. Said there was a fire hazard issue. I told him we'd have our maintenance team look into it, but he insisted it was urgent. I rushed over, and then . . . then . . ." She collapsed into sobs.

A chill went through Hena. Lucinda hadn't stumbled upon Gita. She'd been sent to find her. Someone had wanted to hurt Gita, and they had also wanted her to be found.

But why would anyone target Gita?

"Ms. Mirza?"

Two female officers approached her. One was dark-haired. Her badge identified her as Officer Kraus. The other woman, blond, was Officer Steen.

"Do you mind if we ask you a few questions?" Kraus asked.

Hena hesitated. Her instinct was to grab her phone and call Haris. Ask him to join her. But why? She had nothing to hide.

She followed them to the back of the hotel, overlooking the pool. The swans lazily drifted across from her. Officer Steen pulled out a notepad.

"Where were you this morning, Ms. Mirza?" she asked once they were alone, her pen poised against the paper.

"I wish I'd seen something. I was in my hotel room at that time."

"Can anyone confirm your location?" asked Officer Kraus.

This was protocol, Hena thought. They wanted to verify everyone's location. But the only one who could confirm this was Reza. Her face warmed as she shook her head. There was no way she was telling them that.

"How would you describe your relationship with Gita?" Kraus continued.

"She works for my mother," Hena said. "I met her this week."

Why were they looking at her so closely? Was this a fact-finding mission? Or an interrogation? She needed to play it safe. She fumbled for her phone and dialed Haris's number. When he answered, she quickly explained the situation.

"Ms. Mirza, this won't take long," Steen said. "If you could give us a few moments of your time, we—"

"I'm not saying anything until my lawyer is here."

Moments later, Haris swept into the lobby, hair mussed, shirt untucked. He looked like he'd been yanked out of sleep, but his eyes were alert. He assessed the officers, his mouth a firm line, as Hena filled him in.

"I'm not sure why you feel the need to waste time interrogating Hena," he said, sharply. "The longer you keep us here, the more time we lose finding whoever actually did this."

"This won't take long," Steen repeated.

"I was in my room," Hena told them. "I have no reason to hurt Gita."

The officers shared a look.

"That's—that's not why we're asking," Kraus said, her tone gentler.

"Then what is it?" Haris demanded. His eyes met Hena's. Protective. Wary.

"Do you believe there's anyone who might want to harm you, Ms. Mirza?" Steen asked.

Me? Her mouth went dry.

"Your name came up in our system," Steen explained. "There's a report that you were the victim of an assault several years ago. Attempted strangulation."

"The assailant was not apprehended, correct?" Kraus asked.

"That's right . . ." Hena said slowly as a dread pooled inside her. "Why?"

"We are trying to determine motive," Kraus said. "And we can't help but notice the physical similarities between yourself and the victim."

Hena steadied herself as the implication of their words sank in. They didn't look alike, not really, but Gita wasn't much older than Hena. They had the same build. The same dark hair and olive skin. To someone who did not know them well, they could certainly be mistaken for each other.

"There is also the similar manner of her attack," Steen said.

"She was . . . she was struck from behind," Hena said. "I saw the blood. Was she . . . was she strangled too?"

Steen nodded. "There are signs consistent with strangulation. Our guess is she may have struggled, which led to her head trauma."

Hena drew in a sharp shallow breath. The room blurred.

"Hena, do you need to sit?" Haris watched her worriedly.

Sitting wouldn't make this better. Someone had assaulted Gita. They'd left her for dead.

They'd thought she was Hena.

Rapid footsteps. Reza hurried toward her, his brow creased with worry.

"Hena, what's going on? Are you okay?"

"Gita was attacked," she said in a hollow voice. "A few hours ago."

Reza's eyes widened with alarm. "Where? The premises were deserted when I headed out this morning."

His attention shifted to the officers. Haris.

"Sorry," he said quickly. "I'm interrupting."

He started to turn away, and Haris pursed his lips.

"Where exactly were you heading?" he asked, his tone deceptively casual.

"What?" Reza gave him a startled look.

"You said you were heading out this morning. Where did you go?"

Reza's eyes flicked to Hena, then back to Haris. He slowly shook his head.

"I didn't see anything, if that's what you're asking."

"Not an answer to the question," Haris observed.

Reza frowned. "No offense, but I'm not sure why I need to explain myself to you."

Haris didn't respond, but his eyes didn't leave Reza's. Hena shifted. The tension vibrating between them was so thick she could cut it with a knife.

Reza was new. Sure, he was Khaled's friend, but he wasn't from their community. She understood Haris's protectiveness. Before she could speak up, one of the officers did.

"We'll be asking everyone where they were. It's protocol," Kraus told Reza. "If you don't mind sharing where you were around eight this morning, it would be enormously helpful."

"I was at Publix. Seven miles up the road. Grabbing groceries. I returned shortly after nine o'clock."

"You were at the grocery store," Haris repeated.

"That's right," Reza said. "I needed some ingredients for breakfast."

"Makes sense," Haris said. "It's not as though there's any food to eat on the premises, right?"

"What are you trying to say?" Reza shot back. "Check the security footage. It'll back up what I'm saying."

"Yes," Hena said quickly, hoping to stop this from spiraling. "There should be footage. Lulu's got cameras all over the hotel. If Gita was attacked on the property, it'll show clear as day who did it."

The officers traded a look. Steen sighed.

"Whoever did this got ahead of that. They blocked out the cameras."

"They hacked them?"

"Yes. They vandalized a few as well."

Vandalized.

Her stomach twisted. She bolted outside, racing past the reception desk and onto the pathway she'd hurried down a short while earlier. She scanned the eaves of the building and gasped.

There it was. The camera. It was coated, and splotches of still-wet paint dripped to the concrete below.

Red paint.

Like last time.

The world tilted around her.

She couldn't speak. She couldn't move. Panic filled her system. Because this wasn't random. This wasn't a coincidence. It was now confirmed: Whoever had done this was hoping to finish what they'd started three years ago.

Gita wasn't the target. Hena was.

LUMA AND KHALED

INVITE YOU TO WITNESS THEIR

VOWS AS THEY OFFICIALLY

BECOME MAN AND WIFE

AT THEIR

Nikkah

VISTA DEL SOL

345 EUCLID DRIVE

EVERMERE, FLORIDA

Wednesday, January 14,
at 7:00 p.m.
Cypress Ballroom

Attire: floral

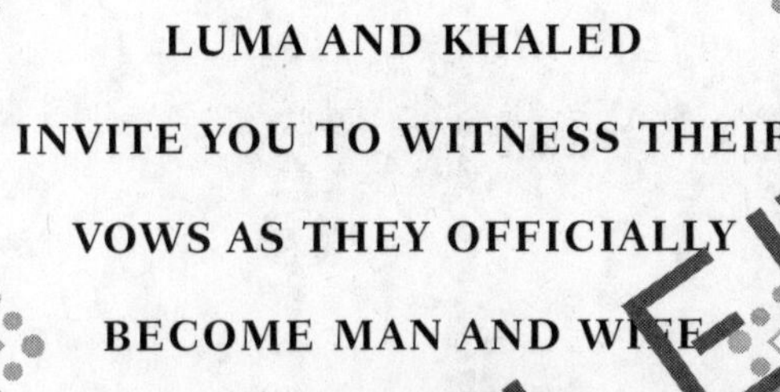

DAY
SEVEN

19

·

The three-hundred-person ceremony planned for the previous night had been canceled. Instead, it was eleven o'clock in the morning on Thursday, and sixteen people were gathered in a simple, unadorned room tucked in the corner of the resort, overlooking the butterfly garden. There were no candles today. No drummers. No Mughal-inspired backdrop.

Khaled wore a cream sherwani, and Lulu a simple ivory shalwar kamiz to match. Her hair was pulled back in a low braid, and a veil was draped over her head. Despite the lack of pomp and circumstance, as they exchanged their vows before the imam and promised to devote their lives to each other, the moment was undeniably perfect.

Khaled took Lulu's hand. He beamed as he slipped the wedding band on her finger. As Lulu gazed at him with complete adoration, a bittersweet sensation welled within Hena. Until now, every event had been a fun house mirror of her own wedding week. But here, their paths diverged. This was a moment she and Nasir had never shared. By this point in her own timeline, Hena wasn't welcoming a future with someone she loved; she was saying goodbye.

After the imam declared them man and wife, there were hugs. Smiles. Happy tears.

Yesterday was a surreal blur—endless trips to the hospital, officers questioning every guest and combing the grounds, and all the while, she and Khala taking turns to care for and calm her distraught mother. But now, at least, there was this. It was now official. Despite all the tension and stress and fear, Lulu and Khaled were now officially married.

As people exchanged well wishes, her eyes drifted to Reza. He lingered off to the side, by the entrance. His posture was stiff, his thoughts clearly elsewhere. Ever since Lulu discovered him in her suite yesterday morning, something had shifted. Hena had texted him last night, asking him to come by. He said he couldn't. A migraine.

"Hey, you," she said, approaching him. "How are you feeling?"

"I'm better. Thanks." He blinked and smiled, though it didn't quite reach his eyes. "And hey—congratulations." He nodded to Lulu and Khaled.

"Thanks," Hena said. "I'm glad it's official."

"How's Gita?" he asked. "Is she any better?"

"It's a serious concussion, but she's stable," she told him. "They kept her overnight for observation, but she'll get discharged soon. She should be back in time for the shaadi tonight. Lulu wanted to call off the rest of the wedding, but of course, my mother wouldn't hear of it."

Worry lines creased his forehead. "It *does* feel a bit risky. Given what happened."

"Unfortunately, Gita sided with my mother."

He hesitated. "Are you sure you're safe here?" he asked. "I heard the officers talking. They said you might have been the target."

"I've double-locked the back door. Staff can only come

and go through the front entrance," Hena told him. "And you saw all the extra security roaming around."

"You think that's enough? Whoever did this to Gita, they're still out there."

"The wedding week is almost done. Besides, whoever is fucking with me, they don't get to run me off."

He smiled at this, and Hena's heart lifted.

"I have nothing on deck until tonight," Hena offered. "Come by?"

He hesitated again. "I'll try."

Try.

"Are you sure you're all right?" she asked.

His eyes met hers. There was something there. Something she couldn't read. It was gone just as quickly.

"I'm good," he said. "Just tired."

Before she could press, Haris walked toward them. Hena excused herself—the last thing she wanted was to risk another confrontation between the two of them.

"Gita's okay," she told Haris. "Hopefully the police can get to the bottom of who did this."

"That's what I wanted to tell you. She spoke to the police."

"And?"

"She said someone grabbed her from behind. She didn't even have time to react before she blacked out. She doesn't remember anything."

Nothing? She pushed down her disappointment. "Someone must have seen something. One of the bellhops or other workers?"

"The police are still interviewing guests, groundskeepers, and other employees to see if anyone noticed anything off. At the moment, we've got nothing."

He shifted his weight, his jaw tense. Hena was afraid to ask. But—

"Is there something else?"

"Milcheck reached out. He wants us to come to the station."

Of course he does.

"I've held him off for now," Haris said. "But you and I should find time to talk through everything. Especially that video."

Something in his expression made her throat constrict.

"I should have told you I saw Nasir the morning of our shaadi," Hena said quietly. "He made me swear not to say a word."

She watched Haris absorb this information. He'd been nothing but professional as each new piece of withheld information surfaced, but deep down, was he furious?

Haris sighed. "Nasir never gave us easy choices, did he?"

"He didn't," Hena said softly. And speaking of Nasir, there was another thing she hadn't had a chance to tell him. Not yet.

She filled Haris in on the gossip about Nasir, the alleged sighting at Las Olas—which meant he must have been trailing the wedding guests.

"I heard that rumor," he said. "I reached out to the PI who works for us on retainer at my law firm and asked him to look into it."

"And?" Hena's pulse quickened.

"He traced everything, but the security cameras didn't clock anyone in the area matching Nasir's description. No phone pings detected either. Makes me think Milcheck is full of it. Something about him doesn't sit right with me."

Of course there wasn't a phone ping. Of course Kiran didn't see Nasir strolling the streets of Las Olas. Hena felt stupid for even entertaining the thought.

The wedding planner interrupted their conversation. It was time for wedding photos.

Hena searched for Reza, but he was gone. As the grooms-men gathered around Khaled, Hena pulled out her phone.

> Where are you? They're taking wedding photos.

Three dots appeared. Then—

> Went to my room to lie down. I'm feeling under the weather.

Under the weather? Hena had just seen him. He was fine. After the photos, her aunt walked over to her.

"Your mother wants to rest," she told Hena. "Do you mind taking her, and I will switch with you once I'm done here?"

"Of course."

"Where did your beau go?"

"My—"

"Reza, right?"

Heat crawled up Hena's neck. "Khala, we're just . . ."

"Friends? Uh-huh." Khala eyed Hena. "You can pretend with others if you'd like, but not me."

The truth was, Hena was a little confused about the status of Reza and herself at the moment. That night on the boat. Her room the next morning. Those moments were so tender. So real. But since then, his evasive behavior . . . how it felt like he was dodging her . . . she didn't want to go there, but she was starting to wonder if maybe their moments together had just led to a hookup and nothing more.

"Reza is nice," she said. "But there's nothing to tell, at least not yet."

"And Haris?" Khala tilted her head. "He's a nice boy too."

"Khala!" She flushed.

"I saw Haris and Reza yesterday. Haris was a bit combative, wasn't he?"

Her aunt had noticed?

"You know how people get about newcomers here," Hena said.

"That's not what it was," Khala said.

"What do you think it was?"

"I *know* what it was. Jealousy." She gave her a sly look. "You can't blame the boy. It can affect the best of us."

Hena fidgeted. Haris wasn't jealous, he was protective. People were always looking for stories where there weren't any. Even well-meaning people like Khala Simki.

Hena approached her mother, who frowned.

"Why are you here?" Ammi asked.

"To take you to your room. You need to rest."

"You should leave. You're not safe."

"They've got plenty of security. Lulu said she's getting more people to come tonight."

"We need one for you in particular. You don't have anyone." She let out an agitated breath. "The marriage is official now. Why stay?"

"You want me to hop on a flight back to California right now?"

"I've heard the chatter. The man who tried to attack you. He's back." She shifted in her wheelchair. "It's foolhardy to stay. Charter a private plane if you must. I'll make some calls. We'll set you up with security back home. It's best to be safe."

"What are you talking about? The shaadi is tonight."

"Hena, be reasonable."

"I *am* being reasonable," Hena replied. "Whoever is trying to mess with me, they don't get to win. I'm not going anywhere."

"You are as stubborn as you ever were."

"Hmm." Hena pursed her lips. "I wonder where I get it from?"

Ammi exhaled, shaking her head, but Hena caught the faintest hint of a smile.

Back in the suite, she helped her mother into bed, then headed to the kitchen to get water. When she returned, her mother was on a video call with Gita.

Gita was raspy, but she was chatting easily.

"The doctor said ibuprofen should do the trick," Gita was saying. "I don't know why they won't let me out already."

"Patience is a virtue, Gita. Hospitals take the time they take."

"Says the woman who was ready to bolt from the hospital room with her IVs still attached?"

Her mother laughed, and Hena felt some of the tension in her easing at the sight of her mother truly relaxed. When Ammi hung up, Hena regarded her thoughtfully.

"You and Gita get along so well," she said.

"She's a good girl."

"I've never seen you speak so easily with anyone."

Her mother considered this. "I suppose I see myself in her," she told Hena. "She was in a bad marriage much like I was, but unlike me, she had the good sense to leave as soon as she realized it."

"Why *did* you marry Abu?" Hena asked, seizing an opening she'd never had before.

A flutter of nerves rose in Hena as her mother considered the question. She waited for a scowl. A sharp retort.

"Why I married him is no mystery," her mother said at last. "He was charming. Handsome. He had a charisma that drew everyone to him. The bigger question is, once the mask came off, why did I stay?"

"It's not easy to leave," Hena said. "Not someone like him."

"Some people leave, though, don't they?" Her mother looked toward the window, then back at her. "Gita did. The one time I tried, early on in the marriage, I barely made it out of the driveway before he dragged me back in and—" She exhaled sharply. "No use dredging it back up. The long and short of it is, after he was done, he let me know what he'd do to my sister if I pulled something like that again."

He threatened Khala? A tremor went through Hena. "That's horrific."

"That was that." Her mother shrugged. "You wouldn't believe how fast I folded."

She tried to imagine her mother then. Younger than Hena herself was now. Stuck with a monster she couldn't leave. She was surprised her mother was telling her. Was it because she was dying? Because there was no sense holding on to secrets anymore?

"You can't blame yourself for staying," Hena told her.

"Well, whose fault was it, then? Besides, I wasn't the only one trapped in that house." She fell into a sudden coughing spell. After a moment it passed, and she sighed. "Thank god we shielded Lulu, but you—you suffered too."

She *had* suffered. This was the moment to tell her mother exactly how much. The words, everything she'd longed to say, pressed against her. But her mother waved a hand.

"There's no changing the past, so why dwell? Still . . ." She took a beat. When she spoke again, her voice was quieter. "When I see Gita, I can't help but think of what could have been. Maybe she'll get the chances I never had."

"It's great that you're supporting and encouraging her," Hena said.

"She's a clever girl. And it's important to have a few people around you who aren't vultures. The guests have been quite something this week."

Hena arched a brow. "If you know how toxic they can be, why do you keep up with them?"

Her mother looked at Hena like the answer was obvious. "Because some are family, and others I've known so long they may as well be."

"But you've said it yourself—they can be awful."

"You think it's so easy, don't you?" Ammi scoffed. "We have history. That counts for something. Yes, they can be awful, but they're mine. When I first got my diagnosis, they were there for me. Set up meal trains. Brought food. Flowers. I'm sure some dropped by looking for gossip—but for better or worse, they're home."

Hena processed her words. This was the most honest exchange they'd had in years.

"I'm glad they've been supportive of you," she said.

"They have. But Hanifa must go."

At least there was that. Auntie Nipa needed to be next, even if she *was* Haris's mother.

Her mother fell into another coughing spell. Hena gave her medicine. She choked it down before resting her head on the pillow again. After a few moments, the coughing passed.

"Now. Let's discuss your suitors," she said briskly, once she'd recovered.

Hena rolled her eyes. "Next topic, please."

"I've heard it's between Reza and Haris. Personally, I favor Haris."

"Haris is a friend," she said. "That's all."

"Well, if you want my opinion, friendship is underrated. It's the best foundation. Haris had a rough stretch, but he's come out of it with sense. That's more than I can say for most."

"Ammi—"

"No need to get defensive on me," Ammi huffed. "All I'm saying is I see the way he looks at you."

Heat crept up Hena's neck. Khala and Ammi had clearly been trading notes. She couldn't blame them—Haris had been a godsend this week. He'd stepped in as her lawyer without a second thought. Because it was the Haris way—it always had been. But even if something more was possible between them . . .

"Haris was Nasir's best friend," Hena said.

"*Was*." Her mother's voice grew gentler, just slightly. "You can't live in the past. At some point, you have to move on."

She stiffened. Ammi was many years late for this conversation.

"I have moved on. I have a whole new life out in San Francisco. A thriving business. Friends."

"You haven't moved on," her mother replied. She tapped her temple. "Not here." Then she pressed a hand to her heart. "Not here. You think I don't see the walls around you?"

Who do you think I learned to build walls from? Hena almost said, but she bit her tongue. They were talking. For the first time in who knows how long, they were having a real conversation. And the truth was, as much as Hena hated to admit it, her mother was right. Her dates over the years were engaging and fun, but most of their conversations stayed surface level—about a favorite movie they'd seen, or what menu items looked most enticing.

Hena liked it that way. Loved it, in fact. There was a reason parents urged their children to stick to the shallows—the surface was where it was safe. The last time she'd dove beneath the surface was with Nasir, and sure enough, she'd drowned, the pressure splintering her heart into a million pieces. Her walls were up for a reason.

Except here, her barricades didn't feel quite so sturdy as they did in California. She'd told Reza things she'd never told a soul. With him it felt as though there were almost no barriers at all.

There was a knock on the door. Haris. Her mother brightened upon seeing him.

"We were just talking about you."

Hena gave Ammi a warning look as he asked how she was doing before turning to Hena. "I was hoping you and I could talk."

She excused herself, and they stepped into the sitting area.

"The police called," he said, cutting straight to the chase. "Look, it's bullshit what I'm about to tell you—but you need to be informed. They found fingerprints on Gita's clothing."

"Fingerprints . . ."

His expression was grim. "They were yours."

The air left her lungs. "I never gave them my fingerprints. How would they even . . ."

"They had them from last time. The attack."

"I did touch Gita. I—I checked for her pulse."

"I told them that. I'm waiting to get more details. I'll keep you posted as soon as I know."

She was breathing fast. Too fast. "So now I go from *victim* to *suspect*?"

"Let's not jump to that yet. They didn't say that."

"What else could they mean? Are they coming to arrest me?"

"Hena, don't panic. It's okay," Haris reassured her. "They just said they want you to stay in town. They may have further questions."

"Stay in town. Lovely."

The knives are out for you.

Those were the fortune teller's words. Hena had dismissed them as absurd. But if everything was absurd right now, wasn't anything possible?

"They want revenge," Hena said slowly. "Whoever is doing this, that's what they're after. It must be tied to the past. To Nasir. To the attack on me that night."

"Did Nasir ever mention anyone he was worried about, even in passing?" Haris fixed her with a worried look. "Anyone he was scared of?"

"He *was* scared, but he wouldn't tell me who it was," she said. "The week of the wedding, he was so jumpy. I didn't push it. I didn't get how bad things were until I got the notification about the empty bank account."

"He must have used the money to pay off whoever was after him."

Here it was. The parts she had not told anyone else. The parts Nasir had made her swear never to tell. It was time for Haris to know.

"He did give them the money," she told him. "But it wasn't enough. They said no dollar amount would do."

He frowned. "It's always money with these people."

"Not this time. This time they said they wanted him dead. I begged him to go to the police. He said he couldn't. He said it would make things worse." Here it came. "Haris, I'm sorry, but . . . I knew he was leaving. I knew he wasn't planning to come back. It's why he came to the boathouse. It's what he'd come to tell me the morning of our wedding."

Haris's jaw twitched. She studied the floor. He was angry. Of course he was. In his shoes, she certainly would have been. This was a big thing to conceal.

"I tried to stop him from leaving," Hena said. "I begged him to think about what he was saying, what it would mean for everyone who loved him, but he was adamant. He made me swear not to say a word. He wouldn't tell me where he was going. Said he didn't want to take the risk of anyone harassing me or his family about his whereabouts."

There was a beat of silence as Haris processed her words.

"That must have been heavy," he said at last. "To know and not be able to tell anyone."

"It was painful." A tear slipped down Hena's face. "Pretending the wedding was on. Acting surprised along with everyone else. He needed time. To run. I don't know if I gave him enough. Or maybe they caught him anyway . . . Haris, I'm sorry," she said, barely above a whisper. "I should have told you sooner."

"Don't apologize. I just . . . Fuck. Poor Nasir."

"Now they're back," Hena said. "I guess if they can't have Nasir, they want me."

"How well do you know Reza?"

Hena looked up with a start. This again? "I met him here. At this wedding. Why?"

He put his hands on his hips, considering his words. "It was strange, wasn't it?" he asked. "Him telling the officers he was out shopping? That's the alibi? Really?"

Hena shifted. She didn't want to go here. But—

"I can vouch for him." Her face warmed. "He was, uh, making us breakfast."

He frowned, then straightened as understanding dawned on him.

"Of course he was," he said, his voice quiet. "Well, there you go. That explains that." He gave her a half smile that didn't quite meet his eyes. "I was grasping at straws anyway."

He's jealous. That's what Khala had said. If that was the case, had she just hurt him? Someone she cared for, who had always been there for her?

When he left, she checked her phone. There was a missed text from Reza.

> **Reza:** Sorry for leaving so abruptly.

> **Hena:** Feeling better?

> **Reza:** A little.

> **Reza:** Do you think we could talk today?

> **Hena:** I'd like that. I'll be around after lunch.

> **Reza:** I have an errand to run this afternoon, but I'll try to swing by your room before the shaadi.

An errand? What kind of errands did Reza have to do while he was here?

She wanted to ask him. She wanted to pick up the phone. To call him. She didn't. Instead, she sent him a thumbs-up. Then she walked back into her mother's bedroom, set the phone on the nightstand, and sat with her. Hena held her mother's hand as she drifted off to sleep. She tried to still her mind, though it wouldn't stop churning.

She was here for only a little while longer. The wedding week was winding down. Until then, she needed to hold it together.

CELEBRATE LUMA AND KHALED'S NUPTIALS TONIGHT AT THEIR

Shaadi

VISTA DEL SOL

345 EUCLID DRIVE

EVERMERE, FLORIDA

Thursday, January 15, at 7:00 p.m.
Celestial Grand Ballroom

Attire: your wedding best

20

.

The shaadi was in less than an hour. Reza never did drop by.

There had been no call. No follow-up text.

Not that she felt a pit in her stomach. Not that she was checking her phone every few seconds like a lovesick teenager.

Maybe he got caught up with his errand. Maybe it was another migraine.

Or maybe if it walked like a duck and acted like a duck, it was a duck.

Maybe their night on the boat meant more to her than it did to him.

Her phone rang. She startled. But it wasn't Reza. It was Lulu. She wanted Hena to come up to her room.

She was seated at her makeup table when Hena arrived. She wore a bloodred ghagra, the fabric fanning around her. Her hair was swept up in a flawless French twist, but her face was bare.

"You look stunning," Hena told her.

"Thanks. The makeup artists are stuck in traffic," she said. "We're running behind."

"The shaadi can't start without you, right?"

"True." A pensive look crossed her face. "I need a favor. It's a big ask."

"I'm afraid I don't do wedding-level makeup."

She laughed. "Noted. No, what I wanted to ask you is— and you can say no, I won't be upset—"

"You're making me nervous."

She took a deep breath. "Will you walk me down the aisle?"

Hena's heart lifted at the unexpected question.

"Ammi can't," Lulu continued. "She's in a lot of pain and—"

"Of course I'll walk you down the aisle, Lulu." Hena reached for her sister's hand. "I'd be honored."

Lulu exhaled, relieved. "Thanks, Hena. And listen, don't worry about safety. As far as I'm concerned, this place is Fort Knox. If someone is trying to fuck with you—I'd like to see them try. The cameras will be fixed by tomorrow too."

"Good," Hena said, relieved. She glanced at Lulu. They had never talked about her reaction upon discovering Reza in Hena's bedroom. Was now an awful time to bring it up?

"I'm sorry I didn't tell you about Reza," she said carefully. "I should have mentioned he was there."

Something shifted in Lulu's expression. Hena couldn't read it.

"That was a surprise," she finally said.

Hena studied her sister. It was more than that, wasn't it?

"Do you not like him?" she asked Lulu.

"It's not that."

"But it's something," Hena pressed. "I know it's a bit impulsive of me, but . . ."

"I was surprised," Lulu said. "I guess I thought I knew what was up at this wedding. You got me. He is cute, though. I see the appeal."

Did she mean it? Or was this a polite deflection?

She had more questions, but Lulu's phone rang. The wedding planner. A seating snafu on the groom's side. The moment was gone. She'd prod later.

The sun had fully set by the time she got back to her suite. Her white-and-gold sari hung on the armoire. On the vanity sat a red box her aunt had dropped off earlier. She opened it and her breath caught. It was her mother's favorite diamond set. The one she'd worn to Haris's wedding.

A note rested beneath it in Ammi's handwriting.

This is yours now.

Tears stung as she lifted out the necklace. The flawless diamonds glittered beneath the lights. She loved it. But right now, holding it in her hands, this piece of jewelry felt like her mother saying goodbye.

Hena changed into her sari. She was fumbling with the necklace's clasp when there was a knock on the door.

"Good news," Haris said when she let him in. "I was able to reach the sheriff."

"The sheriff?" She raised her eyebrows.

"I don't trust Milcheck. Figured I'd go above him and get some answers about what's really going on. He's there for another hour, so I'm going to catch him before he leaves."

"Now?" she asked. "You'll miss the wedding."

"This is important. The sooner we can sort this out, the sooner you aren't forced to stay in town against your wishes. Don't worry, the station's not far from here," he assured her. "I let Khaled know I'll be back as soon as I can. Save me a slice of cake?"

She promised him she would, and nodded to her necklace. "Do you mind helping me put this on?"

"Of course."

They stood in front of the vanity, and his fingers brushed

the back of her neck as he clasped the necklace. She trailed her fingertips along the diamonds, the stones cool against her skin.

"Thanks, Haris."

He lingered for a beat. "You look beautiful. Then again, you always do."

Her heart skipped, but she kept her eyes on the mirror. "You're sweet."

"Just honest."

She met his gaze in the reflection. He was looking at her. His eyes steady. Khala's words came back to her: *I see the way he looks at you.*

She tried to push it away, but the words clung to her now. Her mother and Khala had gotten in her head. That was all. They didn't know Haris like she did. He was always ready to help at a moment's notice. That was the kind of friend he was. It was how he'd always been. That didn't mean she should take advantage of him.

"I need to pay you." The words tumbled out of her as she tried to find her footing.

"Pay me?" he repeated.

She turned to face him. "For your time. You've done all this work and we've never once talked about payment. That's not right."

"Don't worry about that."

"Haris—"

His hand lifted. Gently, he tucked a strand of hair behind her ear. "Nasir left a mess in his wake," he said. "If I can help you, I want to."

Nasir did leave a mess, didn't he? This right here, their shared memory of the man they both loved, was what bound them.

He promised to keep her posted. When he left, she pulled out her makeup bag and set it on the vanity.

She ran a finger along her neck where Haris's hand had been a few moments earlier. The memory of the warmth in his eyes sent a flush to her cheeks.

Which made no sense. She didn't see Haris that way. Not when he was so tied to Nasir. To the past. To this place. She couldn't.

Could she?

There was a knock. Opening the door, she was met by a tall woman with a suitcase in tow. A makeup artist. Bride's orders.

The woman layered Hena with foundation and concealer and eye shadow. When she was done, Hena looked at her reflection in the mirror: Red lips. Highlighted cheekbones. Thick lashes. A jolt of unease ran through her as the bride she had once been looked back at her.

She headed down to the main lobby. Lulu was in a bridal suite off to the side. Twenty minutes to go. The wedding planner invited Hena to wait with Lulu until it was time, but taking in the shaadi hall, the happy feeling bubbling inside her faded. Nasir's parents were attending tonight.

Or at least, they might be.

And if they were here, she needed to get ahead of it.

"I'll be right there," she told the planner.

The last thing she wanted was to be the center of some awful confrontation while trying to walk her sister down the aisle. If his parents were here, she needed to rip off the bandage and get whatever it was they wished to do or say over with.

It was clear why Lulu had saved this space for the most significant event of the week—the celebration following the nuptials. The hall was grand with vaulted ceilings. Red and pink flowers draped the windows. The candle centerpieces glittered gold beneath heavy chandeliers. But she wasn't here to take in the scenery—she needed to confirm if his parents were here.

Judging by the hushed tones and shocked expressions, they were.

Now what?

She hadn't thought this through. What would she say if they confronted her? His mother was unpredictable at best.

Then she saw.

Her breath grew shallow.

The edges of the room grew fuzzy.

Nasir's parents were here. But that wasn't why she was rendered frozen to her spot.

It was because of the man.

He was dressed for the occasion. A crisp gray suit. Silver tie. Polished leather shoes. One would think he was just another wedding guest.

Except he wasn't.

He was Nasir.

21

·

Was it the bass of the music she felt—or the violent thudding of her heart? The room tilted around her. She blinked, but Nasir was still there, standing by the stage. His mother clutched him like a lifeline, sobbing into his suit lapel. His father's eyes were wet with tears. And Irum—she gripped him like she was afraid to let go.

He was thinner. His cheeks were hollowed out, making his face more angular. His hair, once full, was shorn brutally close to the scalp. He looked so different. But it was him.

There was no denying it was him.

Her body moved before she could stop it—one step, then another.

"Here?" his mother said, barely getting the words out, as Hena drew closer. "No call. No messages. All these years I thought you were dead." She was furious, and yet she kept her arms wrapped around him, saying his name over and over, as though to reassure herself that this moment wasn't a dream.

As for Hena, all she felt was cold. Like she was drowning in a dark sea of panic.

Nasir wasn't supposed to be here.

He couldn't be here.

A hand touched hers. She flinched.

It was Reza.

"Sorry I wasn't able to swing by sooner." He was out of breath. "There's something I need to talk to you about. It's kind of important and—"

He cut off mid-sentence when he saw her expression.

"What's wrong?" he asked.

She didn't reply. She couldn't. She could barely stay upright. Her knees felt like they were about to give. Reza caught her arm, steadying her.

"Hena, what's going on?" he asked.

He looked around, taking in the hushed voices. The wide eyes. People were pulling out phones to snap pictures. To share proof this was really happening.

"Everyone's acting like they've seen a ghost," he said.

Because they had. Except Nasir was no ghost. He was real. He was here. At her sister's wedding.

Which was bad. Very bad.

She craned her neck, searching for Haris. He'd know what to do. Except—she winced—he was at the police station.

Nasir scanned the space. At last, he saw her. Time stopped moving.

He took a step toward her, then paused. Unsure.

She gestured to the door.

He nodded. Because he knew.

They needed to talk.

HENA,
Sister of the Bride

66 Three years ago, I was a girl getting ready to marry the boy I loved.

It had been a bumpy journey—from a fairy-tale beginning to the nightmarish years of dealing with his gambling addiction. High-stakes tables. Always. A handful of enormous wins, followed by losses so big they triggered the sale of his cars, his condo. They triggered a broken rib and too many black eyes to count from the people who enabled him. Who expected to be paid.

I didn't give up on him. I stayed by his side. We'd been together nine years, and most of those years were good. Perfect, really. And love isn't love if it breaks at the first obstacle. Or the second. Or the third. And I loved him. So much. No, he wasn't perfect, but he was kind and gentle—everything my father wasn't. Addiction is an illness, isn't it? I saw behind the sickness to the man he truly was—the one I had fallen in love with in college. The man I knew he could be again.

I waited for him to hit rock bottom. And when he did—when he appeared with eyes so beaten he could barely open them, his tibia shattered—he told me this was it. I saw it in his swollen eyes. He meant it this time.

I drove him to his weekly meetings. To his therapy appointments. I saw the work he put in, and I saw the results. He was better. He wasn't hiding his phone from me anymore. He let me check his bank statements without hesitation. We were laughing together. He was dragging me once again to the movies, to concerts, and even if I pretended to complain, I loved it. Loved seeing my Nasir come back to me. He was doing the work, and now he was clean. Which meant we could finally get our life back on track.

We set a wedding date. Sure, there was stress. His parents for starters. But we powered through. All was well. Caterer and photographer deposits paid for. Honeymoon booked. A cute cottage in Coral Gables we were days away from closing on.

And then, sitting at my bridal vanity, getting ready for the professional photographs, I saw the alert on my phone: My bank account was empty. Every cent gone, and along with it, any dream I had of our happily ever after.

The video capture shared for the world to see was not altered. Every word was mine. Yes, I screamed at him that morning. It was bad enough to fall off the wagon, but to steal from me? That was a line he had never crossed until then.

But then he told me the truth. He told me everything.

How they kidnapped him the night before, after the mehndi ended. Covered his head with a sack. Dragged him to a car. He'd lain tied up in the trunk for hours.

He held out his hands. I nearly fainted at the sight

of his nails—gone. Pulled out with pliers. One by one. Only then did I notice him wince as he moved—his shoulder was dislocated. Lifting his shirt, he revealed a sea of purple and black bruises.

"They want to kill me," he said. "They won't stop until I'm dead."

"How much do you owe?" I'd asked.

"I don't owe anything. I'm clean, Hena. I've stayed clean."

"Then why?" My voice cracked. "Why would they do this?"

The lender was upset when Nasir stopped gambling. It's not easy to lose one's best customer. In the ensuing months, they'd grown paranoid, convinced Nasir had turned on them. That he was informing. Preparing to take them down. They gave him one more night to come clean, but Nasir knew no answer would satisfy them. He was a dead man walking.

"I'm calling the police," I told him.

But before I could even press a button, he grabbed my phone. Powered it off. Threw it to the ground.

"If you call the police, you're dead. So is my sister. My parents."

"So now what?"

"I'm leaving." Nasir's eyes grew bright. "I wanted you to hear it from me."

He refused to let me help. He didn't want me involved, even though I would have risked everything to keep him safe. No matter how much I pleaded, he wouldn't say where he was going—only that once he left, he would need to stay gone.

Still, I pulled off my rings. My engagement solitaire, my twenty-four-karat gold bangles. My necklace. I shoved them at Nasir. Leaving wouldn't be easy. He needed all the help he could get.

He drew me to him. Kissed me. And if you don't know what it's like to kiss someone knowing it will be the last time, I hope you will never know it.

"I love you, Hena," he said. "I always will."

I buried my face in his neck. I promised not to say a word.

Then I watched him walk away, understanding that my life as I knew it was over. "

22

·

They slipped out a side door. Hurried toward the conference room at the far end of the resort. Hena reached for the doorknob.

"Hena! Wait!"

Reza. He raced toward them.

Beside her, Nasir stiffened as he drew closer.

"You can't go in there alone," Reza said. "Not with him."

"What are you talking about?" she asked.

Reza didn't take his eyes off Nasir. Stepping closer to Hena, he lowered his voice. "He's gone for years and shows up without warning? You need to be careful."

A funny feeling passed over her. After ignoring her all day, Reza wanted to tell her who she could and couldn't talk to?

"Do you know something I don't?" she asked. "If you do, now's the time to tell me."

"I'm just saying three years is a long time to be gone. And to come back like this? Crashing your sister's wedding?" Reza ran a hand through his hair. "Something's wrong, Hena. You know it is."

That much was true. Something was wrong. Deeply

wrong. Which was why she needed to talk to him. Alone. She turned the door handle. Reza stuck out his hand to stop her.

"Why roll the dice?" he asked. "I'm not saying don't talk to him. Just . . . be careful. Let me come in with you. As a precaution."

"It has to be just us, Hena," Nasir interjected. "Please."

A crowd was gathering behind him. It was growing by the second.

"I don't have time for this," she told Reza. "Stay out here and stand guard if you want. I'm going in and I'm talking to him alone."

They stepped into the room, and she locked the door firmly behind her.

Nasir's breathing was shallow. This close up, she noticed he was thinner than she'd realized. His skin was sallow. There was a scar beneath his left eye. As she took him in, the shock slowly faded—replaced by horror.

"Why, Nasir?" she asked. "Why would you come back?"

"I had to." He studied the carpeted floor. "I'm sorry."

Angry tears blurred her vision. "You're always sorry."

Before she could stop him, he stepped forward and pulled her into his arms.

"Don't—" She tried to shove him away, but her body betrayed her. She melted against him. She hated how familiar this felt. How much she had missed him.

He was here. He was alive.

But—she wrenched herself away—he wouldn't be for long.

"They're going to kill you." She held on to the conference table to steady herself. "You were supposed to stay gone. Stay safe."

"It stopped being safe."

"They found you?"

"No. They found you."

Hena shook her head. "I don't understand."

He scrubbed a hand over his face. "I—I don't check socials. I'm always scared they'll—I don't know, trace me or something. The other day, though, I—god, I'm so stupid—I looked. I saw Irum's posts about the wedding."

He swallowed hard. Met her eyes.

"I saw you. In the background. And I saw . . . I saw them. They were here. I panicked. I created a fake account and messaged them. Told them to back off and leave you alone." His mouth pressed tight. "Stupid, I know. I made everything worse."

"They finally made contact," she whispered.

"They realized you were the way to smoke me out. They started sending me messages. All the ways they were fucking with you. The snakes. The way they coated the elevator buttons with nut residue." He shook his head. "They said it would only get worse until I came back to face them. When they showed me your body, the blood pooling around you . . . I thought you were dead. For a good five minutes, I was sure you were gone."

Gita.

"They called it a preview," he said. "If I didn't come forward tonight, they said they would finish what they'd started."

"Who are *they*?" Hena asked. "Tell me."

He looked away. "I can't. You don't know them like I do. What they can do."

"After everything that's happened, do you honestly think you're protecting me?"

"It wasn't about you," he said. "It was to get to me."

"They've been stalking me all week. I deserve to know who it is. Is it a guest? A staff member?"

She glanced at the closed door. She was afraid to ask, but she had to.

"Is it . . . is it Reza?"

"Please. Don't." He shut his eyes. "If I tell you, they'll kill you. They'll kill my family. You have no idea what they're capable of. They could be listening right now."

She wanted to call him paranoid, except someone had filmed their fight three years ago. Someone had been watching.

A ringtone chimed on the other side of the door. People were surely pressed against it, trying to catch a snippet of their conversation.

She lowered her voice. "So now what?"

"They kill me."

"Nasir—"

"They kill me and it's over. It's as simple as that. Honestly, I'm tired of running."

"Nasir. That's insane. You're not thinking clearly."

"They promised it would be quick. I've made my peace."

They promised it would be quick?

"I don't care if you're fine with it, I'm not fine with it!" Her voice rose.

"This is how it has to be."

He looked serene. Broken but calm. Before she could press further, his phone buzzed. He looked down. His expression darkened.

"What is it?" she asked.

He fidgeted. Then—"You're not safe here."

"What do you mean?" Her pulse stuttered. His expression had gone from weary but calm to tense in a matter of seconds. What kind of message did he get? "You said they weren't after me."

"Should we really take someone like this at their word?" He shoved his phone in his pocket and drew a shaky breath. "There were other ways to fuck with me. Irum's here too. But it's only been you."

He moved to the French doors in the back. The ones leading to the back gardens and pathways. He scanned the scenery before shifting his focus to the conference door.

"Every way out has some risk," he muttered. "Leaving the way you came is the best bet. More eyes mean more safety. Besides, if we step out together, no one will notice you. All eyes will be on me."

"Wh-What are you saying?" Hena stammered.

"Lay low. For a little while. Until this blows over."

"Nasir, do you hear yourself?"

"Look! I haven't—I haven't thought this all through, okay? I just know as long as you're here, you're in danger. Here, take my car, it's not like I'll be needing it."

He fished his car keys out of his pants pocket. His sunglasses slipped out as he shoved the keys toward her.

"It's a black Honda. Toward the back. Make sure no one is following you. They'll be focused on me first. You'll get a head start."

Hena's head spun.

"And then?" she asked. "What next? I'm supposed to go on the run? Hide out in a different motel each night and sleep with one eye open?"

"I don't know. I'm sorry, Hena. I—I just know being here isn't safe."

Her attention dropped to the fallen sunglasses. Leaning down, she picked them up. They were oversized. Tacky. Not his style. Unease crawled up her spine. The man from Las Olas. The one Kiran had mentioned.

"You were at Las Olas," Hena whispered.

He nodded. "I was hoping to catch you at one of the outings. I had to warn you, but I didn't trust calling you on the phone. They could have tapped it."

Hena turned the sunglasses over in her hands. Fragments

of the fortune teller's words passed over her: *Darkness obscures their face . . . someone tried to hurt you.*

The fortune teller's prophecies were a party trick, Hena reminded herself. This was just her nerves. Reza getting in her head.

She didn't care what anyone said. Nasir would never hurt her. There was so much she could doubt, but never his love for her. Yet as he moved closer, she found herself involuntarily taking a step back.

She'd said something else, too, the fortune teller:

They have done dark things to survive. They will do what they must.

She took in the scar beneath Nasir's left eye. The dark circles. When Mariela had said Hena was in danger, was it possible she'd meant from Nasir?

No. She stopped herself.

Those visions weren't real.

They weren't.

But what if they were? There was no way to know for certain.

"Is that really what you want?" Hena asked. "To keep me safe?"

He startled. "What else would I want?"

It's Nasir, she told herself. *I know him.*

And that was the problem. She recognized the fear written across his face. The guilt.

There was something he wasn't telling her. Something serious. She looked past him to the large French doors lining the back room. The garden outside.

Something told her to run.

So she did.

23

·

"Hena!" Nasir cried out as she fled. "Come back. Please!"

She ignored him and hurried down the terrace steps. The sky was dark. Frogs croaked in the distance. Wind whipped against her hair. Glancing back at the brightly lit resort, she prayed she was hidden.

She needed to reach Haris. He had to know Nasir was back. She dialed his number. Straight to voicemail.

She tamped down her frustration. Now what?

Then she saw him. In the distance, striding down the grassy lawn, his back to her—Reza. How long had he been out here? She'd told him he was welcome to keep an eye out while she spoke to Nasir. But he wasn't watching her right now. Instead, phone pressed to his ear, he was slipping into the maze. Why?

Heart thudding, she followed him. Entering the narrow pathway, she crept forward. He was here somewhere. It would have been easy enough to call out his name, but an unspoken dread she could not articulate rendered her silent.

A few paces in, she heard him.

"I'm trying," Reza said into his phone. He was a row ahead of her, his body obscured by the maze. ". . . unpredictable."

She crept closer, flinching at the sound of her heels clicking against the paved pathway. Kicking them off, she turned the bend, straining to hear him, until finally—

"She doesn't suspect anything, but things are moving faster than planned."

Hena faltered mid-step.

"I know what's at stake," he snapped. A long pause. "I don't care. Like I'm just going to walk away?"

The rustle of leaves. Through a narrow gap in the branches she clocked his face. Furrowed. Angry.

"Of course I'm not listening to them. This is serious." Another pause. "Yeah, well, he showed up today!" A pause. "Yes. Nasir is at the fucking wedding."

Hena's blood ran cold. She froze, watching Reza's profile shadowed in darkness.

Reza rubbed the back of his neck. "I told you we should've handled this days ago."

No.

"I know," he said after a beat. "I'll end it now."

He paused again, listening.

"Can we talk about this later? Lulu already gave me an earful."

Lulu? What the hell was going on?

"I'll keep her close," he said. "Don't worry." Another pause. "*Of course* the location tracker is on. I don't trust it, though. The signal's shit out here. We can't afford to wait."

She felt dizzy. A tracker. Her phone burned in her hands. She dropped it. It cracked on impact.

Reza jerked his head at the sound. Through the gap in the branches, his eyes met hers. His mouth opened. Shut. He stuffed his phone in his pocket.

"Hena." He slipped from view, reappearing at the entrance of the pathway where she stood. He started walking toward her.

Hena took a step back.

"Fuck. Hena—listen to me. I can explain."

"Stay away from me."

He moved closer. She raised her palms.

"Don't come any closer." She edged away. The leaves, spiky and calloused, bit into her skin.

"It's not what you think. I want to help you."

"Help me," she repeated. "So you haven't been lying about who you are?"

"No! I mean, it's not that simple." He paused. "I was hired to protect you. It's what I'm trying to do right now."

"Protect me?" she said, her voice tight with fury. "I heard you. You bugged my phone."

"That wasn't me. Hena—"

His mouth was moving, but she couldn't grasp his words over the roar of panic in her ears. Her vision was tunneling. The masked man in the boathouse. The gloved grip against her throat. The one she'd stabbed with a knife.

The scar across Reza's stomach.

"You said . . . you said it was a fireplace poker . . ." she said slowly. "That man. It was . . . it was you."

She had delivered herself straight to him.

Reza fell silent. His face went still.

"You don't understand," he said.

Except she did. A wave of nausea roiled through her. All these years, it was him. He was the one who had haunted Nasir. The reason the last three years of her life were spent in grief and pain.

Their conversations flashed before her. He'd known exactly what to say to get close, hadn't he? He just had to flirt a little and share stories of trauma at the hands of his father. All he needed to do was leave a fucking KitKat bar at her door, and poof—she was putty in his hands.

"Look, we're out of time." He stepped toward her. "I need to get you off the property. Now. You're in danger."

The path felt like it was shrinking around her. Reza was right. She was in danger. Reza was the danger.

"Leave me alone," she said through gritted teeth. She backed into a main artery of the maze. "And stay the fuck away from Nasir. Do you hear me? Don't talk to me ever again."

He stood still. Debating. Then his eyes narrowed. He took a step forward.

"I'm sorry," he said. "But I can't do that."

He lunged for her, his hand shooting out. She jumped back.

Then she ran.

Her feet slammed against the concrete as she flew down the winding path. He was behind her, close on her heels.

Branches scraped her arms as she tore through the narrow hedge openings, her billowing skirt snagging on thorns.

She raced left, feet skidding. Her bridal clothes were bulky, and Reza was fast. So fast. But she was the one who was desperate.

She veered into the next alleyway, praying it didn't lead to a dead end. From there, a hard right. She panted. Her chest burned. The thud of her beating heart so loud it drowned out everything else.

The maze twisted and doubled back on itself. She breathed heavily. Glancing back, she'd lost him. For now. There was only luck in a maze like this, where every turn looked the same.

She heard Reza on the other side of the hedge. His steps growing closer.

She stopped suddenly. A dead end.

Hena pushed down her rising dread. If she turned to double back, he would find her. Grab her. And then what?

He would finish what he'd started.

Her heart skipped a beat. Here: a break in the hedge. Barely wider than her shoulders. She ran her hands along the spiky leaves. She could squeeze through. Maybe. Which meant she stood a chance.

Vines scraped her arms as she fought her way out. The leaves stung, their jagged edges slicing against her skin. At last, she stumbled onto the grassy lawn on the other side.

Reza's footsteps grew louder—then stopped.

"Hena!" His voice thundered in the darkness.

He was still in the maze.

For now.

Hena broke into a run. She reached a gated fence, flung it open, and raced through the butterfly garden.

"Wait!" Reza was out. He was closing in fast. "Don't do this!"

She raced out the other side, slamming the back gate shut and securing the latch, then kept running. Past the gardens. Through the gravel path. Into the parking lot.

She exhaled a ragged breath. Her bare feet burned. She scanned the rows of parked cars. It was only a matter of time before Reza hopped the fence or broke right through it.

What now?

Then she saw the headlights as they cut through the misty night. A silver Range Rover crossed the drawbridge and pulled in.

Haris's car.

She sprinted to it and pounded the window. Hearing the locks click, she yanked the passenger door open.

"I—I called you," she said, breathless.

"My signal's crap out here," he said. "I was going to—" He saw her face. His expression changed. "What happened?"

Glancing back, Reza's shadowed figure loomed in the distance. He'd hopped the fence. Of course he had. Now he was running toward her.

"Nasir. He's at the wedding. And Reza—" She struggled to choke the words out. "He's not who he said he was. I'm in danger, Haris."

Haris clenched his jaw. "Get in. Let's go."

NOMAN,
Uncle of the Groom

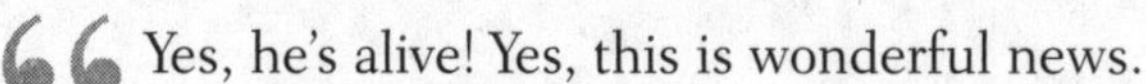 Yes, he's alive! Yes, this is wonderful news.

We'd been so worried. It's awful to say, but with him gone so many years, we assumed the worst. In our defense, his mother said as much. Did you see her? That poor dear. The relief that was written all over her face.

But . . . I have to point this out.

We all saw it.

You saw it too, didn't you?

The look on Hena's face when she realized Nasir was back?

Did you see how disappointed she looked?

And you saw, didn't you? How quickly she fled?

24

·

The headlights of the SUV sliced through the night as they sped down the unlit back roads. Haris glanced at Hena worriedly. She bit back tears. If she started crying, she might never stop.

Reza. All this time. It was him.

The betrayal was so enormous it defied words.

She had trusted him. She had let him into her suite. Her bed.

Her heart.

That evening on the sailboat, she had said she couldn't read him. She'd been right. All this time, he'd been in the background, waiting for the right time to strike.

"Do you want to talk about it?" Haris asked.

She did not. She wanted to pretend it never happened, but that was impossible.

"You were right," she told him. "About Reza."

Through halting stops and starts, she filled him in on everything he needed to know. About Nasir's return. How Reza used her to lure him out of hiding.

"I'm not sure I'd have believed it if I hadn't heard it with my own ears." She wiped her eyes with the back of her hands.

"We'll deal with this. We'll figure it out," he said. "What matters is you're safe now."

"What about you?" The sickening realization dawned on her. "You're helping me, which means you're in danger too now."

"No one knows about my cabin," he reassured her. "Once we get there, we'll tell Milcheck. I know how terrifying this all is, but you're going to get through this, I promise."

She wanted to believe him. She did. But tension coiled beneath her skin all the same as she braced for whatever might come next.

They turned onto Alligator Alley, famous for its darkness and the stars littering the sky. Forty minutes later, his headlights shined against a dilapidated wooden fence. The SUV slowed as his tires crunched against gravel.

Stepping out of the vehicle, Hena spotted the sole cabin a few yards ahead. It was shrouded by trees. A wooden walkway crossed the swamp water leading to its door. Moonlight caught against the peeling paint.

Once inside, Haris lit the lanterns, and the place came into sharper focus. As tired as it looked on the outside, it was cozy and warm inside. There was a worn sofa and a beige rug across from a wood-burning stove. A table for two sat next to a window. She caught a glimpse of a simple bedroom off to the side. An analog clock ticked above the doorframe. Nine o'clock.

She opened the sliding door to the back deck and stepped outside. The waters around them were dark and murky. It should have made her feel wary, but instead—with the silence surrounding them, the sky so bright with stars, the moon shining down like a spotlight—she felt a welcome sense of calm.

A few moments later, Haris joined her.

"I called Milcheck," he said.

"You have a signal out here?"

"Just enough. He told me he's heading to the resort as we speak."

Some of the tension in her body eased. "Good."

"And don't worry about Nasir. He's safe. Reza won't get far."

Reza. Her chest ached thinking of him. She knew she'd have to deal with this, and soon, but for now she wanted to push it out of her mind. She had to recalibrate.

"This is a nice spot," she said.

"I'm relieved you're okay with it. I know it's a bit off the beaten path."

"It's perfect. It feels like a reset after everything."

"I came here all the time as a kid, but there's something about this place that keeps me coming back. The cabin's just always grounded me. Maybe it's because there's no one around for miles, and you can see the entire Milky Way."

"It makes everything else feel small in comparison. More manageable." She looked at the sky and back at him. "Thanks again, Haris. I don't know what would have happened if you didn't show up when you did."

"Anything for you, Hena." His gaze lingered on hers. "I'm sorry for everything you've gone through. Sometimes I get really angry with myself about it."

"Angry with yourself?" She met his eyes, surprised. "Why?"

"Because I knew. I knew how Nasir was. How impulsive he could get. His taste for risk. I could have warned you before you'd gotten in so deep. I didn't know you were together until it was too late. Until he called to brag about finding 'the one.' I didn't want to meddle. Looking back now, I wish I had. I wish I'd at least tried to warn you." He shook his head slowly. "All these years, I wish it could have been different."

It wasn't Haris's fault. She had been in love with Nasir. She wouldn't have listened even if he'd tried. Before she could say this, he spoke again, quieter now.

"I wish it could have been me."

Her heart stopped. Did she hear him right? There was no hesitation in his eyes. He looked at her like he'd finally said something he'd been holding on to for some time.

"Haris, I had no idea . . ."

"That I used to be in love with you?" He gave her a self-deprecating smile. "I was. For years actually. Probably since our kiss when we were kids, when I didn't understand what the word even meant. By the time I worked up the nerve to say something, Nasir had come along, and that was that. You went to the same university, so it's not like I stood a chance. Which was fine. I moved on. Chloe and I had a good few years before things went to shit. But seeing you again this week, I guess it all came rushing back."

His words rippled through her. Khala's teasing echoed in her ears. Her mother's knowing look. Maheen's laughter about her "two suitors."

Deep down, she *had* noticed something shifting between them this week. The way his fingers had brushed her skin when he'd helped her clasp the necklace. The quiet way he looked at her. But his words crashed over her: *In love with me? For years?*

Memories emerged of dinners in Princeton when he'd come to visit Nasir. Their long talks on the drive home when she first moved back to Florida. When Nasir still wanted to stay out, but Haris—like her—was ready to call it a night. He'd make her a latte and they'd kick up their feet, talking into the early hours.

She hadn't thought anything of it. None of this was romantic on its face. Except she'd noticed, hadn't she? The sidelong glances. The way his eyes always found hers, even in the middle of a busy gathering. All those little moments. Her mind hadn't been able to entertain the possibility, but it had been there all along.

He brushed his fingers lightly over hers.

"You've had it rough for so long," he said gently. "Nasir never did right by you, and I've hated seeing you go through it alone. I promise I will keep you safe, Hena."

He rested his hand over hers. Protective. Caring. For one brief second, she was tempted to reciprocate then and there. To take this road. A life with Haris. Something steady. Safe, like he said. He was someone who'd always seen her. Who she could be herself with. Someone who'd known her forever. Who'd always been there, waiting in the wings.

He watched her nervously.

The temptation was real and startling.

But.

Her heart sank. She couldn't. Not now. Not with everything that had happened this week. She needed a minute to process. To take a breath.

She had to say it.

"I'm flattered, Haris." She gently pulled her hand back. "Really, I am. But . . . I can't."

Even in the darkness, she could see how her words had landed, and the brief flash of pain passing across his face before he hid it away.

"Of course. I'm sorry. I didn't mean to make things uncomfortable."

"Don't be sorry. Please. You've done so much for me, and I'm so grateful for you. You have no idea how much I care about you." Her voice was thick with emotion. "It's just . . .

things are so complicated right now. I need a minute. I don't want to make things messier than they already are."

He didn't reply. She blinked hard as she watched his profile, searching his face for something—anger, regret—but he was completely unreadable.

He excused himself. When he returned, he was holding two glasses of water. He handed her one. She took it from him and studied his expression as he took a sip from his glass.

"Are we okay?" she asked, her voice small.

"Of course we are." Haris's expression softened, though she saw the sadness lingering too. "Honestly? I feel better now. At least I said it."

They stood there a moment longer until Haris cleared his throat. He offered her an apologetic smile and excused himself to use the bathroom.

Finishing her water, she walked back into the cabin. She set her glass in the kitchen sink as the dull ache of guilt washed over her. He said he wasn't hurt, but how could he not be? After all he'd done for her, she hoped she hadn't inadvertently led him on.

She winced. A sudden headache. Her hands flew to her head. She realized with a start she hadn't eaten all day. She slid open a kitchen drawer to her right. It was empty. Drawing open the next one, she paused.

There was a framed photo in there. Of her parents. It was a professional picture, the type taken in a studio. They stood before a blue backdrop. Her father in a white polo. Her mother in a pink blouse. Brown bangs swept across her forehead. His hands rested on her shoulders. He looked so young. They both did.

Why did Haris have this photo tucked away in the drawer?

She needed to step out of the kitchen. Wait for Haris. Ask him. But her body was ten steps ahead of her brain. She opened a cabinet door. Tried not to gag at the odor of rotten apples and moldy oranges.

Opening the next one, her mind went blank.

She couldn't process what she was seeing. Instead of food, she was looking at a mini hardware store: There was a plastic bag filled with zip ties. An assortment of coiled rope in a wicker basket. A pack of ski masks and gloves. A variety of knives hung from a magnetic rack like a butcher's arsenal.

But what was inside the next cabinet turned her blood cold.

Matches. Lighter fluid. Brass knuckles. A blow torch. A rusted pair of pliers—blood caked along the tips.

Her breath caught.

Nasir's hands. His torn fingernails.

They had locked him in a trunk. They had driven him far away.

Where no one could hear his screams.

Her pulse quickened. A light glowed on the counter. Haris's phone. She peered at the incoming message from an unknown number.

Reza has been neutralized.

Reza neutralized? Her lungs seized. What did that mean? Another text dinged.

No clear shot of Nasir. Don't worry. He's got to come out sooner or later.

No.
No.
No.

A flush. The sound of running water. Haris stepped out of the bathroom.

"I was thinking . . ." he began. He trailed off as he saw her horrified expression. As he saw the phone she held in her hands.

"Well," he said slowly, his voice low. "Shit."

25

·

"Hena. Please relax."

Relax?

She couldn't relax. Every nerve in her body was crackling. Her pulse pounded in her head. She tried to draw in a breath, but her lungs were tight. Too tight.

"I can explain," he said, his demeanor maddeningly calm.

The image appeared in her mind's eye, unbidden: Nasir's battered face, the shattered look in his eyes, the purple bruises, his shaking hands. His bloody fingers.

It happened here. In this room.

Her insides churned. This couldn't be right. It made no sense. This was *Haris*.

"Fine," she said. "Go ahead. Explain. Tell me you weren't the one hunting Nasir. That you're not the reason he had to go on the run."

"Hunting him?" He looked hurt. "I'd say it was more like he was hunting me. Always crawling back, asking for more money—again and again. Never a thank-you. Not once."

Her guts twisted. This wasn't an explanation.

It was a confession.

"You were the loan shark."

He grimaced. "I don't like that term. I'm there for people when they need me. When they've run out of options. I help them. Like your father did."

My father.

Looking at her expression, he laughed gently. "You didn't know? Yeah, I worked for him. Everything I am, everything I've built—it's thanks to him. He was the best in the game."

The blood drained from her face. She shook her head, her brain fighting to process his words. He watched her with something like pity. His eyes flicked around the cabin before landing back on her.

"I was curious if you'd recognize this place. He never brought you here, did he?"

Hena moved to speak, but nothing came out. Her hands fell to her sides, her fingers curled and digging into her palms.

"This cabin is his. Or it was," he amended. "I helped him with the less savory aspects of the work we did. I dealt with those who took his generosity for granted. After his death, when no one claimed it, I decided to look after it. It's my way of honoring his memory. This cabin looked after me as much as I looked after it."

She felt sick as this information settled in. Haris was one of her father's "kids"?

"He used to terrify me at first, if I'm being honest," he continued. "He was larger than life. You know that better than anyone. But I grew to respect him. I don't know who I'd be without him."

"He taught you how to do his dirty work."

"Careful." His expression darkened. He took a step forward and yanked the phone away from her. "Don't bite the hand that fed you. Everything you have—your fancy townhome, your car, the shoes you wear—it's all because of your father. His sacrifices and his dedication to his family. You were so fucking lucky. Just born into it. And dirty work?" He scoffed. "He taught me how to live in the real world. Lucinda worked for him too, you know. It was good seeing her again after all this time. She was a critical part of this. A bit squirrely at first, but she responds well to direct instruction. She came around."

Lucinda. She'd had her doubts. She'd pushed them away.

"Your father thought we'd be perfect together," he said. "I think it's part of why the idea of you and me had staying power. He said if we got married one day, I'd be family. The son he always wanted. It started as a joke, but he got more serious about it as time went by. He said this way, he could pass everything down to me. To us."

The son he'd always wanted. That tracked.

A sour taste burned in her mouth as she flashed back to the night beneath the lemon tree. She could still feel the weight of her complicated grief, the ache of losing a man she hated but who held the force of gravity with his presence. Haris had sat beside her, so careful, so comforting. She remembered how he'd draped an arm around her and how she'd leaned into him, desperate for something solid to hold on to.

And then—

How his hand had grazed her cheek so tenderly. He'd leaned in and kissed her. So soft. So gentle. It was an impulsive moment, but not an unwelcome one.

Now she realized it had been anything but impulsive.

The room suddenly felt too cold.

"Your father promised me the world," Haris said. "Then he died, and I lost it all. I'd planned to honor his wishes, but you got yourself tangled up with Nasir faster than I could blink.

He took what was meant to be mine. Which is fine. The path got harder, but I kept going. Everything works out in the end, right?"

Tears slipped down her face. She leaned against the wall to catch her bearings.

"Nasir loved you." Her voice broke. "You . . . you tortured him."

"I didn't torture him." When he saw her expression, he clarified. "Right. The nails. I'd told my people to get the information I needed. They got a bit carried away. I had a talk with them."

"You have a hit out on him. You can stop it. Let him be."

"Trust me, I hate that it has to be this way. It hurts me he had to be taught the lessons he did, but I have no choice."

"You were his best friend."

"Best friend?" He let out a low chuckle. "What are we, sixth-grade girls? You think we wore matching heart necklaces too? Look, I loved him like a brother. Still do. But he fucked up. Started talking. There's only so many times someone spits on you before you have to do something about it, friend or no friend. I'm a nice guy, but I have my limits." He checked his watch. "As soon as my people get a clean, clear shot, they're taking it."

"He wasn't talking to anyone. He swore it."

"He lied. Mr. Goody Two-Shoes wanted to help other people. Warned them not to work with me. Word gets around. What was I supposed to do? A damaged reputation is not something money alone can fix, can it? He's the one who declared war." He stepped closer. "If I can be brutally honest for a second? You did him no favors. Your money. Your loyalty. No matter how royally he fucked up, you were always there. I guess you have a soft spot for broken things."

"So your hate for Nasir leaked onto me? You messed with

me this entire wedding. The accusations on the slideshow . . . How could you, Haris?"

His face reddened. "Yeah, the slideshow. I'm, uh, sorry about that." He looked genuinely abashed. "When my people told me about you and Reza . . ." He shook his head, jaw tightening. "Fuck, Hena. Seriously? All I've ever tried to do is be there for you, but you go and hook up with someone you've known all of five minutes. A guy like me has no chance, do they?"

The slideshow was her punishment.

"I shouldn't have done it," he continued. "When I'm emotional, I get impulsive, but that's no excuse."

"Now what?" she asked, her voice low. "What do you want from me?"

"What I want, you cannot give me." The longing plain in his eyes. "But I've had a few days to think about it, and I've decided I will settle for what is my due."

His due. She tried to compute but couldn't.

"Lucinda will bring us the paperwork in the morning once things calm down at the resort. By this time tomorrow, you and I will be man and wife. For a little while, anyway. Your father's wish come true."

Was he insane? Had he absolutely lost his mind?

"Shoot." He pulled out his phone and typed. "We also need to update your will. Your life insurance too. Should be simple enough."

Her head hurt, a pounding that threatened to overtake her senses completely.

"You think anyone would believe this?" she asked.

"Weddings are the perfect place to plant rumors," he said. "At first it was just to mess with Nasir. Really twist the knife. Last I heard, the wedding guests took it way further. Now the story is you and I were secret lovers for years, throughout your relationship with him. Come morning, the paperwork will prove it. It was a happy marriage, even if it was tragically short. It's a shame you took your own life."

His words sent terror down her spine. They should have prompted her to run as fast as she could.

So why couldn't she move?

"What have I ever done to you?"

"Other than not love me back?" His voice was gentle, tinged with regret. "Nothing. I would have rather been part of your family with you."

She felt sick. She needed to escape. She took a trembling step toward the door.

Haris pulled a vial out of his shirt pocket. It was empty.

"You're welcome to try," he said. "But you won't get far."

So that was why she was dizzy. Nauseous. What did he slip into her drink?

"It's been a pain to plan around you," he said. "Reza was a particularly tricky complication I didn't expect. Did you know your mother hired him to look out for you? Seriously. Paranoid much? It was weird from the start. Him and Khaled were friends, but I found it odd he was slotted in at the last minute as a groomsman. I eventually got it out of Khaled, though."

Reza. A tear slid down her cheek. He had told her the truth. He'd been trying to protect her.

Taking in her expression, he smirked. "Yep, never told you, did he? You really know how to pick them. Anyway, once I realized, I knew we had to get you away sooner than later if we wanted to smoke Nasir out, but you slammed into that cake on the island and spooked my guy within an inch of his life."

Black dots clouded her vision. *Focus, Hena.*

"I marry you in secret," she said weakly. "Then I'm dead.

Leaving you everything. You don't think anyone will have questions?"

"I'm still working out the kinks," he admitted. "But I'm thinking I stayed with you because I loved you. Through your depression. Your manic episodes. You must have been manic when you fucked up your sister's wedding. The snakes were weird, but inflicting your sister with an allergy attack? That's sociopathic. My best guess, at least what I'll tell the police, is once you came down from your mania, you saw what you did. You were devastated. Because you're a good person deep down. And, well, you decided to end things. There won't be a body—too many questions—but the suicide note will lay it all out. Shouldn't be too complicated. Disappearances run in your family, don't they?"

Her eyes darted to the windows. The door. Her mind was screaming. Telling her to run. But her body couldn't. Not now. Not when the room was spinning. Then she saw it tucked in his pocket. The black grip poking out.

A gun.

Her lungs seized. She took a stumbling step toward the front door. Her breathing felt ragged.

Haris clucked his tongue. "So glad I remembered to keep a vial in the glove compartment," he said. "After what you did to my guy last time, I knew I'd need it. You've got bite."

A shiver rippled through her.

"I really am sorry for this," he continued. "This isn't personal."

This isn't personal.

The boathouse. The intruder. Haris had sent him.

He took a step toward her. "Let's get you to bed. You're going to crash."

Her vision was blurring.

The memory replayed. That man. His hands clamped

around her neck. How her body slumped against the vanity. He had been there on Haris's orders.

No. She gritted her teeth as Haris's hand went to her shoulder. A surge of adrenaline raced through her. She summoned everything within her, and with her last bit of strength, she kneed him as hard as she could.

His face reddened on impact, eyes widening as he keeled over, groaning.

She shoved open the door. Her heart raced wildly. She stumbled onto the wooden walkway. Darkness churned beneath the slats.

Panic filled her body. Now what?

She took in the gentle sway of the trees. The woods. They were only a few feet away. If she could make it there . . . if she could hide out . . .

Too late. Her body hit the ground.

She heard footsteps. The outline of his boot by her head.

"Well," Haris said, breathing heavily. "I guess I'll have to hurt you after all."

She heard the blow before she felt it.

The world went dark.

DAY

EIGHT

26

·

When she came to, she was tied to a chair.

Her shoulders screamed in pain from being tied for so long—who knew for how long? It was hard to tell at first. There was only darkness and more darkness outside the windows.

She forced herself to sit up straighter. The zip ties around her wrists were tight. So tight they cut into her flesh.

The cabin was silent except for the sound of the ticking clock. Four in the morning. Only now did she notice Haris across from her, half in shadow.

"I'm sorry, Hena."

He said it so sincerely, she wanted to laugh. Except, of course, there was nothing remotely humorous about this situation.

A wave of nausea passed over her. Her head felt woozy—from the impact of his blow, or from the drugs he'd laced her water with, she couldn't be sure. She pushed back a sob. The guests might or might not believe Haris's planted whispers, but her mother certainly wouldn't. Neither would Khala. Would it matter, though? When enough people said a thing was true, it became true, didn't it?

"You don't have to do this," she said. "You can let me go. I won't say anything. We could pretend this never happened. I swear."

"We both know that's not true."

He walked closer. Sat down on the chair near her. Resting his elbows on his knees, he gave her an admiring look.

"The way you fought, I can't deny you have your father's fire," he said. "I think he was right about us. We could have been an unstoppable team."

She looked at his self-pitying expression. As though, despite the facts of the matter—Hena tied up as she was, awaiting her own death—she should be the one comforting him.

It sparked a memory.

Her mother cowering before her father after he'd beaten her. It was a common enough occurrence. Ammi half crumpled on the floor, and that particular moment when he was in the crossroads between remorse and rage. Where the direction of what he chose to do was open. She remembered how her mother spoke to him. As though he were a wounded beast. She soothed him. Made it seem as though his violence was understandable. Inevitable. She promised to not push him to anger again. She said what she needed to say so that she—they—could survive another day.

An idea formed. It might not work. But what did she have to lose? She took a deep breath and channeled her mother. In those perilous moments, Ammi focused on the truth. Because it was hard to call bullshit on what was real. So Hena focused on that. The real.

She surveyed the cabin. The worn kitchen cabinets. She thought of her parents' photo tucked away in the drawer. Her father had been dead for thirteen years, but Haris still held on to that picture.

"You must have come here often with my father," she said.

He was silent for a moment, his attention fixed on the view outside the window.

"The first time, I was fourteen," he said.

Fourteen. "Oh, Haris," she said softly.

"It was an overnight job. Two men. Your father needed someone he could trust."

Hena studied his profile. She'd known him at fourteen. The kid playing football with the other boys. Shooting hoops. Laughing as though he didn't have a care in the world. But it wasn't true. He had been carrying a lot. More than she could have imagined.

"That must have been terrifying," she said.

"It was a bad day." His gaze lingered on a spot by the sofa, covered by a rug spread over the hardwood. "I hated this place at first. But over time, it became a second home. I grew to understand your father. Why he did the things he did."

"I'm not sure there's ever a good reason to kill someone," Hena said.

"When people betray you, sometimes you have to do what needs doing. Your father took no joy in it, but he valued loyalty. Rewarded it. I'm proof. My dad lost his job, and we were weeks from losing our home. Your father stepped in. He saved us."

"What if my father were here right now?" she asked. "If he were looking down on us, what would he say about the situation you and I find ourselves in?"

He flinched at her words. Slowly, he shook his head.

"I won't bullshit you, he'd be pretty fucking pissed. No one messed with his family. It was part of the appeal of joining his family." He broke off. "That's why this is so hard to do."

Looking at his torn expression, she gave him a wistful smile. "Did you know you were my first kiss?"

He didn't reply. A tear slid down her face.

"That was a bad night," she said. "My mother dragged me to that party. Everyone either pretended it hadn't happened or clutched me to them and sobbed, making his loss all about them. I was trying to stay strong for Lulu, but I broke down on that bench. And you. You were there for me. The only one who actually cared."

"I knew what you had lost. I'd lost him too."

"I had no idea."

"No one did," he said. "Officially speaking, I folded linens at his Miramar hotel. When I saw you that night . . ."

"It was a good first kiss."

He looked at her, bemused. Like he was wondering what she was up to.

"I mean it," she insisted. "You don't forget your first kiss."

"I never forgot either," he said. "I'd had this whole plan in my head. To honor your father's wishes. Then, poof, Nasir came and fucked it all up."

"I blame myself," Hena said. "I should have seen it. I should have seen it when we kissed. I should have seen it when you'd drive me home from the parties and concerts Nasir didn't want to leave. I should have seen it during all those late-night conversations. When you made me lattes and watched my favorite rom-coms with me. I should have known."

His jaw twitched.

"You couldn't," he said. "Because of Nasir."

"Because of Nasir. He's a force of nature. I got swept up."

"I spent my whole life playing second fiddle to him."

"We know how well Nasir worked out for me," she said. "All he did was cause me endless pain. You? You're the one who's always there when someone needs you."

His chair scraped against the floor as he moved closer. So close she could feel his breath against her face. The smell of grass and pine on his jacket.

"What are you trying to do?" he asked her.

"Nothing. Just thinking about what could have been."

"Right." He scoffed. "You rejected me. Outside, on the deck. Do you think I forgot?"

"I didn't reject you." When he laughed, she doubled down. "I said I cared about you. I said it was complicated. I said I'd been through a lot and needed a minute. I won't lie, Haris. I'm pretty fucking upset because it didn't have to come to this. You could have told me about your bond with my father. All you did for him. For my family. You never gave me a chance."

"You're right. You deserved the truth. I should have seen how you would've handled it. What's that saying about hindsight?"

"Haris." She locked eyes with him. "You don't want to kill me."

"*Of course* I don't," he said. "But it's too late."

"You make the call, don't you? You decide what comes next. You want my legacy. But you also want me. I can't predict the future—we have a lot we'd need to unpack to move forward, and I can't make any promises. But there's a chance you could have both. Do you want to live with regret about what could have been?"

"Like you'll ever forgive this."

Hena's voice shook with emotion. "You know my capacity to forgive. I forgive to a fault. I forgave Nasir over and over again without any benefit to myself. What I'm offering benefits us both. If you can move past this, so can I. I'm a pragmatist. You know the man who raised me."

She searched his face, wondering if her words had landed at all. For a split second she saw a flash of doubt cross his expression. Just as quickly, he stood up. Frowned.

"You'll say whatever you need to get out of this."

"Of course I want to get out of this. My wrists are killing me, Haris. That doesn't mean what I'm saying isn't true."

"So I untie you, and we live happily ever after?" He rolled his eyes.

"You untie me and we *talk*. We have a real conversation. We see where it takes us. We've always been good at talking, right?"

He didn't reply. Was the air shifting between them? Or was it just her foolish hope? Was it possible he was tempted? Hena knew all too well how fast rationality could fly out the window when feelings were involved.

"You won't run as soon as I let you go?" Haris asked.

Hena looked into his light brown eyes. This man who had comforted her. Who'd held her hand after she'd lost Nasir and let her cry on his shoulder. The man who'd stood by her side for years. The man who wanted to murder her. She told him the truth.

"I'm tired of running, Haris," she said. "I'm tired of betrayal. I want peace. I think in the long run, that's what you might be able to give me." She held his gaze. "You're not perfect, but I see who you can be."

The silence stretched interminably. He was debating. Warring within himself. Hena's heart hammered in her chest.

Haris walked toward the front door, the floorboards creaking with each step. A leaden feeling lodged in her chest. He didn't believe her. Of course he didn't. He was going to sit in his car. Wait for dawn without having to hear her incessant pleas. Or maybe he'd grab his gun from his pocket and end this once and for all.

His hand rested on the doorknob. Then he paused. His gaze dropped. Shaking his head, he walked back toward her.

Wordlessly, he kneeled. His fingers brushed her wrists. He pulled a silver blade from his pocket and sliced through the tie. The tension in her shoulders released.

He held out his hand, helping her up. Hena took it, giving it a gentle squeeze. She hoped he couldn't tell how hard she was trying to keep her hands from shaking.

"Betray me and you will regret it," he told her.

She met his eyes. "Then don't give me a reason to."

He cracked a smile at this. Reaching out, he tucked a strand of loose hair behind her ear. "I know it'll take a minute. We have a lot of trust to rebuild," he said. "But if we can get there, it could be amazing."

"I agree." She forced a smile.

Her hands were free. But she wasn't safe. Not yet. It was one thing to survive this moment. This night, if she was lucky.

How would she survive all that was to come?

She pressed her hand to her throbbing temple. Haris watched her sympathetically.

"You look beat. It's the medicine," he said. "It'll take a few more hours to clear. I'm surprised you're upright, honestly."

Perfect. She'd tell him she was too tired to think straight. She'd pretend to sleep the next few hours away until Lucinda arrived. Until the next part of this nightmare unfolded. It would give her time to figure out what to do next.

"You should lie down. The bed looks uncomfortable, but it's cozy once you're in it."

The bed?

His voice was smooth and low. The way he looked at her . . .

There was no way she was going into that bedroom.

"I'm not sleepy," she managed to say.

"You're trembling like a leaf." His hand pressed against the small of her back. "We don't want you to crash. I insist."

"I think—"

"Don't worry, I'll stay with you," he said. Despite her protests, he was nudging her gently but decisively toward the bedroom. "Just until the meds wear off. Make sure you're all right." A pause. "I promise, I'll be a gentleman."

Her stomach lurched as she took him in. The heat behind his eyes.

Was this the real reason he'd untied her?

And what came next? Would he simply dispose of her come morning? Or operate like her father, who kept her unwilling mother in line by laying a threat to Khala's life— a threat so potent she'd toed the line for nearly two decades?

Hena's breath grew shallow. She had to stall. She needed a way out of this. She opened her mouth to speak. To say something. Anything.

But the words stuck in her throat.

She saw it then: the gun.

It had been in his pocket, but now it rested an arm's length away on the kitchen island. Had he taken it out once he'd tied her up? Had he forgotten it was there? Or was this a test?

Her eyes flicked to the gun—only for a second, but long enough for him to follow the path of her eyes.

"A gun? Really, Haris?" she asked before he could say anything. "Is this some kind of game? You let me go, only to . . . what? Hunt me down?"

"What? Hena. It's not for you. Promise." His expression softened. "I always have a gun on me. It's best to be safe."

This could be her only chance.

There was a brief beat of silence.

Then she lunged, her hands closing around it as he reached for her.

She twisted away from him. Leveled it at his chest.

His hands rose. He backed away.

Which meant it was loaded.

"Don't move," she said. "Or I shoot."

27

·

"Wait!" Panic sharpened Haris's voice. "Don't do this. Please."

Hena kept the gun steady, her arms locked tight, even as her insides shook.

"Familiar words," she said bitterly. "I said the same once. Years ago. When the man you sent tried to strangle me."

His eyes darted between Hena and the gun.

"I get it," he said. "You're pissed. You have every right to be. Like you said, I should have been honest with you from the start. I should've trusted you to handle it."

The gun was impossibly heavy in her hands. Her head was foggy from whatever he had given her. But the adrenaline coursing through her veins kept her upright. Alert.

Haris stepped forward a fraction—slow, careful, his eyes locked on hers. "You don't want to shoot me, Hena," he said. "I know you don't."

He was right. She didn't. She wasn't sure she could physically pull the trigger.

Except this wasn't just about her.

It was about Nasir. It was about everyone she cared about.

And Reza—the text message said he'd been neutralized.

Fury and grief merged and bubbled up inside her. Those words could only mean one thing.

She steadied her grip.

Haris saw the shift in her. His face darkened.

"My people will be here any minute," he said. "You might be able to take me down, but you're no match for what's to come."

"I'll take my chances."

She rested her finger against the trigger.

Breathe in. Breathe out. She braced herself.

A bang echoed in the cabin.

The door had burst open.

He hadn't been bluffing. They were here. His people.

A heavy dread sank through her. It was over.

Then she looked toward the entrance.

She was seeing things. She had to be.

Because it wasn't his people who stepped inside the cabin.

"Ammi?"

Her mother stood at the doorway, her breathing shallow. She clutched her sides as she took a halting step forward. Her eyes swept the room, landing on Haris, who stared at her, shell-shocked. Looking at Hena, her eyes drifted to the gun in her hand. Her mouth pressed tight. She turned to Haris.

"Thank you, Haris," she said. "I heard you helped her escape tonight. I was certain you would take her to safety."

His brow furrowed. She gave him a smile.

"Did you think I forgot about this place? I knew about it. I also knew it was important to you. That's why I staked no claim to it, nor the money he kept tucked away here." At his surprised expression, she nodded. "Ah, yes. I knew about that as well. It was a tidy sum, but considering all you did for us, you deserved it, didn't you? I wanted you to have it. And look how life works. You've used this place exactly as I'd hoped—to protect my family."

Hena's heart raced. Ammi knew. She knew about this place. She knew about Haris. She thought he'd brought Hena here to protect her.

"Ammi, that's *not* what happened. He—"

"It has been so many years." She looked at Haris. "Time really does fly. Remind me what your role was? A fixer, yes?"

Haris didn't answer right away. Finally—

"I was," he said.

"I thought as much." She took a step toward Hena, then another. Each step hurt. Hena could see it in her face. But Ammi kept coming until she stood by her side.

"Uncle and I were close," Haris said. "I . . . I loved him."

"You were the son he never had." Her mother gave him a knowing smile. "He spoke highly of you. I know how you grieved his loss."

Haris's expression softened at the acknowledgment as beads of sweat formed on Hena's forehead. What was going on?

Haris took a step toward her. "Auntie, thank goodness you're here. It's like you said. I wanted to bring her to safety, but she was spooked by Nasir. She thinks everyone's after her."

"You need to put the gun down, Hena." Her mother turned to her. Her words were calm. Commanding. "We don't want you to do anything you'll regret."

"Ammi, I can't. You don't understand."

Ammi looked at her. For a moment she didn't speak. Her eyes filled with tears.

"Honey, I do." Her voice broke the slightest bit. She coughed, then cleared her throat. She was struggling to breathe. Every word was painful. "Listen to me," she said. "I need you to hear me. If I ever meant anything to you, you'll give me the gun."

The crack in her voice. The term of endearment. The fierce look in her eyes. It broke something open inside Hena. Because she recognized that look from the night her father laid his hands on her for the last time. The night she was sure she wouldn't survive.

The night her mother stepped between them and saved her life.

Tears blurred her vision. Suddenly, she didn't see a frail woman before her—she saw the woman Ammi was all those years ago. When she'd walked in on him. His hands in tight fists. When she'd called out his name. When she'd talked him down one final time.

Hena *knew* she shouldn't. Every instinct in her screamed to hold on to the gun. But that look. That voice.

Trembling, she lowered it into her mother's waiting hands.

"Thank you, Auntie." Haris exhaled. He moved toward her. His mouth curled into a sneer. "Now we can—"

But he didn't get to finish his sentence. He didn't even get to take the step that had felt so guaranteed.

Because her mother took the gun Hena had given her, raised it straight at him, and fired. The shot rang out, deafening in the enclosed space.

Haris staggered back, a dark stain blooming across his chest. His eyes sprang wide. He looked down at the wound.

Then he crumpled to the ground.

Ammi watched his still body. She shot again. Then again. Three extra rounds.

"Ammi. Stop." Hena shivered. "He's already dead."

Her mother eyed him with a grim expression.

"With monsters like this, you don't take chances."

28

·

He was dead.

Haris was dead.

Hena swayed as she looked down at his lifeless body, her mind trying to process what had just happened. The cabin door swung open again. Khala, pushing a wheelchair, rushed inside. Hena's mother slumped into it as if she'd been holding herself together on sheer will alone.

Khala adjusted her mother's oxygen, then rushed to hug Hena, crushing her against her soft frame.

"Beta, are you all right?" Her voice was thick with fear and relief.

"Wh-what are you doing here?" Hena stammered.

"You think I dragged myself out here alone?" Her mother tried to scoff, but her words came out breathless. "I'm spent. It's your turn now."

Hena stared numbly at Haris's body. She would need time to unpack. To process.

But right now, there was work to do.

She took the gun from her mother and dropped it next to Haris's still frame. Khala grabbed the matches from the cupboard.

They sprayed lighter fluid over every surface of the cabin.

"I guess if this had to happen somewhere, this is as good a place as one could ask for," said Khala.

"The Everglades are a perfect place for murder," her mother said. "And this place does feel particularly fitting."

"You *came* here to kill him?" Hena's eyebrows shot up.

"There was only one way this could end." Her mother's eyes met hers. "I brought my own gun, but using his is easier. Less messy."

"For the record, I suggested we call the police," Khala interjected. "This could have gone horribly wrong."

"He was never going to suspect an old woman could be the end of him," her mother retorted. "I was counting on that. I blame myself for not realizing who he was earlier."

"You knew he worked for Abu?"

"Your father brought him around the house once or twice after a late night out. He took quite the shine to Haris, but the boy was always so quiet. Scared within an inch of his life. I imagined his family pushed him into it—his father lost his job and things were tight. And, well, once someone accepted work with your father, they did not get to decide when it ended."

"He was so young, wasn't he?" Khala asked.

"It's why I gave him grace," Ammi said. "From everything I'd heard, he put that time of his life behind him. Law school. A partnership. I was clearly very wrong."

"How did you know to come here?" Hena asked her.

"When Reza told us you'd left with him, Nasir revealed everything to us. Once he mentioned a remote cabin, I knew where he'd taken you."

"Reza." A lump formed in Hena's throat. "Haris got a text that said he'd been neutralized. Does that mean he's—"

"Reza's all right," Ammi interjected. "A bit worse for the wear, but he'll make it."

Hena exhaled. He was okay. At least there was that.

"I could have taken care of Haris myself," Hena said. "You didn't have to get your hands dirty for me."

"My hands are plenty dirty as is. Besides, what will they do if they pin it on me?" Her mother let out a chuckle. "I already have a death sentence, don't I?"

My hands are plenty dirty as is.

Lighter fluid dripped from the canister. Hena looked at her mother. She needed to know. A confirmation of what she'd suspected all her life. She debated how to ask, knowing there would be no coming back from it. But it was time.

"You've done this before," she said.

Her mother nodded calmly. "I have."

"*We* did," Khala added.

"It was one thing to hurt me," Ammi said. "He was never to lay a hand on my girls. I told him from the start—that was my line in the sand. Too bad he didn't believe in lines. Once I saw the look on his face, the way he hovered over you . . ." Her eyes flashed with anger. "I knew it was him or us. I chose us."

She sniffled before continuing.

"He's out here too. Your father—or whatever's left of him anyway. He was so delighted when I bought him that stupid boat. An early birthday present, I told him. Your aunt helped me put a big red bow on it and everything. I made him his favorite breakfast. Urged him to head out onto the water. Take a spin. Left him a bottle of his favorite whiskey, a picnic basket of his favorite snacks in the cooler. It's a shame when boats crash. It's a shame when someone is too drunk and drugged to stop themselves from drowning. It's tragic, really. Thankfully, your father had made plenty of enemies. One of them helped me ensure he would never be found."

Hena tried to process her mother's words.

Ammi had killed twice. For her. Khala too.

"You hired Reza," Hena said.

"I knew your attendance at this wedding was a risk," her mother said. "It's why I held off for so long. Time was ticking, though. I had to see you one last time. Lulu thought tracking you through the wedding app would be enough, but we needed you safe as possible. Khaled's friend worked in security, so I hired him to keep you safe."

"Then fired him right when we needed him." Khala gave Ammi a reproachful look.

"He stuck around anyway, didn't he?" Ammi said defensively. "Listen, Hena, I know you fancy the boy, but I was not thrilled with his unprofessional behavior."

"Nonsense," Khala said. "Reza was quite the gentleman. He went from wedding guest to bodyguard without a second thought. It was the perfect cover. Poor Khaled. He was less than thrilled about the subterfuge."

"Well, we needed someone to look out for you," Ammi said.

"Seems he may have taken this a bit too seriously?" Khala shot Hena a knowing look.

Hena flushed.

"I don't like it. Let me be clear." Ammi gave her a stern look. "Mixing business with matters of the heart."

"Don't be such a prude," Khala retorted. "If they get married, they could say you arranged it!"

"Huh. I suppose you're right," her mother mused. "If you have a daughter, could you give her my name? I've heard Frida is coming back in style."

"Ammi!"

"Fine." She harrumphed. "Middle name, then. Children these days give no regard to their elders."

"That *was* a bit rude, Hena." Her aunt shot her a look.

Hena leveled a look at them. "Only the two of you would be matchmaking while we're covering up a murder."

Her mother snorted. Khala started chuckling. Suddenly, Hena was laughing too. It was laughter borne of grief mingled with incredulity. She laughed until tears streamed down her face.

When she wiped her eyes, she felt lighter. Freer.

She wheeled her mother out to the car. With the last of the lighter fluid, she doused Haris's SUV. They'd light it right before they departed—looking up at the sky, the darkness was fading, a hint of light glowing against the horizon—and they needed to get going. Soon.

"We'll have to plant some rumors for why Haris decided to go off grid indefinitely," her mother said.

"It's not a crime to not want to be found," Khala said wryly.

"We have a long ride back. I'm sure we'll think of something." Her mother studied the cabin pensively. "I'm glad everything worked out. Not everyone can say their dying wish came true."

"The wedding was a dying wish too, Ammi. You can't overuse it."

"My dying wish was for closure. I wasn't a good mother. I know that. There was so much I couldn't give you. I was too broken by the time you arrived. But I could give Lulu a big wedding like she'd always dreamed of. Now I can have this. I can leave this world knowing you are safe."

Her words hit harder than Hena expected. It was what Lulu had said. What Khala had said.

Closure.

This was all she'd wanted.

The engine hummed. Khala helped Ammi into the back seat.

Meanwhile, Hena walked over to the cabin. Stepping inside, she paused at Haris's lifeless body. His eyes were open—astonished even in death at what had happened.

She clocked his phone, which lay by his side. The screen was cracked. Her heart leapt. She kneeled down to pick it up, then held it in front of his face. It unlocked.

Hena slid to his texts and scanned his exchanges, hoping she could mimic him well enough. She typed and sent a message:

> The hit is off. Await further instruction.

She dropped the phone by Haris's side. Prayed it worked. Prayed she wasn't too late. She looked at his still form. This man who was her friend. This man she had trusted so completely.

She waited to feel something. Betrayal. Anger. Grief.

Nothing came. Maybe one day it would.

For now, she made her way to the cabin door, then flung the lantern inside.

The glass shattered against the wooden floor, and the blaze was instant. It raced through the cabin, licking the walls, the floors, the evidence. Everything.

Hena torched Haris's SUV. She hurried toward Khala's waiting Camry and slid into the passenger seat. As they drove away, the fire burned bright, glowing against the night sky—erasing the cabin, along with every dark memory it held.

29

·

The police were all over the resort.

Detective Milcheck was there too. She had just finished speaking with him, though there wasn't much to say. Nasir, the prodigal son, had returned, and this new development seemed to have taken the wind out of the detective's sails. It was like he said: Leaving of one's own volition was not a crime. While Hena knew it wasn't as simple as that, for now, at least, she had a reprieve.

No one had made much of Haris's absence. Not yet. By the time they did, there would be no body to find. Thanks to Haris, there would also be no security footage to reveal what had happened and who she'd fled with in the darkness of night.

Lulu was asking questions, though. Hena's disappearance. Nasir's return. So many things demanded answers. Even now, her eyes flicked from Khala to Ammi. She was definitely not buying their story of an urgent emergency room trip in the middle of all the commotion, though she wasn't pressing quite yet.

Ammi was in her wheelchair, frail and exhausted, a shawl draped over her shoulders. The final party of the wedding week was definitely going to be a no-go. Ammi met Hena's eyes for a second. The plea in her eyes was plain: *Stay quiet.*

Hena wished that were possible. It felt kinder, and it would certainly be simpler. But ugly truths left unspoken festered. Even if there wasn't the pressing urgency of accounting for Lucinda and others who were surely staking out the resort at this very moment, Lulu was building a hotel empire in her father's name. She needed to know who he was; she deserved it. Hena would talk to her mother later today. It was time to tell Lulu. Together.

For now, Khala pushed Ammi's wheelchair back toward the hotel. They slipped through the sliding doors.

Hena's gaze lingered on the closed doors. Her mother was no saint, but she had tried as best as she could to protect her children. Maybe Hena could at last forgive her.

Nasir stood near the patio with his family. His eyes found Hena's, and they reunited at a shady corner of the garden, out of earshot.

He took hold of her arms and drew her close. His grip was firm, but she noticed how his hands trembled.

"I thought I'd lost you." His words came out hoarse.

There was no one nearby, but she spoke quietly all the same.

"He's dead," Hena told him.

Nasir gaped at her. Processing.

"Don't ask me how. Don't ask for details. Just know it's done."

"That's impossible. There's no way." He shook his head. "You don't know him like I do. He can shock you when you least expect it."

"Let's say I have firsthand knowledge that won't be happening, and we'll leave it at that," she said. "He's gone. Really."

Nasir swayed. "It's . . . it's over?"

"I don't know for sure. Hard to say how many others worked with him. He definitely had people staking out this property." She eyed the premises, her nerves firing up again. "I tried to stop them, but I can't be positive it worked."

"He was the head of the snake. Once he's silent long enough, word will spread."

"I hope you're right."

"Hope is more than I've had in a good long while." He smiled. The first smile she'd seen since his return.

"Was he ever your friend?" Hena asked.

"I loved the guy," Nasir said. "That's why it took me so long to see what was going on. When he took me to my first high-stakes table, I thought he was being a good friend. He liked gambling too. Said he was getting me into exclusive clubs as a personal favor. When he offered to loan me money the first time, I thought he was looking out for me. The deeper I got, the more things changed. I made the choice, though. I own it. He didn't force me to go to those parties. He didn't make me drop the dice . . ."

He trailed off, lost in thought for a moment.

"Thanks for saving me," he said at last. "Again."

"Let's make this the last time?" Hena gave him a weak smile.

He reached out. Cupped her face with his rough, calloused hands.

"I love you, Hena," he said. "I always have. I always will."

Tears stung her eyes. She thought of their cottage with blooming azaleas in Coral Gables. There had been a whole plan. She'd thought they would grow old together.

But plans changed. Life happened.

Sometimes you couldn't go back in time to the person you once were.

And sometimes that was for the best.

Hena loved him. She always would. But love wasn't always enough. She took his hands and gently lowered them from her face. He understood.

"How's Roscoe?" he asked.

"He's great," she told him. "I'll send you pictures."

"I miss that guy."

"He's yours," Hena said.

"I know he's in good hands. Maybe I can visit him sometime?"

"You can visit anytime, Nasir."

He reached forward and pressed a lingering kiss to her forehead. They hugged. Nasir held on a moment longer than necessary—like he was memorizing the feel of her—before letting go at last.

He walked past the huddled groups scattered across the lawn. They watched him rejoin his family. The gossip about this week was going to be next-level. A scandal for the ages. But Nasir was beloved. The golden child. When all was said and done, he would be fine.

She headed back into the hotel, and her breath caught.

In the lobby, at the reception desk, was Reza.

A suitcase rested at his feet. A garment bag was draped over his arm. He thanked the woman at the front desk and pulled at his carry-on.

When he saw Hena, he paused. A flicker of guilt flashed across his face. She winced at his arm in a sling, his swollen and bruised left eye, the stiff way he was hunched over.

Seeing her stricken expression, he gave her a weary shrug. "You should have seen the other guy."

"You're leaving?"

"My flight's in two hours."

"You weren't going to say goodbye?"

He rubbed the back of his head. "I figured you didn't want to see me," he said. "After what happened, I can't blame you for being furious."

"I've got some thoughts."

"I should have told you. I wanted to from the start. Your mother wasn't having it. Then after you and me . . . When Lulu found me in your room and mentioned it to your mother . . ."

"She fired you?" Hena guessed.

"She was pissed I was still hanging around, but I couldn't leave. Not with everything going on. I had to tell you the truth. I was about to, but—"

"Shit hit the fan," Hena finished for him. "You should have told me, Reza. No matter what my mother said."

"I fucked up." His eyes searched hers. "I hope you can forgive me."

She considered his words. The bated breath with which he awaited her response.

"Was our hookup part of the plan?" she asked with a small smile. "Premium tier?"

"Definitely not." He gazed at Hena intently. "Neither was falling for you."

Her heart fluttered at this last remark.

"How unprofessional." She threaded her fingers through his. "I guess resistance was impossible."

His attention dropped to her hand, then lifted back to her face. "So, you don't hate me?"

"I think that's impossible too."

The lobby buzzed around them. With whispers. The click of heels. The sounds of doors opening and closing. But all she saw right now was him.

"Want to go back to my suite?" she asked him. "I could

use one of those famous omelets. You won't believe the night I had."

His hand tightened around hers. "You sure that's a good idea? Everyone's here. They're definitely looking at us right now."

"Yeah?" She moved closer. Wrapped her arms around his neck. Kissed him. "Good. Let's give them something to talk about."

She took him by his good arm and led him toward the VIP suites. The elevator dinged, and they stepped inside.

When the doors closed, he studied her with a pensive expression.

"What is it?" she asked. "No more secrets."

"No secrets. Just thinking about how far Chicago is from San Francisco."

"It's not too bad, and I've heard those Chicago winters suck."

"They do."

"Good thing you know people in warmer climates."

He drew her to him. "Lucky me."

They kissed again as the elevator doors opened, stumbling into her suite. Hena leaned against the door as it clicked shut behind her. A welcome sense of peace expanded within her. She would always carry the past. There was so much still to unpack. So much grief awaited her around the corner.

But for the first time in years, the walls around her heart were gone.

Which meant, for the first time in years, she was really and truly free.

TANYA,
Cousin of the Bride

66 I, for one, never doubted Hena's innocence. Don't look at me that way, I'm serious. The way everyone gossiped and tore that poor girl apart after all she had been through?

Unconscionable, really.

When it comes down to it, the issue is when things go wrong, people want someone to blame, and the black sheep that doesn't follow the crowd is often the first one picked out for dissection. It may be human nature as one tries to make sense of tragedy, but that doesn't make it right.

It broke my heart seeing the girls at their mother's funeral a few weeks after the wedding. Auntie Frida's decline was precipitous, but Hena had stayed in Florida a little longer to look after her mother alongside Lulu. They were both with her until the end. Both girls looked so forlorn that day, but they are in far better spirits at today's one-year memorial. It was a truly lovely cere-mony. The video commemorating Frida's life was so moving. Not a dry eye in the room. She would have loved it. They held it at Lulu's resort, which is in full swing. I heard she's gone back to culinary school, but she's still doing a wonderful job with this place. I think she was onto something with this whole eco-sheco thing.

Oh, and that boy was with Hena. You know, the one she met at Lulu's wedding? Reza, I think. He's a handsome one. And dare I say, the way they looked at each other, the way she leaned into him, I wouldn't be surprised if there's another wedding on the horizon.

Speaking of marriage, I was so surprised to hear what happened to Maheen. Her poor husband and that horrific skiing fiasco all the way up on Whistler Mountain!

Funny coincidence, though, isn't it? I heard from her cousin's best friend that she had learned he was having an affair earlier that week. And now? He may never walk again.

I'm not saying the two are connected. Coincidences are a real thing.

But if you want my two cents? I think her smiley, bubbly bit is just that—a bit. Because honestly, just look at Maheen. I do not trust her at all. ᱫᱫ

ACKNOWLEDGMENTS

My deepest thanks to my editor, Wendy Wong, for your insight, care, and guidance. Your editorial vision (and the darlings that were killed as a result) made the work stronger at every stage. I'm truly grateful.

As always, my heartfelt thanks to Faye Bender—for your advocacy, your honesty, and for being such a constant and trusted presence.

Thank you to the entire Random House team and everyone at Bantam for their enthusiasm and support, including but not limited to: Vanessa Duque, Chelsea Woodward, Saige Francis, Chanler Harris, Cassie Gitkin, Jo Anne Metsch, and Cindy Howle. Thank you as well to Irene Ng for the beautiful cover.

Many thanks to Justine Larbalestier, Ayesha Mattu, Aqila Zafar, Saba Karamali, and Marcy Franck for your thoughtful feedback. Tracy Lopez and Deborah Halverson, thank you not only for reading—but re-reading several times! All of your perspectives were invaluable.

A special thank you to Mariam Qureshi, not only for reading this book with such care, but helping me name this book.

Gratitude to my husband and kiddos, you are the lights of

my life. And to my parents for always being so very proud of me.

And last but never least, love to my aunties. This book is a love letter to extended families and chosen families and all the drama that lies therein.

THE
WEDDING
WEEK

AISHA SAEED

Random
House
Book Club
Because
Stories Are
Better Shared
™

RANDOM HOUSE BOOK CLUB

Dear Reader,

I grew up in South Florida, on the edge of the Everglades, where community gatherings were large, loud, joyful, and layered with complex dynamics. Weddings especially were epic affairs—days of dancing, shared meals, and of course, the inevitable whispers and gossip.

A few years ago, I returned to Florida for a family wedding. Among the bhangra, and the dancing, my childhood memories came rushing back. As I moved from event to event over the course of the multi-day wedding—reconnecting with relatives, witnessing old tensions resurface and new bonds form—I couldn't stop thinking about how weddings are built-in settings for drama. That tinderbox of heightened emotions, cultural expectations, family history, and sheer exhaustion from nonstop festivities can lead to unexpected—and sometimes explosive—moments. While there was (thankfully) no murder at the wedding I attended, these thoughts stayed with me, and became the seed for *The Wedding Week*.

Within the pages of this novel, Hena navigates complicated family ties while being pulled into something far darker than she ever expected. This book blends my love of big, messy family stories with my passion for suspense—the kind where every conversation feels loaded and every smile might hide something more. I also drew deeply from my own upbringing: the closeness of extended family, the way secrets can linger beneath celebrations, and how cultural traditions can be both grounding and heavy. This story is also, in its way, an ode to Florida, which is not only the land of gators and exotic pythons, but also where I'm from. A place that is truly a character all its own.

I hope you enjoyed stepping into Hena's world as much as I enjoyed creating it. Thank you for spending your time with these characters and their story—it truly means everything.

With love and gratitude,
AISHA

DISCUSSION QUESTIONS

1. *The Wedding Week* unfolds over the compressed timeline of a single week. How does that structure shape the tension and pacing of the story? In your own life, have you experienced a similarly compressed timeline sharing space with people you don't otherwise live with? How did that go?

2. Weddings are joyous occasions, but they often bring out heightened versions of people—their best selves and their worst. Which moments in the book felt most intensified by the wedding setting?

3. How does the book portray love—romantic or familial—as something that can be both sustaining and destabilizing?

4. Hena's relationship with her former fiancé is explored as a plot point but also as a thematic element throughout the story. How does her perception of the relationship and her choices evolve by the end?

5. Hena thinks often about her mother's belief that if people believe a thing is true, then it may as well be. What do you think of this belief about rumors and truth?

6. Which secondary character did you find most revealing or surprising, and why?

7. There are a few love interests in the story. Who were you rooting for and why?

8. There are many misunderstandings of people's intentions within the pages of *The Wedding Week*. How does misunderstanding—not malice—drive some of the conflict in the book?

9. The novel shows how quickly stories can circulate within a closed social environment. How did gossip, observation, and "offhand commentary" within the interstitials shape your perception of the Mirza family?

10. Did your feelings about any of the characters shift over the course of the wedding week? What caused that change?

11. By the end of the wedding week, what do you think Hena understands differently about herself than she did at the beginning?

12. Florida, specifically the Everglades, has a part to play in this book. In what ways did setting serve as character?

AISHA SAEED is the *New York Times* bestselling and award-winning author of *The Matchmaker*. She also writes books for younger readers, including *Amal Unbound, Written in the Stars, Yes No Maybe So* (co-authored with Becky Albertalli), and *Hafsa's Way*. She lives in Atlanta, Georgia, with her family.

AishaSaeed.com
Instagram: @aishacs

Another great thriller from Aisha Saeed

"An intriguing mystery and a heartfelt romance all in one . . .
fresh, original, and utterly charming."
—Liane Moriarty, author of *Big Little Lies*

A society matchmaker realizes she's in danger
when her clients' weddings are sabotaged in
increasingly disturbing ways.

ON SALE NOW!